BROTHER OF DARKNESS

The Blackwood Brotherhood
Book 2

Wendy Vella

ARE YOU SIGNED UP FOR DRAGONBLADE'S BLOG?

You'll get the latest news and information on exclusive giveaways, exclusive excerpts, coming releases, sales, free books, cover reveals and more.

Check out our complete list of authors, too!

No spam, no junk. That's a promise!

Sign Up Here

www.dragonbladepublishing.com

Dearest Reader;

Thank you for your support of a small press. At Dragonblade Publishing, we strive to bring you the highest quality Historical Romance from some of the best authors in the business. Without your support, there is no 'us', so we sincerely hope you adore these stories and find some new favorite authors along the way.

Happy Reading!

CEO, Dragonblade Publishing

Additional Dragonblade books by Author Wendy Vella

The Blackwood Brotherhood Series
Brother of Sin (Book 1)
Brother of Darkness (Book 2)

CHAPTER ONE

L ORD TOBIAS CORBYN arrived at his front door after a long and surprisingly restful sleep. Usually, he never slept well without the noise of a London street outside his window, but he had this time.

It was a dream that had brought him back to Hawthorne, a property he'd barely set foot in since turning eighteen.

Two weeks earlier, he'd awoken in his London townhouse, unsettled by a dream in which his father had been angry at his son for abandoning his heritage. Not normally one to do anything he had no wish to, selfish bastard that he'd become, Toby had been unsettled enough to travel here four days later.

Hawthorne was the estate his parents had loved most of the three his father owned. Toby had his happiest years here, but after age fourteen he'd never found happiness again.

The last ten days had been spent wandering the halls, and his lands, reacquainting himself with his staff and estate. It wasn't exactly enjoyment he felt being back here, but there was a form of contentment in the memories Toby relived. The tightness that was a constant companion inside him eased slightly.

"Good morning to you, my lord."

"Good morning, Collins," he said to his butler, who appeared from beneath the stairs behind him.

As a child Toby thought this man had eyes everywhere, as he always seemed to know where the family were situated. A serious fellow, Collins rarely spoke unless he had something important to say.

"If I may have a word, my lord."

"Of course."

"I've been hearing murmurs about goings on in the village, and none of them good, Lord Corbyn. As yet, I'm unsure what's at the root."

Hearing the name of the local village made Toby tense, but it did not show on his face.

"What have you heard, Collins?" Toby watched his butler work through what he needed to say. He always got to the point and never dithered. He thought a few people in London society could take lessons from his butler.

"Masked riders coming into Bidham brandishing guns at night."

"When did you hear these rumors, Collins?"

"A month ago, my lord. I went into Bidham myself, but no one there is willing to talk on the matter. In fact, they appeared fearful when I pressed them."

Toby respected his butler's opinion, and knew he was not prone to exaggeration.

Like many things from his childhood Bidham village was a raw wound inside him, but Toby knew what he needed to do, even as he wished otherwise.

"Then I shall stop there on my return journey to London, if you think it necessary, Collins?"

The shock on his butler's face was quickly masked, but Toby had seen it. He'd not visited Bidham since his return from school. He knew Collins like the rest of the staff still here at Hawthorne, who had been here when he'd grown up, were horrified by that. Corbyns had been aligned with the village for centuries. Toby had turned his back on it, like many things.

"I would be grateful, Lord Corbyn. Something is not right there."

"Very well, and perhaps it is time," he added.

His butler bowed. "Safe travels to you, my lord."

"Should you need me, then send word, Collins." Another look of surprise flashed across his butler's face. "Good day to you."

He left before he could say anything else to shock the man and went to the carriage that awaited him at the impressive entrance to Hawthorne. Turning, he looked up at the pale stone facade a last time. There were so many memories, good and bad inside those walls; the worst part was, he'd forgotten the good ones until now.

Climbing inside, they were soon rolling away from his family's home. The short ten-minute drive to the village was undertaken, with Toby looking out the window at the landmarks he knew so well. The tree split in half by lightning that he, Liberty, and his brother Mathew had climbed all over. They'd waded barefoot through the thin stream that ran into the village all year round, and nearly lost their toes to frostbite in the winter months.

The memories were accompanied by a deep pang of sorrow. Toby had turned his back on all the good in his life because he'd not known how to deal with the hell he'd endured.

When the carriage stopped, he stepped out, taking a deep steadying breath. He was a viscount and had endured many things. This was just another.

"I will return soon, Rory. Please wait here," Toby told his driver.

"As you wish, my lord."

He walked along the narrow, cobbled road and down into the village he'd grown up running through as a boy.

The day was cool and clear, and still early enough that a few wisps of mist were clinging to the hills behind him. Beyond the small village were cliffs, below which swirled the sea. Another place he'd spent his childhood.

His mother had thought Bidham quaint. A handful of shops catered to the needs of those who lived here or nearby, and when you stepped foot in the village there was someone wanting to chat or offer well-meaning advice. Toby doubted much had changed, but again, it had been years, so he had no notion of what had taken place within its borders. One thing had always struck him about this little nest of houses and shops, and that was happiness. Whenever he'd been here, someone had been laughing. Had there been anger and sadness? Definitely, but his dominant memory of this small village was happiness. It was an emotion that hung in the air, but something he'd never been able to reach again since the day he'd entered Blackwood Hall as a child.

Toby inhaled the familiar tang of the sea as his eyes moved from left to right, taking in the scene before him. Like everything good in his life, he'd shut this place out, too.

His years living in Blackwood Hall, where he boarded during his school days, had shaped the man he was today. Hard edged, cynical, and a libertine, or so his mother had called him just last month. She despaired of him ever taking a bride as no woman would have him, and then there would be no future Lord Corbyn, as he had not supplied her with a grandchild yet.

Just the thought of caring for a child made him queasy. He could barely care for himself. *How would he keep it safe?*

Toby walked until he reached the first house in the village. As if it had only been a week and not years since he'd seen him, Mr. Jasper was bent, tending his vegetables. He raised his head as he heard Toby's footsteps, and the smile fell from his lips to be replaced by a scowl.

It surprised him to see the man had aged, and why it should as it had been so long since last they'd met, he had no notion. Perhaps he'd wanted Bidham and its inhabitants to stay exactly as it had been in his memory. A place he'd once been happy.

"Good day to you, Mr. Jasper," Toby said.

Mr. Jasper nodded once. He then walked away, up the stairs and into his house, closing the door behind him.

He'd once smiled at Toby when he saw him, and spent time

teaching him things, like when was the best time to plant vegetables. Now, they were strangers, and from that greeting, he guessed his refusal to fulfil his family's obligations to the village of Bidham had left a foul taste in the mouths of many.

Stomping on the kernel of guilt, Toby walked on.

The Bodkin sisters were the next house, and both seated on their front porch. Toby had thought at least one if not both would have passed by now, but there they were watching him approach. They stared at him, nodded, and then rose too, and went inside. There would be no thick wedge of bread slathered in jam for the young lord and his brother today.

What had he expected? He'd refused to frequent the businesses in the village, or open the annual fair, which a Viscount Corbyn had always done since its inception. So wrapped up in his own hell, he'd given no thought to those he was hurting.

Like her.

He continued to walk, stomping down the guilt and pain, looking at houses, naming the owners in his head, and wondering if they were still living there, while he struggled to come to the understanding that the people who had embraced the young heir once, now ignored him.

As he walked, Toby recalled his butler's words. *Something isn't right, my lord. There's something sinister at foot in Bidham.* He felt the change. There was no longer happiness here. He could hear no one laughing or people talking together on the street.

"Am I seeing things?"

He turned at the words, sure they'd been spoken to someone else, and saw her sitting there. Miss Ainsley had been the Corbyn boys' nanny for many years until Toby had gone away to school. She'd seemed old when she'd joined the staff.

"Harry," he said, crossing to where she sat on a wooden bench outside the home her family had owned for as long as Toby could remember. "At least someone is speaking to me."

"Did you expect different?" she asked. "You turned your back on everyone in this village, and they relied on your patronage.

The Corbyn family has been linked to Bidham for many years."

"My mother has not come here either?" Toby had never asked her, and she'd not spoken of the village since the day she'd begged him to do his duty as Lord Corbyn, and he'd refused.

"She has not." Harry's face was worn like the pages of an overused book. But the woman who had been his first love was still there in the green eyes and lovely smile.

Toby and Mathew had worshipped her because she'd given them everything their parents hadn't. It had been Miss Harris who had really shown the brothers how to love. How to laugh and be happy. She'd also taught them that because they were rich, titled and in her words, "one day would be more handsome than was good for anyone," they also had to be humble.

"Your father passed the year before you returned, and since then, no Corbyn has entered Bidham until today."

"What of the Talbots? Surely a duke and duchess are an adequate replacement?" Toby asked, battling his shame.

"It is the Corbyns who are linked here, my lord, not the Talbots. For all, they have been constant visitors to the village," Harry said in a sad voice.

He looked across the street and saw the curtains in the Taylor house twitch. Toby was being watched.

"Why are you back here now, my lord?"

She'd always asked whatever question was in her head. Regardless of the fact he ranked far higher than her on the social ladder his peers savored so much.

"How are you, Harry?" he said, instead of giving her the reason.

"I'm well, because you make sure of it by sending me money, which I've told you I don't need."

"Give it away then," Toby said, wondering how he felt so comfortable with this woman, even here in Bidham. There were only two people in his life who usually laid claim to that.

She turned in her seat then and looked at him, which meant he had to look at her. Her eyes ran over his face, and then a soft hand patted his cheek.

"I am as well as can be expected, considering," she said, but her voice had dropped to almost a whisper.

"Considering?"

"You'll not want to ask me any more on that," she added.

"Harry—"

"Have you been to the cemetery, my lord?"

Toby nodded. It was the first place he went to when he came back. He visited his father's grave, and then, for the first time since his death, he sat beside his brother's for hours.

"Let him lie now, my lord. Find your peace, as he has his. You will never be happy until you do that." She studied him. "But I suspected there was more than just your brother's death haunting you when you returned from school," Harry added. "But as you sent me away, along with everyone else you cared about, I did not know what."

He hadn't spoken about that time in his life with anyone, and had no wish to start now. Regaining his feet because he didn't want to discuss this further, Toby prepared to leave. Fingers on his arm stopped him.

"Make your peace with her and your brother's death, and leave the past there," Harry said.

He didn't respond, just bent to kiss her soft cheek. "Take care, Harry."

"One more thing, my lord."

He looked down at her again.

"There's evil about. Have a care," Harry whispered.

"Evil?"

She looked left, and then right. "I can't say more."

"Is someone threatening you, Harry?" He would not stand for that.

"Not me, but us," she whispered. "It will take someone brave to fix it." Her eyes held his steady now. "Someone who has known evil to root it out. You are brave, Lord Corbyn; never forget that."

Toby stared at her for long seconds as the hair on the back of his neck rose. She then pulled herself upright using his arm and walked away without a backward glance. Opening her front door, she closed it softly behind her.

What the hell is going on here?

Chapter Two

TOBY FELT EYES on him as he walked, but no one approached. The cobbled road opened to face the sea. To the right and left were little cottages and small gardens with an abundance of flowers. They soon gave way to shops as he walked down the road. A sign caught his eye.

He'd never entered the Gill, and it was a whim that made him do so now. Besides, he could do with a shot of something to dislodge the lump in his throat after seeing Harry. Opening the scarred wooden door, he stepped off the cobbles and into the dark interior of the tavern.

It was early afternoon, and the place had a few patrons, all of whom looked at him as he entered, and then just as quickly away. He recognized some, but others were strangers. As a boy he'd peeked in the mullioned windows, but never entered. The scent of wood smoke and alcohol hit him as he made his way to the bar.

"Good day to you, my lord," the large man behind it said solemnly.

Toby studied him, and the recognition came as he saw a scar just under his right eye. He'd received that one day from his sister, who was fighting him with a branch.

"Liam?"

He nodded. "What would you like, my lord?" The words were cool and had every right to be. What bothered Toby was that it burned deep in his chest. Since when had he cared what people thought about him? He'd hardened himself to that long ago, and yet there was no doubting he was feeling something for how he'd treated the people of Bidham. *Regret?*

"Do you work here now?"

"I own it," Liam corrected. Once, he'd been a skinny boy, all elbows and knees, who liked to get Toby into trouble. The nobleman's son had been a prime target for the village kids, but Toby had been up to the task, and soon won their respect. He and Mathew had played here often before Toby had been sent away to school.

"Congratulations," Toby said.

The man nodded, but his face remained emotionless.

"How can I help you, Lord Corbyn? Seeing as you've not stepped foot in Bidham for many years."

"I thought it was time," Toby said, and the words sounded lame to his ears. "I'd also like a whiskey, please."

While Liam filled his order, Toby let more memories of his childhood spent here come and go. He'd been innocent then, and unaware of the hell that had been about to descend upon him.

"Will there be anything else, Lord Corbyn?" Liam asked after lowering a glass to the bar before Toby.

"No, thank you," he said, picking it up and taking a sip. The liquid slid down his throat. "This is excellent," Toby added, looking at Liam.

His old friend had no wish to speak to him, but he owned the local tavern, and chances were he knew exactly what was going on in his village, so he was a good place to start. First, he had to soften him up a little. Toby was usually excellent at getting people to talk. "Can I purchase some of this whiskey from you?"

Had he not been looking at Liam, he wouldn't have seen his eyes shoot to the left, but he did. Toby resisted the urge to glance over his shoulder and see who he was looking at.

"I'm unsure who the supplier is."

Which was odd. How could he order more if he didn't even

know who he'd bought it from in the first place?

"So, this is not your usual supply of whiskey?" Toby lifted his glass.

Liam looked nervous now.

"No, it's not."

"Can I ask you a question, Liam?" Toby leaned closer as he lowered his voice.

The man nodded, but his eyes shot behind Toby again.

"Is everything all right in Bidham?"

If he'd asked the man to dance with him, the shock would have been the same. Liam reared back, eyes wide.

"Not sure why you would ask such a thing, my lord, seeing as you've not cared about us for years."

"I understand that, but—"

"Everything is as it was in Bidham since you last visited, many years ago." Liam cut off Toby's words.

"I've just heard a few rumors—"

"Rumors?" This time it was Liam who leaned in closer so only Toby could hear his words. "Not sure why you would. Everything is well here, my lord. You can leave again with the knowledge we need nothing from you and your family, Lord Corbyn."

He was panicking, Toby was sure of it.

"If there is ever any need for me, you've only to send word and I will come," Toby said.

"I won't have need of you," Liam said quickly. "It's best you just leave now, my lord."

Toby drank the last of the liquid in his glass and lowered it to the bar gently. "Good day to you, Liam."

"Lord Corbyn." Liam nodded.

Turning, he saw a table to his right. Seated there were two men. Both looked at him. Toby nodded and left the Gill. Who were they, and had he been imagining that Liam was nervous around them?

Once he was back on the street, he studied the scene before

him. Where were the children? He saw none running about the place shrieking. Nor people milling or laughing. His father used to say Bidham villagers were the jolliest he'd ever met, yet not today.

Why did I leave it so long to come back here? Toby had no answer for that, other than he'd wanted to shut out his past. He'd drawn a line between before he'd left to live in Blackwood House, and after.

He shouldn't have come here. It was opening him up and making him feel. Looking around, he thought about leaving, but then what did that say about him? Nothing good, that was for sure.

Toby went into the blacksmith's next. Heat from the forge slapped him in the face as he searched for whoever was running it. He found a man seated on a three-legged stool.

"Good day to you, sir."

The man lowered the file he held, and rose to his full height, which was a few inches above Toby's.

"My lord," the man bowed.

"Good Lord, Mr. Bentley?"

"Indeed, it is me, my lord," the man said in a solemn voice. From memory, he'd rarely smiled but had been kindhearted. "Is there anything I can help you with, my lord?"

"Just reacquainting myself with Bidham, Mr. Bentley. How have things been?"

The man rocked back on his heels, still clutching the file in one hand. "Well now, Lord Corbyn, it's been a good many years since you were here, and much has changed."

More guilt. "I shall make sure to return often then," Toby said.

The man looked from left to right, and then directly at Toby. "We'd be grateful, as things are not as they were, my lord."

"What has happened, Mr. Bentley?"

He clamped his lips together, looked right and left again, then shook his head, which told Toby precisely nothing. But he knew he would learn no more here today.

Toby left the blacksmith's. He got nothing from the grocers and only hostile stares from the apothecary, so he decided it was time to visit Potter's bakery. Some food may sweeten his mood, although he very much doubted it. In fact, he couldn't rule out someone putting something in it at this stage.

Moving to one side, he watched a cart roll toward him. The man who drove it looked at Toby, touching the brim of his hat. The eyes beneath then widened in shock… or was that horror? He searched his memory for the name to go with that face but couldn't find one. The cart rolled by. Looking at the back of it, he saw a cover tied over what was beneath. Barrels was his guess by the shape of them. Toby wondered what was inside?

Shaking his head for no other reason than he felt a need to, he walked on as another memory slid into his head.

He'd been seven when his father had given him some money to buy a treat for him and Mathew. They'd run down to the bakery, eager to get a wedge of warm gingerbread. A group of children had been outside. Four boys and two girls. The boys were teasing a girl about how ugly she was. She was crying. The other girl had stepped in front of her, drawn back her fist and punched one boy hard in the nose.

Toby felt a smile tug his lips at the memory. The boy's rage had him charging at her. Toby had stopped the boy and demanded he apologize. It was the first day of his friendship with Liberty. A friendship born of two children from the same world of privilege.

Looking to the bakery, he watched two women walk out the door laughing, and he suddenly couldn't move.

Her.

Lady Liberty Talbot was with her maid, Helen, who had been the girl the boy had been teasing that day. Toby watched as she pushed her glasses up her nose. *When had Liberty started wearing eyeglasses?* She certainly hadn't when he'd seen her in society. As if sensing him, her head turned, and their eyes locked on each other.

Liberty was a duke's daughter, and she'd once been his best friend. The shock of seeing her had him stopping right there in the middle of the narrow street, his eyes taking her in.

Dressed in soft mint, over which she wore an emerald velvet pelisse, she was every inch a lady now. Her bonnet was matching, the ribbon tied in a bow to one side. Under that would be hair the color of burnished copper. Hair she'd always passionately disliked. He couldn't read the expression in her cool glacier-blue eyes, but knew it would be empty.

After Toby had walked away from their friendship, he'd not seen her again until she'd entered society, many years after she should have. He'd wondered what stopped her from coming to London when she came of age to do so, but had not asked after her. Toby had ensured he had no rights to this woman ever again.

This was her third season, with no engagement forthcoming. He wasn't sure why, as the girl he'd known had a sharp wit and intellect. She'd drawn people to her, and he'd been one of them until leaving to attend school.

Once, Liberty had been his best friend, and someone he'd believed would always be in his life. Now they were strangers.

He'd watched her from afar and this Liberty was nothing like the hoyden he'd known. Toby knew age had to have changed her like him, but she'd seemed almost a different person. He knew why he was now like he was, but not her, and hated that she may have suffered as he had.

They'd not spoken, just a nod occasionally, but for the most, they'd avoided each other.

Toby watched as she said something to her maid, and then they were walking toward him, which was the only way out of the village. Reaching him, both women dropped into a curtsey.

"Lord Corbyn." Liberty's voice was so cold it was amazing he didn't turn into an ice sculpture.

"Lady Liberty, Helen," Toby said, bowing. "I hope you are well?"

A flash of pain, which she quickly masked, accompanied the

surprise on her face.

"I am, thank you." There was a tense silence before she added, "I'm sure the villagers are as shocked as I to see you here, my lord."

Before Toby could answer, she'd walked on leaving him feeling raw and exposed. He'd heard the anger in her words, and they were justified. He resisted the urge to watch her walk away from him.

Toby kept his expression blank and entered the bakery to purchase a wedge of gingerbread from a young woman he didn't know, thankfully, so there was no censuring look accompanying his purchase. He then walked slowly back up the street, eating it as he took in everything around him. Of Liberty, there was no sign.

Reaching his carriage, he climbed inside and began the long journey back to London, knowing he now had many hours to think about seeing her again, and the flash of pain on her face.

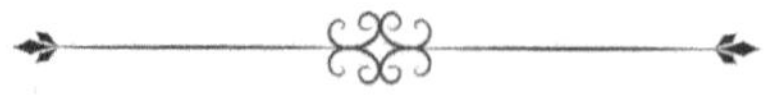

CHAPTER THREE

LIBERTY KEPT WALKING with her head high, eyes focused on the road ahead. Beside her, her maid did the same. To anyone watching, they were just two women strolling. Not that anyone was watching. Something felt wrong here. Usually it was a bustling hub of activity. Even for a small village there was someone waving or calling out, but not today.

Liberty held two pieces of gingerbread in a gloved hand, but the thought of eating them now made her feel ill. *Damn you, Tobias Corbyn.* She hated when he suddenly appeared like that. Usually, she could walk the other way, or at least force a fake smile onto her lips, which was expected in society. But the shock of seeing him here had reduced her to a mute statue for long seconds.

Why was he in Bidham after all this time?

Lord Corbyn was a rake who seemed to relish in shocking people. He'd also once been her best friend.

"Lady Liberty, how wonderful to see you, and here of all places."

"Lord Michael," Liberty said surprised to find this man at the entrance to the village of Bidham. "My father's estate is nearby, my lord, and what is your reason for being here?"

His smile was genuine. They'd had many conversations on a variety of topics while dancing. The man was always interesting to chat with, and unlike other men, actually thought she was capable of intelligent conversation.

"Of course, I had quite forgotten you live nearby. I am here visiting Mr. Landon. We hoped to see the Great Comet through his telescope."

"I'm sure it was spectacular," Liberty said, and meant it. She'd always wanted to see the night sky through a telescope.

"Unfortunately, we could not see it due to cloud cover. But I have not given up hope and will be returning until I do."

Not overly tall, the man had a smile that reached all corners of his face, and made his eyes twinkle. Unassuming, he was not flamboyant in his dress like many.

"Well, good day to you, my lord. We are to return to London now."

"Good day, and I will look forward to our next dance. But right now, I shall get a slice of the gingerbread you are carrying, as it smells delicious."

"Indeed it is, and I highly recommend it."

He raised a hand and walked toward the village.

Thankfully, there were no further sightings of the perfidious Lord Corbyn as Liberty and Helen made their way to the carriage. She was not looking forward to the hours cooped up inside, and yet her family insisted she return to London today.

They had left two days ago as her parents had an important dinner they had to attend, and as she'd been suffering from a stomach upset, it was decided that Liberty recover completely first. So, today, accompanied by Helen, a footman, and driver, she would start the day long return journey to London.

Liberty, however, had no wish to reenter the horrid and treacherous waters of society, which she passionately disliked, and had for the three years she'd been forced to endure them. At eighteen, just before she was to enter society, Liberty had a horse-riding accident. It had taken her three years before she was ready to contemplate society. By then she'd been twenty-one, and too old to be a debutante.

Her mother had, of course, insisted, never giving up hope

that one day her daughter would wed, and wed well. That, plus by some odd anomaly, become a diamond in society at age twenty-one. What Liberty had been was uncomfortable and a failure. She'd coped by being scrupulously polite and aloof.

"He's a very handsome man," Helen, her maid, said dragging her from her thoughts. Seated across from Liberty, she sat, as she would for the entire journey. Upright, hands folded neatly in her lap, looking immaculate. Unlike Liberty, who hated sitting still for long periods because the muscles in her bad leg seized up.

"Lord Michael?"

"Lord Corbyn," her childhood friend said. "He's a handsome man, my lady."

"I do wish you would call me Liberty in private."

"Absolutely not. If I started that I may slip up while we are in public." Helen shook her head. She was more of a stickler for society rules than Liberty.

"It was lovely to see him back in Bidham," Helen said with a tenacity Liberty usually admired.

"I'm not sure why. The man is no longer a friend."

Helen frowned. "I still believe there was more to what he did, turning from you. Something wasn't right about that."

Liberty dismissed the words. She's spent far too many hours wondering what she'd done to turn Tobias from her.

"I don't want to discuss him, as he no longer plays any part in our lives. But I do want to discuss Bidham. Mrs. Dibby was right in what she said to me, Helen. All is not well, and we both felt it. Have your family said anything?"

"They live just outside, but my youngest sister Betty did say that one of her friends who lives in the village is not allowing her children out after dark anymore."

"That's odd, because Bidham has always been a happy safe place for children." Liberty looked out the window as the carriage drew close to the cliffs. Gulls swooped and squawked, and she had walked every inch of those paths as a girl, and usually with Lord Tobias Corbyn. *Don't think about him.*

Seeing him here had dredged up all the hurt again, because the last time they'd been together outside Potter's bakery, they'd been friends.

"I felt it, Helen. Bidham locals are some of the happiest people I know, but they weren't today. If I had to give one word for what I felt, it would be fear. But no one is talking."

Helen added, "Because I saw old Mr. Toms, and he loves a good gossip, but he wouldn't stop and speak to me. Something isn't right I tell you."

"We need to find out what. I'm going to have a talk to my father about it and see if he will do some investigating," Liberty said.

They chatted a while longer, and then Helen fell asleep, as she was wont to do when in a carriage. It was the only time she wasn't immaculate. Her mouth fell open, and she snored. It was at these moments that Liberty wished she could draw. But she soon felt her own eyes closing. She'd not slept well last night because she knew today she must return to London.

Liberty woke as she fell sideways. Pushing herself upright, she could feel the carriage gaining speed.

"What's going on?" Helen asked, her voice thick with sleep.

"I don't know." Wrestling the window down, Liberty looked out and quickly pulled her head back in as a bullet whistled past her ear.

"I believe we are about to be robbed, Helen," Liberty said with a calm she was far from feeling.

"Oh dear," was her maid's response.

As the carriage slowed, Liberty felt about under the seat for her father's rifle, that he always kept there.

"You'll make matters worse with that," Helen said.

"Or, I'll shoot one of them and scare them away."

Liberty went to the window just as a rider pulled alongside. She pointed the rifle at him and fired. The man yelled, clutching his arm.

Another shot rang out, and the carriage slowed, and then

lurched sideways suddenly. Liberty fell into the door. It flew open and her out of it. She hit the ground hard, her head connecting with something. Stunned and breathless, she lay there as mayhem broke out around her. She heard the thunder of hooves, and then Helen arriving, turning the air blue with her curses.

"My lady!"

"Th-the men?" Liberty wheezed out.

"Gone. Jasper shot one of them, and you the other. They fled. Are you all right?"

"Yes," she rasped, not feeling all right at all, but not wanting to scare her maid. "Can you see my glasses."

Helen dropped to a crouch and searched. "Here." She handed them to Liberty.

"My lady, are you well?" Jasper, their footman, appeared to look down at her. "We scared those rogues away."

"Excellent. I just need to sit up now," Liberty said not liking the idea of moving, but knowing she had to do so, as she could not sleep here for the remainder of her life, no matter how appealing that thought was right now.

Hands eased her upright, and her vision blurred.

"She's bleeding!"

"I'd be excessively grateful to you if you stopped shrieking, Helen," Liberty gritted out. "I am alive and well, as you see. There is no need for hysterics."

"No need! You could have been killed falling from the carriage like that," her maid said. "And there's your body still not right from your accident."

"My body is right," Liberty said, and then hissed when she moved.

"What if she's broken a limb!"

Helen was usually the epitome of calm and no nonsense, unless someone was hurt; then she fell apart completely. Edward, Liberty's brother, had once fallen down some stairs and broken his arm. Helen had fainted.

"Blood," Helen whispered.

Lifting her hand, Liberty's white glove came away red after touching the side of her head. "It is a scratch and nothing more. Go to the carriage and find something to blot it with," she said with far more strength than she was feeling.

"Are you really all right, my lady?" Jasper asked when Helen had gone.

"Hurts like the devil, Jasper, but I will live. I would, however, like to lean against the trunk of that tree for a bit until I no longer see two of you."

Between them, they got her to the tree.

"I have a blanket, and the flask your father always keeps in the carriage," Helen said returning.

Liberty tugged off her gloves and took the flask.

"How is the carriage?" Liberty asked.

"Dudley didn't see the large rock, and unfortunately one wheel rolled over it, so we'll need to get it fixed before we go anywhere," Jasper said.

"What will we do?" Helen whispered, sounding like the heroine in a book.

"I'll unhitch a horse and ride to the Thorny Thistle, which is not far. I'll get help and back here as soon as I can, my lady."

"Wait. I hear a carriage," Helen said clutching her hands to her chest. "They could be coming back!"

"They were on horseback. It is a carriage that approaches; calm down," Liberty gritted out. "Get me upright at once." Her head felt light and her body odd, but she was a duke's daughter, and she would be damned if whoever approached found her seated on the ground. There was also the fact that after the pain she'd suffered already in her lifetime, this was manageable.

"My lady, you should—"

"Now, Jasper."

She knew all sorts of silent signals were firing back and forth between her maid and footman, but she didn't care. Grabbing the hands Jasper held out, she let him pull her up, and bit back the moan of pain that felt like an axe blow to the back of her head.

"Steady," Helen said as she listed sideways.

"I'm all right. Get my bonnet please, Helen."

"Lady Liberty—"

"At once."

"We've just been nearly robbed, and you are hurt. Please stay seated, my lady," Jasper pleaded.

"I want to stand, thank you," she said in a tight voice.

Her maid hurried to the carriage and returned with her bonnet. Liberty put it gently on her head, and with hands that she noted shook, tied the ribbons.

Relieved when a carriage appeared Liberty released the breath she'd been holding. When the vehicle had stopped, the door opened, and her relief turned to despair as the man stepped down.

CHAPTER FOUR

VISITING BIDHAM AND seeing Liberty there, in the place they'd once been friends, had unsettled him, and it had been a long time since he'd allowed anything to do that. He'd forced down any emotion that made him weak.

Toby had seen Liberty many times in London since she entered society. He'd been curious as to why she had not done so until the age of twenty-one, but he no longer had the right to ask.

They'd avoided each other for three seasons, but he'd watched her.

His childhood friend, like him, had changed. The girl who had laughed freely was now serious and reserved. He rarely saw her smile or talk in groups of young ladies like others. No, Liberty had a single friend, Miss Alice Hamner.

She'd never spoken to Toby, nor he her. Not once had the situation arisen where there was a need to interact, other than a curt nod, or muttered, "my lady," on his part. Toby told himself he was happy with that. Had to be happy with that, as this was the path he'd chosen, and could not afford to deviate from. This is how he stayed safe.

But sometimes, when she slid under his guard, even now, years after he'd turned from her, Toby remembered things. Times they'd spent together all those years ago, and conversations they'd shared. Promises they'd made for the future. It was then he distracted himself, usually with his business interests.

When his father died leaving the Corbyn finances in excellent health, Toby knew it was up to him to ensure that continued. With money came control and safety, and he needed those in his life.

He'd increased his portfolio with two mills and a factory, but nothing ever completely satisfied him, and he always wanted more. Sometimes he wondered if one day his demons would end him. That he'd lie in his bed and let the past he'd fought to rise above consume him, descending Toby into madness. If he were honest, it would be a relief.

It was never good for him to spend too much time alone with his thoughts, but as the dream about his father had spurred him on, he'd gone to Hawthorne and now Bidham, many years too late. But it was a start.

Will I go back there? The answer had to be yes until he knew what was going on in the village. He'd ignored it for too long.

Looking out the window, Toby watched the flashes of light and dark as they followed the tree line in the fading afternoon sun. Deep in thought it took him a minute to realize the carriage was slowing and then it came to a complete halt.

Lifting the hatch above his head, he said, "What's wrong, Rory?"

"A carriage appears to have broken down, my lord."

Toby sighed. He couldn't very well drive around it, even if he wanted to. So he opened the door and stepped down. He saw a carriage listing slightly to the left ahead of him. Walking toward it, he then saw the people. Toby focused on the women in the middle of the group of three.

"Hello," he said when nothing else came to mind.

"Go on your way, my lord," Lady Liberty said, glaring at him through her round eyeglasses. "My footman is about to ride for help. We have no wish to hold you up."

Did her voice sound shaky?

Toby focused on the woman who had once climbed trees and run endlessly over the hills and valleys of their families' estates with him. She was pale, and her face pinched as if in pain.

"How can I be of assistance, Lady Liberty?" Toby asked, staying where he was and ignoring her order, because that's exactly what it had been, even if the delivery was weak.

"I want no assistance from you, Lord Corbyn," she said slowly.

"And yet your carriage wheel is broken, and I am here ready to help, as I fear it will start raining soon, and the air is cool. So perhaps we could relocate to the next inn and wait there until your carriage is repaired?" He kept his voice calm and even. In truth, he would like to obey her and leave, as any time spent with this woman was as comfortable as dancing in stinging nettles because of their history. But if there were one thing he excelled at, it was hiding his thoughts.

"No," she said. Just the one word as she started toward her carriage, believing that was the end of the matter. Her steps appeared slow and unsteady.

He'd noted that about her too. The agile and elegant girl he'd known wasn't that anymore. She barely danced, and when she did, Toby could tell she wasn't comfortable.

"No?"

"No, thank you," she added.

Toby watched as she stumbled and was steadied by her maid.

"Liberty—" Before he finished his sentence she appeared to sway, and then was falling.

Her maid shrieked. Both the footman and Toby ran, but it was he who caught her just before she hit the ground. Toby cradled her limp body as he made his way to his carriage in long strides.

"What's going on, Helen?" Toby demanded as ice sluiced through his veins, fear for someone he'd long since thought he'd stopped caring for.

"Men tried to rob us. Lady Liberty shot one, and Jasper another, but when the wheel broke, she fell into the door, and it opened and threw her out."

He couldn't remember when he last felt the panic that was gripping him. Liberty's hands hung limp at her sides, and her head lay against his chest. The dark crescents of her lashes were a stark contrast against her pale cheeks.

Not dead.

"She hit her head but made me and Jasper help her upright when she heard your carriage. She's a stubborn one, and even had me fetch her bonnet," Helen added.

Toby remembered Liberty Talbot's stubbornness all too well.

"My lord?"

"I will let you know when to move, Rory," he told his driver, who was now standing looking worried. "For now, stay seated," he said to his driver. "Be alert in case those who tried to rob Lady Liberty return."

Climbing inside his carriage, he lowered Liberty onto the seat. Taking the blanket Helen handed him, he bundled it into a pillow and then eased her head onto it. He took off her eyeglasses next and slid them into his pocket. Toby then tugged the satin bow open and removed her bonnet.

"Liberty," he rasped, bending over her. "Wake up now." Toby hadn't been this close to her in a long time. His eyes went to the ridge of a scar beneath her chin. How had she gotten that? It hadn't been there when he knew her. Before he could stop himself, he ran a finger down one pale cheek. So soft.

"Open your eyes, Liberty." Toby put more force into his words.

Her lashes fluttered open, and those pretty blue eyes looked up at him, dazed and confused.

"How do you feel?"

She clenched her eyes shut and opened them again.

"Liberty, how do you feel?" he persisted.

"What happened?" she rasped.

"You fainted."

"I did not." He wanted to snort at her words as they sounded more like the old Liberty he'd known.

"You certainly did, and I caught you," Toby said.

She pushed at his shoulder, and he eased back slightly. Liberty then struggled to rise. Toby held her down with a hand.

"Release me," she hissed.

"No, because if you faint again, then I'll have to catch you."

"I don't faint," she whispered.

"I beg to differ."

Her lips clamped into a hard line.

"I want to sit up now, Lord Corbyn."

"Very well, but I will help you." Toby slid an arm under her shoulders and sat her upright.

"Thank you."

"Let me look at your head now, Liberty."

"I am Lady Liberty, or my lady," she said slowly as clearly she was in pain, and any movement hurt. "I don't need you to look at my head. Helen can take care of me." She shrank back into the seat to evade the grip he had on her shoulders. When that didn't work, she said, "Unhand me."

Ignoring her, he eased her forward and then used his free hand to part the thick copper locks. Matted with blood, they were stuck to her head, and there were so many pins holding the thick mass of curls in place, he wasn't sure how her head didn't ache. Toby began to ease them out.

"Ouch," she whispered with no strength. "Stop that. Where is Helen? She can do it."

Ignoring her, he continued until the last one lay on the floor of the carriage where he'd thrown them. Toby then studied the cut. It was deep, but not too long, and still bled sluggishly.

"It needs cleaning and dressing," he said, easing her back onto the seat.

"And I will see that done when we reach the next inn. I'm going to get out of your carriage now, Lord Corbyn."

"No, you're not, because you are too weak to do so."

"You can't—"

"Get in beside your mistress, Helen, while I speak with Lady

Liberty's footman and driver. Do not let her out of this carriage."

"At once, my lord," Helen said, doing as he asked when he'd climbed out.

He shut the door behind the maid and then approached the footman and driver. "I will take one of you to the next inn, and you can organize someone to come and fix that wheel. I will ensure your mistress is safe until you can collect her."

It was decided the driver would stay with the horses and the footman was soon seated up beside Rory, which his driver would not mind, as he loved to talk.

Opening the carriage door again, he stepped into a tense silence.

"Trouble?" He looked at Helen. The maid shook her head.

"Stop berating your maid for doing the right thing, my lady," he then said to Liberty.

"Go to hell," she replied. Then closed her eyes. She was now resting her cheek on the side of the carriage.

They started moving as he took the seat opposite the two women.

Toby watched Liberty and saw every wince or exhale as they hit a bump in the road, but she didn't make a noise. That too was different. Liberty had been loud and once spoke every thought that came into her head. She'd laughed louder than anyone he knew.

Had he played a part in changing the girl into the woman before him today?

Toby let his eyes run over her.

Her hair was the color of sunset and had once been the bane of her existence because no one else had locks like it. He'd heard men call her beautiful, in a cool, aloof way, but none so far had captured her hand. Hers was a face that made you look again. Want to study the soft arc of her brows and long dark lashes. See the flashes of emotion in her blue eyes. Her top lip was slightly fuller than the bottom, and he wondered if any man had kissed it... her. The bolt of anger told him not to think about that or her too much again.

Her eyes opened suddenly and caught him staring. She then squinted as if to bring him into focus.

"Where are my eyeglasses, Helen?"

"Please," Toby said, taking them from his pocket and handing them to her.

"Why are you doing this?"

"Helping you?" She nodded at his words. "Because I was there, and you needed my help."

"We loathe each other, and I would have been fine waiting in my carriage, as you very well know, Lord Corbyn."

"I don't loathe you," Toby said slowly, knowing that was the impression he'd left her with many years ago.

Her laugh held no humor. "Of course you don't, which is why you told me you never wanted to see me again."

He saw it then, the hurt in her eyes he'd inflicted all those years ago with his cruel words. Helen shifted in her seat, clearly uncomfortable with their conversation.

"Liberty—"

"Lady Liberty," she said, raising her chin. "We are not informal, you and I, and never will be again. For three years we have avoided each other. It is my hope that continues."

He didn't speak, just kept his eyes on her face.

"Leave when we reach our destination, my lord, as we have nothing further to say to each other," she added, dismissing him.

No one dismissed Toby. He'd earned respect in the business world, and in society no one dared speak to him in such a way. *Only her,* he thought. She'd once challenged him constantly, especially when she thought he was being overbearing.

"I am not leaving you in this condition," Toby said in a cold, hard voice.

"Why? Don't try to tell me you care," she scoffed, which held no strength as her cheek was still resting on the side of his carriage.

"It is done, and I will see you to the next inn."

She looked at him then. Stared into his eyes, and he suddenly felt stripped bare. As if she could read everything he kept locked away inside him. All the dark, angry scars and pain.

"Why?" she whispered. "I know who you've become, and that you care nothing for me or anyone."

"What have I become?" He mocked her, when deep inside he was reeling from her words. Reeling from being this close to Liberty again.

"A womanizing rake and a wastrel." The words had no strength, but each one sliced through him with the accuracy of a knife.

"And you," he gritted out, striking back at her. "What have you become?"

"Why don't you tell me?" Her lip curled, enraging him further.

Toby fought for control. No one slid under his guard, ever. But she had.

"I see a cold and emotionless woman as yet unwed," he said, deliberately cutting. The words were out of his mouth before he could stop them, and like her, he'd spoken them to inflict pain. More pain on someone who didn't deserve it from him.

They glared at each other, and then he watched the single tear spill over her eyelid, and trail down her cheek.

"Liberty," Toby rasped, completely undone by the sight. "I'm sorry. I should not have—"

"I hate you." The words were whispered, but he heard them, and then she closed her eyes again, and he had to sit there and watch that tear trail down her cheek.

CHAPTER FIVE

"You can come inside now, Lady Liberty," Lord Corbyn said from the doorway of the carriage. "The Thorny Thistle is busy, but the proprietor is willing to accommodate a duke's daughter and a viscount."

"How lucky that you could throw about your title," Liberty muttered, rising from her seat.

There was so much anger and tension between them after the hateful words they'd thrown at each other. Her head hurt, and she had the ridiculous urge to lower it into her hands and weep more foolish tears.

"Take my hand," he said. "You are unsteady on your feet, and I do not want you to faint again."

Don't show him what you are feeling. You are strong now, Liberty.

She looked at the large hand gloved in tan leather with loathing.

"I don't need your help to get out. Step aside, if you please."

His sigh was loud enough to be heard inside the inn.

"I have no wish for you to fall on your face and injure yourself further," he said, his calm, unfeeling facade firmly back in place.

Liberty had glimpsed a flash of pain in his brown eyes, in the carriage. It had gone so fast she'd thought she'd imagined it. This man cared for no one.

"Now, my lady. I will carry you in my arms again if you do

not take my hand." He beckoned her with his fingers.

This was her absolute nightmare. Being this close to a man who had hurt her, like Tobias had. Yes, it had been years ago, but Liberty remembered it as if it were yesterday. At the time, it had broken her, and then made her strong, and with strength, she'd vowed never to forgive him.

"Come, you are tired and hurting. Inside is warmth and food, Lady Liberty."

She took his hand as there was no other option and allowed him to help her down. She then dropped it as if it were a burning coal. Liberty started walking to the inn and the welcoming lights and warmth it would provide.

A large hand settled on her back. She didn't have the energy to tell him to remove it, plus she couldn't discount completely that she wouldn't fall on her face like he'd suggested. For now, Liberty would tolerate his presence, but soon he would be gone again.

Once inside, they were ushered into a small parlor. She nearly wept when she saw the large comfortable chair before the fire. He nudged her toward it and then she was sinking onto the blissfully soft cushion.

"Excuse me while I see to refreshments," she heard Lord Corbyn say, and then the door closed behind him.

Liberty worked hard on unclenching her muscles, as that was not helping the pain in her body. This nightmare would be over soon, and he would once again be a stranger in her life.

"It is kind of Lord Corbyn to come to your aid, my lady," Helen said from behind her.

"Helen, would you find a cool cloth for my head, please?" Liberty said instead of addressing what she'd just said.

"Of course, my lady."

Liberty had told no one exactly what happened that day on Tobias's doorstep many years ago, but they knew something had, no matter how hard she'd fought not to show her pain.

Resting her head on the side of the chair after her maid left, she closed her eyes and tried to shut out thoughts of the man who had once been her best friend. Her head hurt, and her body ached. She just wanted to reach London and sleep for two days, not deal with him when she felt unarmed to do so.

"I have tea and brandy," a deep voice said.

"Brandy, please," Liberty said, opening her eyes. Exhaustion rolled over her, but she'd experienced that, and pain so fierce you wondered if it would kill you, before. So this was nothing by comparison.

She'd always considered herself brave, but two life events had truly tested that belief. The day Tobias told her he no longer wanted to be her friend, and when she'd fallen from her horse and broken parts of her that had never really healed.

Tobias held out a glass, and she took it. He then dragged a chair closer, so he was soon sitting in her line of sight. Liberty closed her eyes again, cradling the glass in her hands, having no wish to look at him.

"I need to discuss something with you, Lady Liberty. I would be grateful if you could put aside anything that lay between us until I have done so."

"You say that like it is my fault." This man had hurt her, and she'd never forgive him for that.

"I know where the fault lies, my lady." His eyes held hers, but she could read nothing in their dark depths.

She nodded for him to continue.

"Something is not right in Bidham."

"In what way?" She'd felt the same but wanted to hear his thoughts on the matter before acknowledging that.

"My butler told me there was something sinister afoot in Bidham. I then talked to Harry when I arrived in the village, and she too said, 'there's evil about, have a care.'"

"I have heard rumors," Liberty said. "Helen also."

"I could get no information when I was there today—"

"As no one would speak to you?" Liberty cut him off. She wanted to hurt him. To strike out and inflict pain as he had on her.

It was years ago, Liberty. You should have moved on by now.

"Yes." His eyes held hers steady.

When the pain and anger over what Tobias said to her had eased, Liberty wondered why he'd said what he had. What prompted the boy, her friend, who loved the village of Bidham, to cut her and them from his life? She'd never found the courage to ask him, and then it was too late, so she'd held onto her anger instead.

"What have you heard?" he asked her.

Liberty watched him sip his brandy, the muscles in the throat working as he swallowed it down. Many women of society believed him handsome. They twittered and spoke about him behind their hands. She knew their words for the truth.

Tobias had grown into a man that drew eyes. Tall, broad shouldered, with thick brown hair. His face was usually impassive, but when he smiled, he changed completely. Softened, and seemed almost like the boy she'd once known. Liberty had spent far too many hours watching him in ballrooms. Flirting, dancing, and being the man she'd never believed he would be.

"Please, my lady. If there is trouble in Bidham, I want to know."

"I'm not sure why you would now, but as I too believe something is not right, I will tell you what I have learned," Liberty said.

He nodded, his dark intense gaze locked on her.

"Mrs. Dibby came to my father's house last night and said her brother, who lives in Bidham, is behaving oddly. That while she was visiting him, a man knocked at the door. Mrs. Dibby did not overhear everything that was said, but she heard the words, 'you know what will happen if you don't do as we tell you.'"

"Did she get a look at the man?"

"No. When I asked her, she said the conversation felt threatening, so she stayed hidden until he and her brother had left," Liberty said. "When she questioned her sister-in-law about who the man was, the woman had seemed terrified, but she wouldn't speak on the matter."

He sipped from his glass again before speaking.

"I saw Liam in the Gill, and while I understand he had no wish to speak with me, I felt as if he was nervous because of two men who were seated at a table," Tobias said. "When I asked him if everything was all right in Bidham, he said of course, but shot the men another look, as if he'd not wanted them to overhear our conversation."

"I have some water to wash your head," Helen said, returning.

"That can wait until we reach London," Liberty said. "Come and listen to what Lord Corbyn and I are discussing please, Helen."

"I can do both. I won't be cleaning your head with my ears."

Lord Corbyn snorted at Helen's words, and Liberty ignored him. She wanted to feel no familiarity with this man.

Her maid draped a drying cloth over her shoulder as he began to tell Helen what he'd just told Liberty.

"You're a great deal braver than you once were," he said watching.

"She's had reason to be," Helen said.

"What reason?"

"It matters not. The question is: What is to be done to find out what is going on in Bidham?" Liberty said. She wasn't about to discuss her accident with this man.

"I will send someone to ask questions," Lord Corbyn said.

"Strangers will get nothing out of the residents in Bidham," Liberty added.

"I have a man who is excellent at blending in, and also at striking up conversations with strangers. He has ferreted out a lot for me over the years."

She did not ask why he would need such a man, because Liberty told herself she didn't care.

"I would be grateful if you hear anything that you let me know, Lady Liberty."

"As would I," she added.

"Of course." He nodded.

Liberty had a feeling that he was lying and wouldn't come to her at all, but she said nothing further, and allowed Helen to finish cleaning her head.

They then ate a small meal in heavy silence, which even her maid did not try to break. Liberty wished he would leave, and when he had eaten everything on his plate, she said as much.

"As you can see, I am safe, and my carriage wheel is being fixed as we speak. There is no further need for you to stay here any longer, Lord Corbyn."

He studied her for long seconds. "I am not leaving yet. Excuse me, I wish to speak to the innkeeper."

"Thank you," Liberty made herself say as he regained his feet. "For helping me today." She could be gracious. After all, without him she would have been sitting with a sore head on the side of the road for hours.

He turned with a hand on the door and faced her. "You are welcome."

"Well," Helen said when it had closed behind him.

"Well?"

"There was so much tension between you it nearly choked me."

"That was not tension, it was animosity. As you heard on the carriage ride here, we are no longer friends," Liberty said.

"I never understood what happened between you."

"Everyone changes when they grow up," was all Liberty wanted to add to that. She then closed her eyes and slept again.

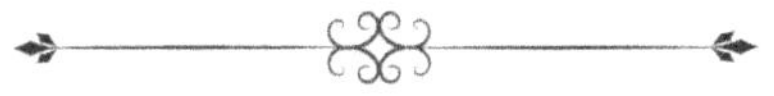

CHAPTER SIX

"I NEED TO return to my family," Liberty said when Toby walked back into the parlor. "My head is steadier, and there is no need—"

"The wheel will not be fixed until the morning, and you are not fit to travel for another four hours to London, my lady," Toby said wishing it were different. Wishing he could put her into her carriage and send her on her way, so he could do the same.

"I have secured rooms for you and Helen, and your driver and footman will have lodgings in the stables. I have also sent word to your family that you are safe, and what has happened."

"How dare you make decisions on my behalf without consulting me," she said, every inch her father's daughter in that moment, even if she looked like a stiff wind would blow her over. "I don't need you looking out for me. I am more than capable of doing that."

"Yes, I can see how strong you are," he drawled. Exhaustion was in every line of her face. "Come, I will show you to your room."

"I will hire a carriage, Lord Corbyn."

"There are none for hire. I asked," he lied.

"Then you leave and I will stay, my lord."

"If I leave now, I will not return until late, and have no wish to rouse my staff from their warm beds. Therefore, I will do so in the morning," Toby said.

She couldn't fight him over that. Liberty was always championing the staff in her father's houses, or had once. He watched as she rubbed her temples.

"I will ask if the proprietor has a powder for your head."

"Thank you, that is unnecessary, as not much will help it, and my medicine is in London."

"Medicine?"

She waved his words away and rose. He steadied her as she wobbled, and that she let him told Toby just how tired she was.

"What if someone were to see us?" Liberty said as they climbed to their rooms.

"I have checked who is here and recognize no one."

She nodded.

"Your reputation is safe, my lady." He'd said the words to reassure her.

She muttered something he didn't hear but Toby left that alone and walked her to the room the innkeeper had shown him earlier. It was small, yet clean, because he'd checked that too.

"I know your things are with the carriage, but a nightgown was found for you to sleep in."

She turned in the doorway to look at him. "Thank you for all of this. I'm not sure considering… well, thank you." She then closed the door in his face.

Considering the bastard you were to me, he finished off her words.

Toby went back down the stairs to the bar and ordered a whiskey. Sleep would not come tonight after the day he'd had, and being this close to Liberty again. Sipping the drink, he let the liquid roll around inside his mouth.

"Where is this whiskey from?" Toby asked after he'd swallowed. "It's good." He knew whiskey and would bet a great deal of money it was the same as the one he'd tasted in the Gill.

"We have a new supplier. Plentiful and a good price, too." The barman tapped his nose. "But I'll not say more."

"Irish or Scottish?" Toby asked after another sip.

The man didn't answer as he was called away, and Toby was left mulling over what he'd learned today in Bidham, which wasn't a great deal, but when you added what Liberty and Helen had said, it was something. He thought about the barrels he'd seen on the back of that cart in the village, and how Liam had been nervous when he'd asked about the whiskey.

"Evening."

Toby nodded to the man who took the stool beside him. Large and menacing were his initial thoughts.

"I overheard you asking about the whiskey," the man then said.

Toby had spent a lot of time in his life watching people, and this man had thug written all over him right down to the sneer on his face. But there was also something familiar about him, he couldn't put his finger on.

"It's very good. I would like to procure some for my private cellars," Toby said taking another sip.

"Don't believe that would be possible, Lord Corbyn."

Studying him more closely, Toby realized then where he'd seen the man before. He'd been in the Gill earlier today, and one of the men Liam had been looking at nervously.

"I am happy to pay, of course. Are you the supplier?" He didn't ask how it was this man knew his name. Everyone in Bidham knew Toby, even if they didn't like him.

"You're best to mind your business, my lord. Safer for everyone."

The words were a threat, and there was no other way to take them.

"Mind my business?" Toby asked, swallowing the last of his whiskey. He'd never taken well to threats, and especially not after his time at Blackwood House, as they'd been constant there.

The man smiled, but it held no humor.

"A word of advice, my lord. Don't meddle in what doesn't concern you."

"I'm a viscount. What is it you think you can do to me, and I'll add why to that? I don't know you, or what it is you allude to, but I know I don't like the threat in your voice, especially as I asked a simple question about the supply of whiskey."

"All is well, my lord?"

Rory, his driver, and Liberty's footman, Jasper, were now standing beside Toby's stool.

"All is well," he said, holding the man's gaze. "Two of your whiskeys for my men, if you please," he said to the barman.

Toby watched two others rise from the table near the bar.

"I've always found that if someone is guilty of something, they are likely to be aggressive for no apparent reason. You were that from the moment you sat next to me, sir, but what I don't know is why?" Toby said.

The man leaned in, and his foul breath washed over Toby. He never moved, just held his gaze.

"My boss doesn't like people asking questions about things that don't concern him."

"You'll want to back away from Lord Corbyn now," Rory said.

The man grinned as he straightened.

"Why do my questions about whiskey in both Bidham and here bother you, sir? Perhaps because you are obtaining it through nefarious means?" The man frowned. "Nefarious means criminal or wicked," he added to annoy him.

"You'll want to be careful how you speak to me." The man's words came out a growl now.

"And you'll want to be careful how you speak to me," Toby repeated. "Where before I wasn't curious about the whiskey and its origins, I am now more than that, and what you should know about me is I can be tenacious when my curiosity is roused."

"Another big word I don't think he's grasped, my lord," Jasper said.

"Tenacious, in this instance, sir, means I will not give up until I have the answers I now seek." Toby said the words as he rose to his feet. "I'm a nobleman with a lot of connections and power. Perhaps you should remember that?"

He saw the moment the man's weight shifted. It was a subtle movement, but Toby was ready when the fist swung his way. He ducked and punched him hard in the jaw.

In seconds, the man's friends and Jasper and Rory were involved in a fight. Toby heard the barman curse, but he had no time to apologize, and he was soon engaged in a wrestling match.

People yelled their encouragement as the men grappled, punched, and tried to beat the other. Toby took a blow to his jaw, and one to the ribs he knew would hurt tomorrow. Throwing a hard right at the man's face, he sent him stumbling backward.

"Enough!" the innkeeper roared, having just arrived.

The man Toby had thrown to the floor regained his feet. He then glared at him, and along with his men, fled outside, and into the night.

"Are you both all right?" Toby wheezed as he looked at Rory and Jasper. They nodded. Locating the innkeeper picking up a chair, he headed for him.

"When those three come to drop off a delivery, there's always trouble," the man said running a hand over his bald head. "I'm right sorry, my lord."

"No need, and I will pay for the damages," Toby said. "Tell me, how long have you been receiving your whiskey from these men, sir?"

"Coming up two years now. Good stuff too, and a good price. Patrick," he waved a hand to where the barman was sweeping up broken glass, "he was the one who contacted the supplier."

After handing the innkeeper some money, he told his men to seek their beds and then climbed the stairs. His face and ribs ached, but at least now it was likely exhaustion would allow him some sleep.

The door to Liberty's room opened as he passed. She stood there in a white nightdress that was too big, with a blanket around her shoulders. Her hair was loose, and she still looked pale and vulnerable. Something inside Toby's chest squeezed, but he ignored it.

"What was all that noise?" She raised the candle she was carrying and studied him. "What happened to your face?"

"Nothing. Go to bed, Liberty."

He walked by her to his room. Opening the door, he closed it behind him. Toby shrugged out of his jacket and waistcoat and then fell into the seat before the fire.

"Hell of a day," he muttered. He could still hardly believe that Liberty was in the room next door. The woman who had not been part of his life since he'd sent her out of it many years ago. A tap on the door had him rising with the hope it was another glass of whiskey and something to put on his throbbing jaw.

"Go back to bed," he said when he saw Liberty standing there. "You can't be seen in the hall in your nightdress, near me."

"A maid brought me some salve. It might help."

"I don't need your help." His well of politeness had run dry. Toby wanted to be alone with his thoughts, not be tended by sweet, innocent Liberty Talbot.

"And yet I had to take yours?" She placed a hand on his shoulder and pushed. Toby didn't move.

"You abhor me, and we're not friends. You're here because you had no other option but to take up my offer of help. So don't make more of this than it is, my lady."

She sighed. "All true, but I had the supplies, and saw you were hurt, so here," she thrust them at him.

Toby had no right to feel that deep ache of need when he looked at her.

"What happened?" she asked as he took what she held out to him.

He struggled with what to do for a few seconds, and then opened his door wider, and waved her inside, as clearly she wasn't about to leave.

"No."

"No?"

"I'm not coming in there. I know your reputation."

He snorted. "In my current state, and because you hate me, I'm thinking you're safe."

She just stood there looking at him out of those cool blue eyes.

"I think that whoever is supplying the whiskey for the Gill is supplying this inn," Toby said. "And if you want to know more than that you have to come inside, because I need to sit down."

Toby walked away from her and fell into the seat he'd recently left. He heard her move, and then she was standing a few feet to his right.

"A man approached me downstairs wanting to know why I was enquiring about the whiskey, and I recognized him as he'd been in the Gill earlier and made Liam uncomfortable. He wasn't happy that I was asking questions and threatened me."

"He threatened a viscount?"

Toby nodded. "He took exception to something I said, and we fought. Jasper and Rory were there too."

"Are they all right?" Concern was clear on her face.

Her worry was for them, not him.

"They are. I think whatever this business with Bidham is, it's dangerous and concerns the whiskey in some way, my lady. I think you should—"

"I know what you think, and I'm not interested." She gripped the blanket tighter. "Bidham is my village too, and I will not shy away from helping the people who live in it, as you have."

He ignored that comment as it was true and instead said, "This is not a game, Lady Liberty."

"Oh, because I thought it was, clearly," she said in a mocking tone, which made him grit his teeth. She'd always been able to annoy him into a response, but he was no longer that boy.

"Anything you hear, you must tell me," Toby said deliberately making his words sound threatening. "Take no risks."

"I am nobody's fool, my lord." She then walked out of his room slowly, closing the door softly behind her.

"When did my life become so complicated?" He knew the answer to that question. This morning, when he'd seen Liberty walk out of that bakery.

Deciding that tomorrow was soon enough to think more about what he'd learned regarding Bidham, Toby stripped off his clothes, washed, and fell into bed. Tomorrow he would reiterate once more that Liberty was to take no risks. For now, he needed sleep, and he would get it with his old friend in the room next door.

He woke six hours later, to be told by Rory that Lady Liberty had left for London as the sun rose. Ignoring the anger he had no right to feel, he was soon following.

CHAPTER SEVEN

A WEEK AFTER he'd found Liberty injured on the side of the road, Toby was still struggling to get her out of his head. *Was she healing?* He'd not seen her at any society functions and could not simply turn up at her door asking after her, when he'd ignored her for years.

Was her head actually worse than he'd originally thought?

Toby wanted to knock on her father's door and demand an explanation why she'd left that inn without telling him. Then he wanted an assurance she was indeed healthy.

The woman had not crossed his mind in years, other than when he saw her at a society gathering, but one encounter and he could think of little else. She believed him to be a womanizing rake and a wastrel, which in part was true, but it bothered him Liberty thought of him that way.

"Because you're a fool," he muttered, gripping the rope tighter, and beginning to climb. Beside him his friend, Lord Jamieson Stafford, was doing the same, and faster, which annoyed Toby excessively. He'd always been fiercely competitive.

"Yes, you are, but why are you more of a fool today than others?"

"Shut up and climb, Jamie," Toby said.

Since he'd been plunged into the brutal hell that was Blackwood Hall in his youth, Toby had done whatever he could to outrun his demons. Like the two friends he'd met there, they did what they needed to stay sane and shut out the darkness. Jamie chose exercise. He walked, ran, and rode everywhere as fast as he could. Toby often wondered if one day he'd hear his friend had died due to the extreme lengths he went to in pursuit of good health.

"You can go faster than that, Lord Corbyn."

"I'm trying, Professor Voelker," Toby said to the man instructing him. Gritting his teeth, he climbed as the muscles in his arms begged for mercy. "That man is evil."

He'd allowed his friend to drag him from his bed this morning, and to an open-air gymnasium he'd been a member of since its inception a few years ago. There was a fence around a grassed area, inside which had masts and ladders for climbing, mats for wrestling, and plenty of other evil forms of exercise. Jamie had got him at a weak moment, and now Toby was suffering. It would not be happening again.

"Why did I agree to this?"

"Because you are lazy, and wish to have a physique like me," Jamie said, reaching the top of the mast before him.

"My physique is equivalent, if not better than yours," Toby gritted out. "My arms are certainly stronger."

"Perhaps then, if I may suggest you try harder to keep up with Lord Stafford, Lord Corbyn," Professor Voelker said from below.

"You think I'm not trying to?"

The man showed no emotion at Toby's attempt at levity. He was relentless and drove those who were foolish enough to enter this hell hole mercilessly.

"What surprises me is that you actually came today," Jamie said, sitting on the wooden pole above him now.

Toby had come because he'd been unable to sleep and woken foggy. He'd felt forcing thoughts of Liberty out of his head with exercise was an excellent idea… until it wasn't.

Reaching the top, he gulped in air and then descended behind his friend.

"Next you will climb the ladders," Professor Voelker said when Toby landed back on the ground.

"Excellent," he rasped, bent at the waist. "I can't believe you would willingly choose to do th-this, Jamie."

"I like to stay strong and healthy. It keeps my mind clear. I don't want to pickle myself nightly with alcohol."

"I don't pickle myself nightly," Toby protested, glaring at his friend, who was not even breathing hard.

The Marquess of Stafford was tall, with dark hair and piercing green eyes. Women loved him, and he tolerated them back, but like his two friends he didn't let any close. Correction, that had changed for one of them, Anthony, who had married the love of his life recently. The first of them to fall, he'd said, to which Jamie and Toby had replied, the only one to fall.

"I can't work out if you two are idiots, or to be commended for what you are doing."

These drawled words came from his right. Straightening while attempting to force air back into his lungs, Toby found a man leaning on the fence, watching.

"Anthony, have you come to join us?" Jamie asked.

"Absolutely not," he replied with a wide smile.

"Get away, you lovelorn fool," Toby muttered. The man never used to smile.

"Jealousy is an ugly trait in a gentleman," Anthony added.

Ignoring him, Toby gripped the ladder.

Tall like he and Jamie, the Earl of Hamilton was dark haired with amber eyes, and had lost the savage air he'd once carried. As if marrying the woman he loved deeply had cleansed him of his demons. Toby had to say he almost hated him for that.

"Up those ladders now!" Professor Voelker barked.

"Yes, do get up those ladders," Anthony goaded them safely from the other side of the fence, where he and a handful of spectators watched. "I could do with a laugh."

Jamie ran up his, and Toby followed wheezing. He'd believed himself strong and healthy, but this had convinced him he needed to do more, not that he'd admit that to anyone, and especially not Jamie and Anthony.

When they were back down, with his hands now raw, Professor Voelker said they were done with their exercise that day but felt it would be best for Toby to return frequently.

"Well, that's telling you," Anthony said when they joined him.

"You should join us. I'm sure your middle is thickening," Toby said.

"Good Lord, why would I want to do that?" He didn't add anything about the thickening waist, as they all knew that for a lie.

"Because it's good for you," Toby wheezed.

"I can see that by the pained expression on your face," his friend drawled. "I can't believe you finally agreed to join Jamie, Toby. Didn't we decide never to do that?"

Toby grunted something that made no sense.

"Now wash in that cold water, and then we can eat," Anthony said.

"Where is your wife?"

"Shopping with her sister."

"And so we are fit company for you now she doesn't want you?" Jamie asked.

"Exactly that," Anthony agreed.

Shaking his head, Toby went to the trough of cold water and jar of soap behind the screen. He washed and then pulled on his jacket. Jamie did the same. They then left to join Anthony.

"You are preoccupied, Toby," Anthony said as they walked in the late morning sunshine. The streets were alive with vendors and people. Horses and carriages added to the cacophony of noise, and to some it was loud, but not to him. Toby enjoyed it. He didn't like silence.

"Am I?"

"Yes, you are," Jamie added. "And the fact that you came with me today points to you needing a distraction. At least that bruise on your jaw that you have not been truthful about obtaining is fading."

He'd seen them both since his return to London. Toby had just not mentioned about Bidham, or seeing Liberty. Neither of them knew exactly what had taken place between them, but they knew she had once been his friend.

"Actually, I do want to speak with you both about..." His words fell away as he watched the man running toward him. "Is that one of my footmen?"

As he drew closer, Toby saw it was indeed Nigel.

"My lord," the man rasped when he reached him. "A note has arrived, and the man who delivered it said you must read it urgently."

"Have you just run all the way here?" Jamie asked.

"I have, Lord Stafford."

"That's quite a distance. Well done."

Toby opened the note while his friend congratulated his footman on his fitness. Reading the first words, he noted it was from a solicitor. He read on.

"Christ," Toby hissed when he'd finished.

"What?"

"Thank you, Nigel. Please do not run home, and find something to eat or drink on the way," Toby said handing his footman some money. Only after he'd left did he read the words on the note before him.

"'Lord Corbyn, it is with my deepest regret that I must inform you of the death of your cousin and his wife, Reverend and Mrs. Hereford.'"

"I only met him once, when he came to London, but I remember he was a nice man," Anthony said.

"He never gave up on me, even when I wanted him to," Toby said, his eyes still on the words before him. He continued reading. "'Because there are no other living relatives and you were appointed guardian to their daughter, Miss Florence Heresford, the child will arrive in five days at your townhouse.'"

They stood in stunned silence after Toby had finished reading. Lowering the note to his side, he looked at them.

"Are you her guardian?" Anthony spoke first.

Toby nodded. "Timothy wrote to me every Christmas, usually six pages long of what had happened in his year. I responded with a single page of what a selfish bastard I was, and that nothing had changed."

"Toby—"

"Then the year you met him, he came to London to tell me Melissa, his wife, was carrying their babe," Toby continued, cutting Jamie off. "He asked if I would be its guardian, and I agreed, because I never thought I'd have to do more than send a gift occasionally. I was invited to the christening, and went, but it was the only time I saw the child." He could feel the panic welling up inside him now.

"How old is she?" Anthony asked.

He thought back and came up with a number. "Five years I believe."

"You are going to be guardian to a five-year-old child when you can barely care for yourself?" Jamie said.

"I object," Toby said weakly. "My staff do an admirable job of caring for me."

"But seriously, Toby. What are you going to do?" Anthony asked.

"I feel ill," he whispered.

The three men looked at each other blankly.

"Tea, I think. We will strategize, and if that doesn't work, ask someone who has children what you should do," Anthony said.

"I am not telling my mother yet. She will take to her bed for a week," Toby said.

"Evie can help. She helped raise her sister," Anthony said.

"I can't be responsible for a small child... a girl," Toby whispered.

They walked and all he could think was how could he protect a child from hurt and suffering, because no one had protected him when he'd needed them to? Was he strong enough to do that? Be a parent?

"I can see the panic clawing at you, Toby. You need to take a deep breath now," Jamie said. "You are not alone, and never will be. We are there for you as we always have been, and will help you."

"Agreed," Anthony said sounding grim.

We will never walk alone, Toby thought. They'd made that promise to each other many years ago when there had been no one else to turn to.

CHAPTER EIGHT

"RIGHT, SO REMEMBERING back to when my sister was younger. Your niece—"

"Florence," Toby added. "Do you think they call her Flo or Florence? What is her favorite food? Does she—"

"Stop now," Jamie said. "Let Anthony continue."

"She will need a nanny if she doesn't come with one, which she possibly will. Also, rooms made into a nursery. Is there a nursery somewhere in your townhouse, Toby?" Anthony asked.

"Yes. I haven't been into it for years. Surely I am not fit to have a small girl child in my house. She will be mourning the loss of her parents. How can I care for her?" The panic coursing through his body had words pouring out of Toby's mouth. "I am not fit for a child to live with."

"Why?" Jamie demanded. "You're a good and fair man. You have questionable waistcoat habits, but other than that, you are normal."

He didn't acknowledge the waistcoat comment. His mind was working through and discarding thoughts with the speed of a runaway carriage.

"We need Evie. You must bring her and her sister to my house at once. I need to find someone to take the child, but until then, I will have to care for her," Toby said.

"You cannot toss her into an orphanage surely?" Anthony said.

"Or send her away to a school," Jamie added.

"Hell no," Toby said. "Our school life was enough to cure me of sending any child associated with me to one."

"Hello!"

They turned at the greeting to find Anthony's three aunts on the opposite side of the road.

"We could make a run for it. We're faster than them," Anthony said.

"But we all know that they'd make us pay," Jamie said.

"True," Anthony added. "But talking to them will take precious time away from the discussion we need to have over food."

"You've done nothing to deserve food like Toby and me," Jamie protested.

"I can't believe you're talking about food after what I've just learned," Toby said.

"It will be all right, Toby," Anthony said.

"How?"

"Anthony!" one of his aunts called.

"We can't discuss this with your aunts or anyone yet," Toby said quickly. "I want to keep it quiet until… Christ I have no idea what I'm saying. It's like throwing a lamb among the wolves handing a child into my care. How is it my cousin never realized this could be a possibility?"

"Or he did, and believed you a good man who was more than up to the task of raising his child," Anthony said solemnly as they crossed the street.

"Ladies, how wonderful to see you," Jamie said.

Toby, Jamie, and Anthony owed these three women a great deal, because it had been they who saved the three boys from the hell they'd been living, and they would never forget that. For now, he would put his impending guardianship to one side and force down the panic. Later he would allow it back out.

"I do believe that you get more handsome every time I see you, Tobias," Lady Petunia said, patting his cheek. "Although I do believe you look a little tight around the eyes today. Is something amiss, dear?"

Toby thought of her as the leader of the three sisters. Lavender was her color, and she always spoke the loudest. "I stayed up too late last night and have not had enough sleep," he lied.

Next came Agatha, whose dresses were always apricot. Lastly was Lavinia, who favored the colors of green.

Older now, they had silver hair, and soft paper-thin skin, and smelled of a potpourri of scents that were as familiar to Toby as any others in his life. They were to Jamie and him the aunts they'd never had, and he loved them very much.

"And you ladies just get more beautiful," Jamie said, dragging the conversation away from Toby. "Where are you off to?"

"To the lending library. We have book club tomorrow and the selection is ours, so we are going to try to agree on something," Agatha said.

"I didn't know you belonged to a book club." Anthony frowned. "How is it I have never been told this?"

"We don't tell you everything, nephew," Lavinia said fussing with the lapels on Anthony's jacket. "It's quite fun."

"Who is hosting this book club?" Anthony demanded.

"It will be at our place this time," Petunia said.

"And who is in attendance?"

"Well," Agatha said. "There is Lady Sowter, and Miss Hamner. The Duchess of Talbot and her daughter Lady Liberty. Plus, Miss Williams. Have I missed anyone?" she then asked her sisters.

"No," Lavinia said. "Although sometimes Mrs. Little comes with her niece, but only if she has the time."

"Why wouldn't she have the time?" Anthony asked.

"Apparently, she and her husband play chess most evenings. And their niece, Miss Hamner, said sometimes well into the night. If a match has started, neither will leave until it is completed," Petunia added.

Liberty went to a book club with Anthony's aunts. On the heels of that thought came another one. She would know how to take care of a child because he'd seen her with her little brother.

Dear Christ, he was going to be guardian to a five-year-old girl. *This cannot be happening.*

"I believe the Duke and Duchess of Talbot have their estate close to yours, Tobias?" Lavinia asked.

"They do, yes."

"Then you must know their lovely daughter well," Petunia added. "Wonderful gal. Forthright and sweet natured."

"I do, yes," he said, still working through the problem that had just landed in his lap.

Petunia frowned. "I don't believe I've even seen you dance with Lady Liberty, Tobias. Why is that if she is your neighbor?"

"Aunt Petunia, Toby—"

"I'm speaking to Tobias not you, nephew."

"Hardly neighbors," Toby said. "And I do not dance with everyone."

"Have any of you seen them talking?" Petunia then asked.

"I do not speak with everyone all the time," Toby said, feeling his necktie tighten. "Just because our estates are close, does not mean we are," he said hoping that stopped further conversation, because he really had no time for this. He needed to get home and open the doors to his nursery and hope a flock of bats did not fly out. Did bats live as a flock? Such was the state of his mind this bothered him.

Lavinia leaned closer to Toby, her face now inches from his. "Why are you sweating profusely?"

"I've just exercised." At least that was the truth.

"No, I think talking about Lady Liberty has you unsettled."

All three women were now staring at him.

"Leave him alone please," Anthony said. "He is not himself today."

"So it would seem," Petunia said. She then patted Toby's cheek. "A good night's sleep will fix that, and a dance with your old friend, Lady Liberty."

Like hell.

"Excellent. Well then come along, Lavinia, Aggie. We have a book to select, and perhaps we shall have a wee chat with Lady Liberty at the book club."

"There is nothing to talk about. She and I are very different people, thus we were never friends," Toby lied, but they ignored him and wandered away.

"That went well," Jamie said. "I find I'm famished. Come along and we will put our heads together and work through the problem of your niece's impending arrival." He then walked in the opposite direction with Anthony.

"Hurry it along, Toby, as I cannot discount they will not return," Anthony said, sounding testy now. "Put your cousin to one side, as you still have five days to work through what is to be done."

"My life is about to change beyond recognition. How is it you expect me to put things to one side?" Toby thought about just going home and locking the door but knew his friends would follow and demand he open it.

"Is that cart selling spiced cake?" Jamie said, veering left. "It smells like it."

Minutes later, with large wedges of delicious cake, they continued walking. Yes, his insides felt like a butter churn, but he could still eat.

"So, Lady Liberty," Anthony said.

"We are not discussing Lady Liberty now," Toby snapped.

"We're taking your mind off your niece until we sit down and work things through," Anthony said. "Lady Liberty is an excellent topic to do that as clearly she unsettles you with that history between you."

"She does not unsettle me, and there is nothing further to discuss. Now there is something else I need to ask your advice on," Toby said. "It is to do with Bidham."

"The little village close to your estate?" Jamie asked.

"Yes. I have not been there for many years."

"For so long, it was Jamie, or me, that had a problem we

needed help with. It seems that is all about to change, along with your life, Toby," Anthony said.

"I am going to be the guardian of a five-year-old girl. I doubt anything either of you do could improve on that for a problem."

"True," his friends both agreed.

Toby explained what his butler had told him, and then what he'd seen in the village. Lastly, he spoke of what happened in that tavern he'd spent the night in with Liberty. He didn't mention the fact she was there, however.

"So, finally, we have the reason for those bruises you returned to London with," Jamie said.

"Why have you stayed away from Bidham for so long?" Anthony asked.

"And why did you not take us there when we visited Hawthorne years ago?" Jamie added.

"Are you sending someone to investigate what is going on in the village?" Anthony said.

"Which of those questions do you want me to answer first?"

"Mine," Anthony said before Jamie spoke.

"I am sending someone to the village to investigate, and had planned to go back in a few weeks for the Bidham festival, but now that is uncertain because of Florence." Silence greeted these words, so he took another large bite of spiced cake.

"Bidham festival?" Anthony asked with his mouth full of food.

"You should swallow that before you choke. And you're only eating like a barbarian because your wife is not here," Toby said.

"True. But we digress. There is a Bidham festival?"

Toby nodded. "It has been going for many years."

"Do they have sweet foods there?" Jamie demanded.

"Of course."

"I'm exceedingly vexed that you never told us about this, Toby, or for that matter, took us to this festival. That will change this year, as Florence will wish to go, and we will accompany you," Anthony said.

"I don't think so, and you make that sound like she already

knows you, or for that matter will like you."

"She will. We're likeable, and there are always sweets to bribe her with," Jamie said.

Did Florence like sweets? He didn't know a child who wouldn't, but then Toby didn't know any children, so there was that. Would Liberty be attending the festival, and if so, did he want to?

"A Corbyn has opened that festival for hundreds of years," Toby added softly.

"And that stopped when you refused to go?" Anthony asked.

"The year I returned from Blackwood, I refused the three years following. They never asked me again."

"Your mother—"

"Couldn't make herself go there after my father's death," Toby said.

"I feel like Lady Liberty plays a bigger part in all of this. However, as you have more than enough to deal with considering Florence is arriving shortly, I will leave that for now," Anthony said.

"There is nothing to discuss. Now shut up. Look, it is the chocolate house." If there was anything that could distract his friends, it was food, drink, and most especially chocolate.

CHAPTER NINE

"G OOD MORNING, MY lady."

Liberty groaned at Helen's overly cheerful greeting. Then winced as she threw open the curtains and allowed the sun to stream in.

"Gah," was all she could muster.

"Are you well, my lady? It is not often I have to rouse you from your bed," Helen said.

Liberty forced herself upright and into a seated position. "Is there a reason you are waking me with the sun?"

Helen deliberately looked from Liberty to the window, where the sun had clearly risen.

"Oh, very well. I read late into the night as I could not put my book down," Liberty said. "But in fairness that does not happen often."

"Not anymore, but it used to," her maid said.

The problem was she'd had to stay home due to the injury on her head, and that had allowed her time to think about Tobias, which she'd not wanted to do. Therefore, she'd read.

Liberty thought she'd dealt with her feelings toward Tobias Corbyn. Stomped down the anger and resentment over what he'd done to her, but spending time in his company once again had brought it back to the surface.

For years she'd seen him, but they'd not spoken a word to each other. She'd been more than happy with that. Now, however, that had changed. He'd carried her to his carriage and looked after her.

Perfidious man.

"Your family is at present sitting down for their morning meal, and your father wishes you to join them," Helen added.

"Is my house confinement over, then?"

"It would appear so," her maid added.

She washed and dressed. Helen looked at her head and declared it was a great deal better. Liberty left her room and went to see her family.

Elegant and stately, as befitted a duke's household, her father's townhouse was decorated in the subtle tones of celestial blues and soft creams with touches of gold. Her mother had commissioned the renowned decorator Ludlow last year to completely redecorate the entire house.

Passing the two tall windows that looked down to her favorite garden seat, Liberty saw the day was at least fine, even if her mood was not. Opening the door, she walked into the breakfast parlor.

"She's frowning. Everyone, run for cover," her brother Edward said by way of a greeting.

"Very amusing," Liberty said, poking out her tongue.

"Manners if you please, children," their mother said. "How is your head this morning?"

"Much better, thank you." Liberty loaded her plate from the sideboard and sat next to Edward.

"Excellent. It is the Potter ball tonight. You can attend."

Shorter than her daughter, the Duchess of Talbot had a sweet round face, and gentle nature unless she wanted something. Then she was tenacious. She laughed often and was more than happy with her life exactly as it was. And who wouldn't be when you had pots of money and servants to run hither and yon for you?

"Wonderful, I can hardly wait," Liberty said.

"Such enthusiasm, sister."

Edward was younger than Liberty by eight years, and a surprise to the entire family when he'd arrived. Their father had been ecstatic, of course, that he had an heir.

He would be tall, like the man seated at the end of the table behind a newspaper. Dark-haired, with her eyes, he was turning out to be strong-willed, much to his father's delight. Apparently it was acceptable to be strong willed if you were the heir, but not the daughter.

"I had a chat with Morris this morning, Liberty," her father said lowering his newspaper. "You omitted a few pertinent facts about what happened that day when the carriage wheel broke and you were forced to stay at that inn."

"What happened?" her mother demanded.

"It's really nothing—"

"Two highwaymen attempted to pull over Liberty's carriage, and she shot one, and Jasper the other, and the men fled. Then she fell out of the carriage, which appears to be the only truthful part of the story she told us."

"Dear Lord," her mother whispered.

"Nothing exciting like that ever happens to me," Edward said.

"It seems Lord Corbyn stepped in to help you to an inn," her father added, eyes narrowed with anger. "And stayed there with you over night to ensure your safety."

Silence greeted those words. Liberty did not speak and simply picked up the crumpet on her plate and took a large bite. She hadn't wanted to worry them, and so had not told them the entire truth. Liberty had hoped the staff who had accompanied her would not discuss the incident with her father. Clearly, they had.

"Tobias Corbyn?" her mother asked. "Our neighbor, and your old friend?"

"Are there other Lord Corbyns in society then?" Liberty asked.

"There is no need for that tone, daughter," her father said.

"How terrifying for you, Liberty," her mother added. "I'm sorry you went through that, darling, but how lovely you and

Lord Corbyn have reconnected. I never understood why you were friends one day and not the next."

"Not one day, mother. He went away, and we grew apart," Liberty lied. No way was the truth ever coming out.

"Lord Corbyn took you in his carriage. What did you talk about?" her mother persisted. "You must have had much to catch up on."

"Nothing. I had just hurt my head. Besides, we have been in society together for three years."

"But I have yet to see you speak or dance together," her mother persisted. She was good at that. Talking at a person continuously until they broke down and told her exactly what she wanted to know.

"We should have taken you with us, even ill," her father said.

"It could have happened if I was in your carriage too," Liberty said, reaching over to pat the hand that was clenched around his newspaper.

He was a good man, and life in their family during the early years had been wonderful. Things changed when Liberty came to London for her first season with the expectation that her focus was now on marrying, and marrying well. The carefree life she'd once lived was over. Now she had to always dress perfectly, and must at all times behave like a lady.

Pushing her glasses up her nose, Liberty wondered who she could get to tighten them, as they had definitely loosened since that tumble she took out the carriage.

"It will not happen again," her father said ominously. "And I will thank Lord Corbyn when I next see him."

"Oh, there is no need—"

"There is every need. You will also not be traveling alone again, Liberty, and that is my final word on the matter."

"I was not alone. I had three of your staff with me."

"Yes, well, it is done, and you are safe. Now our focus this year is finding you a husband," her mother said.

As it was every year, but Liberty didn't mention that.

She'd been a failure from the first society event she walked into. Her mother had refused to let her wear her eyeglasses, so she had to squint a lot, and when you coupled that with nerves it had not gone well. By the end of the first evening she'd hurled the entire contents of a glass of champagne over Miss Hamley and walked into a butler bearing a tray laden with glasses, sending him, and it, flying all over some guests. It had been an inauspicious beginning. But she was a duke's daughter, and with time, Liberty had learned to play the society game.

She'd subdued her personality, raised her chin, and carried on.

"We are to host a ball," her father said suddenly.

"What? Why?" Liberty asked.

"We have not hosted one for a while, and it is time," her mother said, not meeting her eyes.

"You told me that hosting a ball takes so much effort, and there are others in society who seem to enjoy it, so let them," Liberty added.

Her mother waved a hand about. "I've changed my mind."

"What aren't you telling me?" Liberty asked her father.

He was still a handsome man. In fact, she'd overheard Lady Gulliver say a few weeks ago, that it was deucedly unfair that the man did not appear to age a jot. His hair was black and shot through with gray, and he used his dark brows to maximum effect when scowling, which he usually was at her and Edward at least once in every day.

"Nothing at all," he said also not meeting Liberty's eyes.

Something was off here, *but what?*

"What are you not telling me?" Liberty said again more slowly.

"Nothing, dear," her mother said far too quickly. She then laughed nervously.

"Definitely something."

"Your mother and I have been talking—"

"Seven words that never go well for either of us," she said to

Edward, who snorted.

"It's time, Liberty, to prepare yourself for the future before it is too late," her father said.

"Future?" Liberty asked, feeling her stomach sink.

"Marriage, of course, dear," her mother said.

"Our fear is you are not putting your heart into securing a match," her father added. "I've had some offers, but foolishly discussed them with you—"

"Foolishly?" Liberty's voice rose.

"I am your father and know what is best for you. Your mother convinced me you would not marry without first finding love. I agreed with her, but clearly that is not going to happen so things must change."

Edward was applying himself to vigorously buttering a crumpet now and not making eye contact.

"I don't want to marry, and after my time in society thought you understood that," Liberty said with a calm she wasn't feeling. "I was on the back foot from the day I entered, older than every other debutante, and already on the shelf," she added.

"We want you to be happy, Liberty. We want you to have a family and—"

"I can be happy looking after Edward's children," she cut her father off.

"It would be an honor to have you living with us, sister," he said, nodding his head regally, like he already had a wife and six children.

"You need to marry, Liberty; it is for the best," her mother said. "I know you will be a wonderful mother."

"I understand your need to find the right man, but this is your fourth season, daughter, and of the four offers you've received thus far, none have been suitable as far as you were concerned," her father said.

"They were all fools, and older than you, father."

"There is nothing wrong with marrying a man older than you, surely?" her mother said. "Your father is older than me."

"By six years," he drawled.

"I know I wished love for you," her mother said, ignoring him, "but if you have respect and tolerance, that will come."

Liberty knew they loved each other, and that her parents' marriage was a happy one, but that was not always the case in society.

"So to help you along, we have decided to host a ball, and all the eligible men will be there."

"Why will hosting a ball help me along this season when the hundreds of society events I have already attended haven't?"

"Yes, well, your mother and I have decided to help you with that also," her father said calmly.

Liberty stared at him. "Exactly how are you both going to help me?"

"This afternoon I have someone coming to meet with you," her mother said, looking like she'd eaten something off now. "Someone who will help you toward our goal."

"Of marriage?" Edward asked, as confused as Liberty now.

"Mrs. Battlemore is paying you a call."

"Dear Lord, tell me it isn't so," Liberty whispered. "She dresses the season's debutantes, and has a fierce reputation for sticking pins into people, mother. Surely, the gowns we get from Madam Claudine are fine?"

"Yes, well, it seems something is not working—"

"I am a duke's daughter," Liberty snapped, which had her mother wincing. "Apparently, I am tolerable to look at, if a little long in the tooth. My dowry is surely adequate?" Her father nodded when she looked at him. "I do not need assistance from Mrs. Battlemore."

"She will simply change your style slightly. Annabelle said she did wonders for both Penny and Sybil," her mother added.

"Penny and Sybil are young debutantes. I am not, as I believe I have already noted," Liberty gritted out.

"It is done, and you will meet with her here today," her mother added. "Isn't that right?" She looked at her husband, who quickly nodded his support of her comments. "I also think you need to try harder to mingle, Liberty. You cannot simply spend the evening with Alice."

The silence following these words was deafening. Edward shot her a look, but Liberty kept her eyes on her mother.

"You cannot be serious," she said. "It is a miracle that I have not fallen over more, as I cannot see my bloody peers, because you forbid me to wear my eyeglasses!"

"It is not right that you wear them in a social situation," her mother said, lips in a tight line. "And don't curse, it is unbecoming."

"So I stumble about, unsure who I am speaking with and appear half-witted," Liberty said with remarkable restraint. "Because it is not right?"

"Now, Liberty—"

"Don't you *now Liberty* me," she cut her father off. "Do you know that most evenings I stay in the same place, and barely speak because I am terrified of walking into someone."

"Now, now, your mother knows best, daughter."

"Father, you can't be serious?"

"Liberty, your mother and I love you very much, but we want you settled and happy."

"I am happy."

"Are you really?" her mother asked.

"Yes."

"You will be happier running your own household," her father said.

"Just meet with Mrs. Battlemore, Liberty," her mother said. "You can work on the designs together."

"I can't see the bloody designs!"

"No need for such language," her mother tutted. "And of course you can wear your glasses around Mrs. Battlemore."

"And when I'm married, then what? I put on my glasses and my husband recoils in horror?"

"You will be married by then. There will be no going back,"

Edward said.

Ignoring him she glared at her parents. Neither looked away, and she knew her fate was sealed.

"Very well." She got to her feet then, and left without speaking another word. Reaching her room minutes later, she closed the door quietly behind her. Walking to the window, Liberty looked down at the street below.

Her parents were good people, and she'd thought as they'd not pressed her lately, that they'd come to the understanding she didn't want to marry, but they'd not given up hope it seemed.

"My lady."

"We are going for a walk, Helen."

Ten minutes later, dressed in a pelisse, gloves, and a bonnet, she reached the front entrance.

"Where are you going, Liberty?"

Turning, she looked to the top of the stairs and found her mother there. She rarely questioned her actions. It seemed that was about to change too, and no doubt at her father's orders.

"Out for a walk, mother. Do you wish to come?"

"No, but thank you for asking. Have a nice walk, ladies, and Liberty, you will not wear your eyeglasses, as someone may see you."

She bit back the sigh. "Of course, but it will be all right if I fall and break a bone, I suppose?"

"Take them off please," her mother said unmoved by her words.

Liberty removed her eyeglasses, and dropped them into her reticule.

Letting herself out the door, Liberty realized she would have to think long and hard about her next steps, because she had no wish to marry now, or ever.

CHAPTER TEN

WALKING ALONG THE street, Liberty wandered for a while, not that she could see anything up close clearly. Distances were not too much of a problem, blurry, but mostly, she could navigate about the place easily, especially with Helen at her side.

Her mind whirled with the problem of how to stop her parents putting pressure on her to marry. Yes, she knew that a woman in society had one goal. To wed and wed well. There was no greater shame than being a spinster and living off your family. Liberty had understood this but as time went on, she'd thought her parents had accepted the fact she would not marry.

"I don't want to wed just anyone, Helen."

"As you shouldn't," her maid said. "But it's your duty to do so."

"Duty to whom?"

"Your family," Helen said with no hesitation. "A little to the left, my lady, as there is a raised cobblestone.

"I am not completely blind, but thank you for the reminder," Liberty said, walking left. "And I understand it is expected of me to wed, even if I have no wish to," she muttered. Helen wisely chose not to comment further.

Liberty walked, looking in shop windows and at passersby, but not really seeing as she contemplated her problem.

"Good Lord," Helen said suddenly.

"What?" Liberty looked at her maid. The woman had a

shocked expression on her face, and she was staring at a cart that was rolling away from them. "Helen, what is going on?"

"I'm sure Sydney was driving that cart."

Helen and Liberty had known each other for years, as they'd both grown up close to Bidham. Helen was two years older, and far more responsible according to her parents, which is why she was chosen to accompany Liberty to London.

"Your brother Sydney? I thought he lived and worked a few miles out of Bidham?" Liberty squinted to focus on the cart, and then thought to hell with it, and took out her glasses.

"He does. I'm not sure why he'd be here," Helen said, still following the cart with her eyes. "But I'll tell you one thing, my lady. I don't like this."

Liberty remembered what Tobias had discussed with them that day he'd taken her to the inn.

"Helen, do you think it could be something to do with what Lord Corbyn talked about?"

"That all is not right in Bidham?"

"Yes."

"I don't know, but it's possible."

"Do you want to follow that cart?" Liberty asked.

"I would if you please, my lady."

"Excellent. I could do with a distraction. Let's go."

"I don't understand," Helen said keeping pace with Liberty. "Sydney's wed now, and has a child back in Bidham. He works for a local farmer, so what would bring him to London and not then tell me he was coming?"

"I'm sure there is a reasonable explanation. Perhaps he is helping someone out, and is planning to call on your brother Norman, and then notify you he's in London."

"Perhaps." But Helen didn't sound confident.

The cart turned and then continued on down a narrow lane until it reached a building that had two large doors. It was definitely Sydney, Liberty realized, as he climbed down from the driver's seat. She knew Helen's family well.

They watched the doors open and someone walk out of the warehouse and join him. The man had dark hair and was dressed as a gentleman. He spoke to Sydney, but from this distance they could not hear what was being said. He pulled back the covers on the cart and revealed barrels. Two more men walked out from the warehouse dressed like Sydney, and soon they were unloading them.

"There you go. He's doing a delivery for someone, Helen," Liberty said.

"But who, and why don't I know about it?"

"Perhaps you need to ask him what he's about."

"I'll wait until he comes out of the lane, I think."

"Why?"

"I don't know, but after what we've heard about Bidham, I don't want to make trouble for Sydney," Helen said, which made sense to Liberty.

They retreated to the beginning of the street.

"You'll stand back if you please, my lady. I don't want you involved in this."

Looking around her, Liberty wondered where she was meant to stand, but took a few steps to the right, which put her against the side of a building. The clop of hooves seconds later had Sydney and his cart appearing. The man spotted his sister but did not look Liberty's way. She'd heard the saying, the blood drained from a person's face, but she'd never witnessed it until then.

Helen's brother looked like he'd seen a ghost, not a family member. She moved closer as he pulled the cart to a halt beside Helen.

"Why are you here in London without telling your brother and sister you could be so, Sydney?" Helen said.

"H-hello, sister. How lovely to see you," he said in a high, strained voice.

"I want the truth, and I want it now," Helen said with her hands on her hips.

She was the eldest of her five siblings and Sydney was number three in the sibling line up.

"There ain't nothing to tell. I-ah, I was doing a delivery," Sydney said, looking ready to toss up the entire contents of his stomach. "Now, I need to go home."

"You're lying to me, Sydney," Helen said. "You work for Mr. Hatcher. What reason would he have to send you to London?"

"Be quiet," he snapped down at her. "You don't know what you're about, Helen, and for your safety, you need to stay out of this." Sydney's voice had lowered.

"This doesn't concern you, sister." With these words, Sydney flicked his reins, and his horse and the cart rolled away.

Liberty moved to stand with her maid. "Are you all right, Helen?"

"Something is wrong, my lady. Very wrong, but I don't know what."

"Do you wish for me to go back to where your brother unloaded those barrels and see what is happening?"

"We will both go back there." Helen marched away before Liberty could stop her. She hurried to join her maid and soon they were in front of the warehouse that Sydney had delivered to.

"Do we knock?" Liberty asked.

"I think we could, but not come right out and ask what Sydney was doing here. I feel it was something nefarious, my lady. I don't want you to walk into trouble."

"All right. How about I knock and ask if this is the building that has those Greek sideboards mother wants with the saber legs?"

"Do you think they'll believe you?"

"Possibly not, Helen, but as we are out of options, we shall try and see what happens." Liberty knocked on the door. It did not take long before the man, who was the better dressed of the two they'd seen talking to Sydney, opened it.

He nodded, but didn't speak.

"Hello. I just noticed you received a delivery and was hoping it was what I was after."

"Pardon?"

"The cart that just rolled in there. I did not see what was unloaded, but I'm hoping it is what I am looking for. My mother has tasked me with selecting a sideboard from you that is in the Greek style. But it must have saber legs, you see. She was most insistent on that."

He looked at her like she had two heads and an eye in the middle of her forehead.

Liberty looked up the side of the building, as if searching for a name, and then back at him. "Is this not Mr. Malcolm's warehouse?"

"It's not. On your way."

"Well then, what do you sell? I am in need of a gift for my mother. It is her birthday, you know," Liberty added.

The man's lips tilted up condescendingly as he looked Liberty over. "I sell nothing a lady like yourself would wish to buy."

She frowned. "Well, what do you sell? Surely, I can decide if I want to purchase it or not."

His eyes narrowed suspiciously, and Liberty thought it was time to back off.

"Spirits," he growled.

Liberty wrinkled her nose. "Can't abide the stuff. Good day to you." She then turned with Helen and left.

"My lady, there was a man in the window above watching us," Helen said as they walked away. "Don't look!" she whispered, as Liberty did just that. "I couldn't make out his features, but he did not move the entire time you were speaking."

Liberty wasn't sure why she felt cold suddenly, but she did.

"Come along, I think we need a cup of something to fortify us," Liberty said when they reached the end of the street. Something made her turn, and she saw that the man she'd spoken to was watching her. Raising a hand, she then kept moving until he could no longer see them.

"Well," Helen said.

"Well indeed. I'm not sure what that gained us other than it is spirits in that warehouse."

"Take off your glasses," Helen whispered suddenly, as two well-dressed young ladies walked toward them.

"I'm sure I don't know why I have to," Liberty muttered, whipping them off and putting them in her reticule once more.

"Because your parents wish for you to do so."

"Why is it wrong for me to see where I am going?"

"I have no idea, but it is," Helen hissed.

As far as her maid was concerned, every word that spilled from Liberty's parents' lips was to be obeyed.

They walked, and she left Helen alone with her worrying thoughts about Sydney, and hers went to her own brother.

Thus far, Edward had done nothing that was overly taxing on the family. In fact, unlike her, he was a model child and brother. She was sure that would change after he went away to school next year. It certainly changed Tobias Corbyn.

He had come home at eighteen, nothing like the good-natured boy who left. He'd been cold and hard, and dismissed Liberty as if she had not once been his best friend. The boy she idolized.

She'd noticed the change in Tobias after his first year, when his brother Mathew had passed away, but put it down to losing someone he loved. But when he came home four years later, she knew he was nothing like the Tobias she'd once known. This one was mean and hurtful. The old Toby had never been that.

"And here we are. Come along, Helen," Liberty said, happy to be distracted from her disturbing thoughts.

Blundell's Chocolate House looked as it normally did. Busy. Liberty pushed open the door and entered to the delicious smells and chatter of patrons.

"I'm sure I don't know why you can't take tea like everyone else," Helen said.

"It seems I'm not alone in my love of chocolate," Liberty drawled, looking at the tables of people. Helen harrumphed.

"Lady Liberty." A man rose from his chair as they walked through the tables.

Drat, it was Lord Patterson. Nice enough in a bland way. He danced well, and didn't appear to have any noticeable faults. That didn't mean she wanted to marry him, however, and after that conversation with her parents, everyone was now a prospective husband they would hurl into her path.

"Lord Patterson." Liberty dropped into a curtsey, her eyes going to the two women he sat with. His sisters. Both smiled at her. She smiled back, and then, with a nod, went to the farthest table from where he sat and pulled out a chair.

"Sit, Helen."

"I'm your maid and shouldn't sit with you."

"I don't care about that, as I've explained before. Now sit. It has been a trying morning, and I wish to drink lashings of chocolate and eat those delicious small round discs with marvelous flavors."

Helen sat.

"We're going to Dobson's after this, as I am in need of a new book," Liberty added.

"That place smells," Helen said wrinkling her nose.

"Old books," Liberty sighed. "I love that scent."

"How can I help you today?" A young lady approached.

"Two cups of hot chocolate, and some of those citrus peel and vanilla chocolates please."

"I won't be able to do up your gowns soon," Helen said.

"Well then, your job will be a great deal easier if all I do is loll about on my bed all day like a whale."

Helen didn't have a sense of humor, but that wasn't to say Liberty hadn't tried to make her laugh over their years together. Her maid had a sturdy, dependable soul.

"Lady Liberty, do you believe Sydney was smuggling those barrels into that warehouse?"

"That thought crossed my mind, Helen. The village is on the coast, and there has been smuggling before. My belief is that it could have something to do with what's going on in Bidham."

"We need to tell Lord Corbyn, because he asked us to inform

him of anything we learned regarding the village, and this could be that," Helen said.

"If we mention Sydney, that implicates him," Liberty said. She'd also rather choose to spend the day stitching than speaking to Tobias again, and she loathed stitching.

"I would rather he was implicated if it meant stopping this... whatever it is," Helen said, her face tight with worry.

Liberty sighed, knowing she was right.

"Oh, now it's as if we've conjured him up," Helen said, her eyes on the door.

Liberty turned, dread slithering through her, and saw Tobias, Lords Hamilton and Stafford entering Blundell's Chocolate House.

He saw her and nodded. Tobias then hesitated, and something passed across his face before it was gone.

Go to another table, she begged silently. She watched him lean in and say something, then Lord Hamilton shook his head and walked toward her. Lord Stafford followed, and lastly, Tobias.

"Lady Liberty." The three men bowed after Lord Hamilton addressed her.

"We shall take this seat," Lord Stafford then said, pulling out a chair at the table closest to the one Liberty and Helen sat at. Tobias took the one near hers. He then looked directly at Liberty, eyes intent.

"Are you well, my lady?" he asked abruptly.

"Have you been unwell, Lady Liberty?" Lord Hamilton asked, clearly overhearing.

Her eyes went to Tobias, who looked resigned.

"Lady Liberty's carriage broke down after someone attempted to rob it. She was then thrown from it and injured her head. I arrived and took her to the nearest inn."

"When did this occur, my lady?" Lord Stafford asked, his eyes going from his friend to her.

"A week ago." She wondered why that mattered.

"Really, and yet we are only hearing about it now." Lord

Hamilton looked at Tobias, who in turn rolled his eyes.

It wasn't a gesture she would expect this Tobias to give, but it was one her old friend would have made.

"My lord, regarding what we discussed the other day," Liberty said. Helen was right. She needed to tell him about this, no matter how much she wished to have no further interaction with him.

"About Bidham?" He raised a dark brow, his eyes going from her to Helen.

"Helen, you tell him," Liberty said.

"My friends are aware, as I have explained to them, of our concerns. So speak freely," Tobias said.

"It's my brother, Lord Corbyn," Helen said, looking nervous as she stared at the powerful lords behind him.

"Don't be nervous speaking before them, Helen. They're both idiots. Your wealth may not be the same as theirs, but your intellect far outstrips them," Tobias said with a gentle smile on his face.

And Liberty saw more in that smile of the boy she'd once known, but couldn't allow herself to care for. Never again would anyone hurt her the way he had.

CHAPTER ELEVEN

"Wʜᴀᴛ ɪs ɪᴛ you wish to tell me, Helen?" Toby said, turning his seat to face the women.

Liberty didn't want him here, as she'd not wanted his help when she was hurt, but like him, Bidham was important to her, so she'd put up with Toby's company.

"It's regarding what we discussed, and your and Lady Liberty's worry for Bidham," Helen said.

Liberty sat still, her eyes on her maid. Anyone watching her would not think she was overly concerned to have the man who had ruthlessly ripped her from his life, without an explanation, sitting a few feet away. But he knew her well enough to see the signs of her agitation.

"It's my brother, Sydney, my lord." Helen's eyes went from him to Liberty, and then over his shoulder to Anthony and Jamie again. She was clearly uncomfortable in their presence.

"Continue with your story, Helen," Liberty said, patting her maid's hand.

He looked at her fingers tipped with short nails and felt something uncomfortable settle in his chest. A longing for his old friend he had no right to feel.

Their drinks and food arrived while Helen began her tale about Sydney and how they'd seen him earlier, and he made himself focus.

"And you say there were barrels on the back of the cart your brother drove?" Anthony asked from behind Toby.

"Yes, my lord." Helen bobbed her head.

"I think it's likely something to do with smuggling," Liberty said. "We knocked on the warehouse door and—"

"You are not serious?" Toby demanded, now glaring at Liberty. "Why would you do such a bacon-brained thing?"

"I beg your pardon. You do not get to speak to me in that manner," Liberty snapped back. "I did what I felt was needed, as Helen was upset about her brother. The man was not suspicious, as I stated. I thought it was the warehouse where I could get my mother's Greek sideboard."

Tobias rolled his eyes, feeling his anger rise. "God save me," he hissed.

"I love those sideboards," Anthony said. "Especially with the saber legs."

"She should not have gone, is the point here," Tobias snapped.

"Excellent cover, though, it has to be said," Jamie added. "I too like saber-legged chairs."

"Shut up," Tobias hissed, knowing what his friends were doing. Deflecting away from the fact he wanted to roar at Liberty for her foolish actions. "It was a risk you should not have taken, Lady Liberty."

"We now know that it is indeed spirits they sell or store in that warehouse," Liberty gritted out. "I did what needed to be done to confirm that."

They glared at each other, so much more than anger over what she'd done simmering between them. There was also the fact he'd learned he was to be guardian of a small child riding him, which was making Toby irrational, but he'd deal with that after this… her.

"There is something else," Helen said, shooting Liberty a look.

"Something you've not shared with me yet, Helen?"

Helen nodded at Liberty's question.

One look at her cool blue eyes told him nothing of what she was thinking. Liberty had learned to hide as Toby had. He wondered why? She then squinted.

"Where are your glasses?" Toby said before thinking better of it.

"Continue with your story," Liberty said, ignoring him.

"Mother sent me a note from Bidham, just yesterday," Helen said. "I was going to tell you, Lady Liberty, but I knew it would be upsetting for you."

"What has happened?" Liberty said calmly. "You know you can tell me anything, Helen."

Toby knew Anthony and Jamie were also listening intently.

"It's Sally Ackers, my lady. She went missing one night while walking home from Pippen farm. She was found dead the day after we left Bidham."

Toby thought through the people he'd once known in Bidham. The Ackers were a large family who lived a two-minute walk from the entrance into the village.

"She was the youngest?" Toby asked Helen. "From memory, a sickly child."

"She was," Liberty whispered.

"I'm sorry, my lady."

He was missing something here, Toby was sure of it. Yes, Liberty would be upset if someone died from Bidham, but he had a feeling there was more to this.

"Did you know Sally well, my lady?" Anthony asked Liberty.

"Not well—"

"Lady Liberty sent a doctor to care for her when she was poorly. Then visited regularly to ensure Sally got everything she needed to get better," Helen whispered.

"How did she die?" Liberty asked, her voice brittle now.

Helen looked down at the cup before her, and Toby knew she wasn't really seeing it. "She was found with her hands and feet bound, and it is believed she was strangled," Helen whispered.

He kept his eyes on Liberty as her maid spoke. He saw her flinch and then lower her eyes too. He wanted to touch her but had lost that right. When she raised her head, she was every inch the duke's daughter she'd been born to be. No emotion showed on her face.

Toby knew he played the part well. The carefree peer, the charming viscount women adored, who kept everyone but a chosen few at arm's length. But watching Liberty struggle to mask her pain twisted something in his chest. He didn't want that. Didn't want to feel.

"Poor Sally; her family must be devastated," Liberty said with a calm he knew she was not feeling. One hand was clenched into a fist in her lap.

"Yes, they are," Helen said.

"Did your mother say anything else, Helen?" Toby said working through what he already knew about Bidham.

"She didn't."

"I think someone is threatening the village," Liberty said.

"Why do you think that?" he asked. It had been the conclusion Toby had come to as well.

"After seeing what Sydney was unloading today," she added. "Whoever is behind it must be using the route through the village, and perhaps—"

"You can't know that, and nor should you involve yourself in this," Toby interrupted her. His voice came out harsher than he'd intended, and the narrowing of Liberty's eyes told him she'd heard it.

"You have no say in what I do." Her chin didn't lift at these words, but to him it was implied.

She then reached for her cup and knocked it sideways. Toby caught it just before the contents spilled.

"Where are your eyeglasses?" he demanded. "Why, if you need them, don't you wear them?"

She glared at him, picked up the cup and sipped without answering.

"Just watch you don't walk in front of a carriage," he snapped.

"I would have thought that would be a relief to you, Lord Corbyn. After all, we know how coldhearted and ruthless you can be around people who you once pretended to care for." Liberty regained her feet after delivering these terse words. "Come along, Helen. There is a tea shop on the next street. I believe the company will be more preferable."

Toby also rose. "I want to be informed if you hear anything." His words were as cold as hers now.

"I'll tell you what you can do, Lord Corbyn." She then leaned in close. He took a deep breath and instantly his head was filled with her scent. Soft, subtle, but with a hint of something stronger. Orange blossom, Toby thought. "You can go to hell."

"Again? I believe you've already told me to go there, my lady?"

They were close now. He could see the rapid beat of her pulse in her throat, and the flare in those pretty eyes. Made brighter by the matching ribbons of her bonnet, tied neatly under her chin.

"Such a shame you do not take orders well then, Lord Corbyn." She turned and walked away with her maid on her heels.

Toby watched her, his eyes on the straight line of her spine until she'd left the chocolate shop. Only then did he sit once more.

"Seeing as they didn't touch their food, we could—"

"Absolutely not. You're a bloody marquis," Toby snapped, interrupting Jamie. "You cannot eat off another table."

Jamie raised both hands in the air in a gesture of surrender. Toby ran a hand over his face. *Damn it to hell.* Now the inquisition would begin.

"Now before we discuss what needs to be done for Florence, will you tell us what happened with Lady Liberty Talbot, Toby," Anthony said. "Clearly there is anger between you, and a great deal more than what you told us earlier. I would go so far to say that there is a lot of history between you."

"I don't share my entire life with you two," he said as the server brought their order. Three large mugs of steaming bitter chocolate, and a plate of food.

"Well, perhaps it is time you do," Anthony said.

"We were once close," Toby said, looking at the two men who knew more about him than anyone else. Men who had been beaten and tortured in the name of fun at Blackwood Hall. Tortured by older boys, a housemaster, and others who should have known better.

"And now she hates you," Jamie said.

"Yes, and with good reason. I came home after Mathew's death, which was a year after I arrived at Blackwood. Liberty visited me, but I didn't speak with her, and she understood that was due to my brother's passing."

"But it wasn't, because you'd changed, as had we all," Anthony said solemnly.

Toby nodded, and then sipped his drink, needing it to ease the ache in his throat. He'd gone home bruised, broken, and grieving for the little brother he'd no longer see. His parents hadn't realized what he'd become as they'd been deep in their own grief, and he'd not told them. Liberty would have listened, but he'd refused to spend time with her.

"But you saw her when you came home after your father passed away?" Jamie asked.

"Yes. She found me leaving the house one day. I'd sent her away the previous times she'd called. I said some things, and she left, and I don't regret that our friendship ended," Toby added. "Only the way I did it."

They fell silent, and for a few minutes, the only sounds were of them eating, which they all did well, and often.

"All right, so we know some of your history now, but surely you were young when you and she were friends?" Anthony asked. "Was your bond that strong?"

"It was, but I severed it." Liberty was a raw wound inside

Toby, no matter how much he'd denied it to himself.

"Back to this business in Bidham then," Jamie said.

"When is the fair?" Anthony asked.

"Three weeks," Toby said.

"First, you need to write to whomever you need to write to and tell them a Corbyn will once again be in attendance," Anthony said.

"They may have no wish for me, too."

"You're a Corbyn; of course they will," Anthony added. "Then send in your man to snoop around. You also need to speak with Lady Liberty again and find out where those barrels were delivered. We must search that place. If, as you both suspect, there is smuggling going on."

"We need to investigate Sally Ackers's death too, because someone murdered her, and that kind of thing just doesn't happen in my village," Toby added.

"Oh, so it's your village now?" Anthony raised a brow.

"Smuggling is happening up and down the English coast," Jamie protested. "Why is what's happening in Bidham a threat to the village... if it is?"

"We need to visit there," Anthony said. "I'm quite sure Evangeline would like a nice trip to the country. She has a way of getting information out of people."

"Only you, because you are so pathetically in love with her," Toby scoffed. His friend smiled, and in that moment, he could have leaned across the table and plowed his fist into his face, because that look of genuine love and happiness was something Toby knew he'd never achieve. He wasn't worthy of it.

"Considering Florence is arriving this week, I'm unsure we will attend the fair," Toby added gruffly.

"She is a child, and it's a fair. Of course, she will love it, and by then you will be comfortable with each other," Jamie said. "You'll see."

Liberty slid into his head again, and he pushed thoughts of her aside. Once, he'd wondered if she'd be his wife one day even though they'd been children. She'd always seemed to understand him. Seemed to fit, which was an odd way to put it, but the minute he'd met her, she'd felt like part of him.

"Toby, you need to make amends with Lady Liberty," Anthony said.

"No, that will not happen, and I will soon have little time for anything."

"She will help you find peace," Anthony added.

Jamie's snort held no laughter. "There will be no peace for some of us, Anthony. Just because you found it, does not mean we will. You have to understand that."

"I know that I have someone in my life who helped me to find it."

"But that is not for us," Toby said, *and never will be.*

Jamie raised his mug in agreement.

"Very well, if you say so, but tonight is the Pilkington ball, Toby. At least you can be cordial to Lady Liberty, because if whatever is taking place in Bidham is dangerous, then we must ensure it is snuffed out," Anthony said. "I'm sure over the years the village has relied on protection from both noble families living on its borders, and now more than ever will need it."

"The Corbyns were there many years before the Talbots," he added.

To his shame, Toby had walked away from Bidham because he'd wanted to shut out every aspect of his life that made him feel, but in doing so, he'd turned his back on those that needed him most. Anthony was right. The village should be under his protection.

"I will do better once I settle Florence… if she settles," Toby said. "I'll add to that. I'm not sure how she can when the only life she's known is gone forever." Now Liberty had left, the weight of the responsibility he now faced settled again on his shoulders. How could he care for a child's needs?

"We will ensure she settles," Anthony said. "All of us will be there to help."

That humbled him, so he drank a mouthful of chocolate to wash down the emotion clogging his throat.

"From your memory of Lady Liberty, is she one to take a risk? To throw herself into this investigation without a care for her own safety?" Jamie asked.

"She is quite capable of doing that," Toby said.

"Really? That does surprise me," Jamie added. "I've never seen an overt display of emotion from the woman. I've danced with her a few times, and her smile is usually polite, if a little chilly. I believed until today, she was a reserved type, and the epitome of a proper society lady."

Toby barked out a laugh. "She was never that once." The smile fell from his lips. "But yes, that is how she portrays herself in society."

"Right, we have a way forward regarding Bidham and Lady Liberty. Now let's talk about Florence," Anthony said.

And they did. Through two pots of hot chocolate, and numerous plates of food, they worked through what they believed needed to happen. It helped that his friends had sisters, and Toby would be leaning on them heavily for guidance as he had no clue what to do. But one thing he now knew was that Florence's welfare was his only concern.

CHAPTER TWELVE

THE DAY OF Florence's arrival dawned, and with it absolute panic from Toby. He'd not slept well and was now up before the sun and in the nursery. The walls were a stale brown, but he'd not had enough time to do anything but hang pictures to change that.

He'd opened this door five days ago, and the smell hit the back of his throat. Toby had gagged. He'd flung open windows and with the help of his staff, they'd removed dust covers and set about making it habitable.

The bedroom was next door, with, much to his relief, a good-sized bed. Next to that another, smaller, for a nanny, which he hoped came with her, or he'd have to get one of his staff to watch over Florence until he acquired one.

They'd thrown out mattresses, and he'd brought new ones and bedding. Toby had then purchased books and dragged Evie to a shop to buy other things a small girl child may like.

There was a doll's house and two dolls, plus a small table and chairs.

"What do you think, Chadders?" he asked his butler, who arrived with the mug of black coffee Toby had asked for.

"It's a room any child would be happy to sleep in."

"This particular child has lost both her parents and been wrenched from the only life she's ever known to live with me, a stranger, and not a terribly nice man, Chadders."

He alternated between fear that he'd raise the child to be cold and heartless like him, and wonder that he now had someone that relied on him for his existence.

"If I may say, Lord Corbyn, I've never thought of you as cold and heartless."

"You're too kind, even if you are lying, Chadders."

But in this, he likely believed he wasn't. John Chadderly had been the son of the cook at Blackwood Hall. Those who believed themselves better than him had treated him terribly. It had been Anthony and his friends who protected him. Ever since, he had worked for one or the other of them, and eventually became Toby's butler. He was short, solid, and fiercely loyal to the men who had saved him.

"I shall see about refreshments for when the young miss arrives, my lord."

His butler then left to do butlering, and Toby wandered around the nursery trying to remember his time here. He couldn't. In fact, he'd blocked out much of his past, and that had included the good times he'd spent with his parents and brother.

I must do better for Florence's sake. Must be a better person.

Evie and her sister, Prudence, had arrived the day after he'd found out he was to be Florence's guardian, and started making lists of things he needed to do. It had been a relief, because she had given him a direction. If he was busy, he didn't have time to think about the fact his life was soon to change beyond recognition.

There was also Liberty who he kept running into. She was a distraction, along with Bidham. In fact, he'd told Jamie last night while they sat in his study drinking brandy, that in a matter of weeks, his life had turned completely on its head. His friend had said perhaps it was time.

Time for complete chaos when for so long your life had order? Toby didn't think so, but it was done, and he could do little but deal with what was before him.

He washed, dressed, and went to his study, hoping that working through the papers his business manager had sent would distract him. It didn't. By the time Chadders appeared in the doorway to tell him a carriage had arrived, he was pulling his hair out as the tension inside him climbed.

Toby didn't run to the entranceway, but he walked at a clip. He saw the hired carriage as he stepped out the front door and hurried down the steps. Reaching the door, he opened it and found the face of a large golden dog staring at him. Beyond that was a young lady, and next to her was Florence.

"Hello," Toby said as his throat went dry. She was so small. Her bonnet was white, as was her dress and her face pinched tight with worry.

"I am your Uncle Toby," he said to the child, even though they were cousins. Uncle sounded less intimidating to his mind. "I was your father's cousin, and we were great friends when we were your age."

She looked at him with big sad brown eyes, worry in every line of her face. His heart broke for the pain this little girl had suffered. Losing a parent at any time was hard, but two that you loved, devastating.

"Good day, may I have your name?" Toby said to the young lady with Florence.

"I am Miss Haigh, Miss Florence's nanny."

Well, at least that was one thing he did not have to worry about. A large pink tongue ran down the side of his face then. Toby found a smile. He'd always loved dogs, but hadn't had one since he'd returned home from Blackwood Hall. Yet another thing he'd allowed that place to rob him of.

"And who is this handsome fellow?"

"His name is Barnaby, my lord. He and Miss Florence are inseparable."

It wasn't a threat exactly, but Miss Haigh's chin rose as if to say, you will not remove this grieving child from one of the few things she has left to love. Toby found in that moment he liked Miss Haigh very much and was relieved that at least Florence had her.

"Well then, let us hope he likes his new home."

He hadn't planned on a dog, but now it seemed he must. Turning, he found his butler behind him. "Chadders, Miss Florence has a dog. His name is Barnaby, and I'm sure after his long carriage trip, he needs a drink, some food, and a run in the gardens. Would it be acceptable to you, Florence, if Chadders took him into the house?"

The solemn brown eyes studied him, and then she nodded.

"Right then, out you get, Barnaby. It is time for you to explore your new home," Toby said.

The dog bounded out, unaware of the tension the others were feeling, or perhaps he was and that was why he was happy to be removed from it.

"Now, Florence, may I call you that?" Another small nod. "Would you like to come inside too and see my house?" She looked like she wanted to refuse.

"Of course she does. After all, we cannot simply sit in here all day now, can we? Plus, we are hungry, aren't we, Miss Florence?" Miss Haigh said smiling at the forlorn child.

Toby moved out of the doorway and took a deep, steadying breath. Looking skyward, he thought about his cousin and the precious child he had loved. *I will keep her safe.* For the first time in many years, he had another responsibility, and that terrified him, but he would not let Timothy down.

Miss Haigh appeared in the doorway first and stepped down. Behind her came Florence. So small and vulnerable. He wanted to help her down. Tell her it would be all right but was sure she wouldn't want comfort from him.

"Come along," Toby said with as much enthusiasm as he could muster.

He let them go first and saw Florence's head swivel from left to right, taking everything in. There were no flowers in the narrow beds on either side of the path, and hadn't been since he'd become Lord Corbyn. Looking at his town house with fresh eyes made Toby realize just how austere it was.

Stepping inside did not change that opinion. No flowers, no light, just dark colors and furnishings. His butler had obviously handed Barnaby off to another staff member as he stood there watching them approach.

"Florence, this is Chadders. A wonderful man who if you need anything and I am not nearby, will be only too willing to help.

Something odd happened then. His butler softened, and his shoulders lowered, and he was bending at the waist smiling at the child. "How wonderful it is to meet you, Miss Florence. We are so very happy to have you with us."

Clearing his throat, Toby introduced Miss Haigh.

"Well then, let me show you the nursery," Toby said when they all fell into an uncomfortable silence.

They trooped up the stairs past large austere paintings of his ancestors. If a small child were to live in this place, he needed to do something about it. They entered the nursery in a silent procession, with Chadders at the rear.

Toby stood just inside as Miss Haigh and Florence entered.

"Oh now, isn't this lovely," the nanny said, looking around her. "Don't you think it's lovely, Miss Florence?"

The girl didn't speak, just walked across the room to the windows, beneath which sat the doll's house. She then dropped to the floor and picked up a doll with golden hair and hugged it close.

"Miss Florence is probably tired so she will need a sleep, Lord Corbyn," Miss Haigh said.

"Would you like a tray sent up before she does?" Toby asked.

"Yes, please." Miss Haigh hesitated.

"Please speak freely, Miss Haigh. Now is not the time for anything else, as Florence's welfare is at stake," Toby said.

"She is scared, sad, and unsure what this new life is, my lord."

"Completely understandable. I feel the same way and I'm an adult who has not lost his parents recently."

Miss Haigh nodded. "It will take her time to adjust."

"Luckily, she has you to help her with that. I would be grateful for any guidance from you as to how I should proceed."

"Of course. If I may suggest before you leave, my lord, you say goodbye to her."

Toby moved to stand behind the little girl. "I will leave you to your nap, Florence, and will not be far away should you need me."

She didn't look at him, just one solemn nod again.

Toby walked from the room, vowing that Florence would never want for anything. Love, however, she would likely have to get from others, as it had been a long time since he'd given that to anyone, and was no longer sure he knew how.

CHAPTER THIRTEEN

TOBY FOUGHT THE urge to walk out of the house instead of in through the doors of Lord and Lady Manwaring's.

How was Florence?

He knew, of course, it was late and she was no doubt sleeping. He'd spent the days since her arrival in his household standing outside the nursery door and listening a lot. It had mainly been Miss Haigh who was talking or singing. In fact, he'd not heard Florence speak in his presence yet.

He'd taken tea with her in the nursery. Walked outside with her and Miss Haigh, and the child had stayed pressed to her nanny's leg as far from him as she could get. He didn't know how to get her to trust him. How to get her to like him, and it bothered him deeply.

Toby thought he wasn't fit company for a five-year-old girl, but the long dormant feelings she roused inside him made him want to try for her.

Time, Miss Haigh had said. It would take time. He'd not had his friends over in those days and only left the house when necessary. He'd simply walked the halls waiting until he got word of how Florence was doing. Waiting until he could take tea with her.

It was hell. She carried his blood, and wanted nothing to do with him. So tonight he'd made himself return to society.

After greeting the hosts, he entered the ballroom.

"Corbyn."

The drawl had Toby's back stiffening, but he turned with his usual social mask firmly in place.

"Lord Michael." Toby bowed. He tried not to hate too many people in his life. This was one person he had no qualms about doing so.

This man had been a benefactor at Blackwood House. He'd known what was going on. Toby had once asked him to do something about it, and he'd laughed, saying it was just a rite of passage, and harmless fun.

Tall, elegant, with silver hair pomaded into the latest style, Michael was the epitome of a society gentleman. His clothes were expensive, and his friends rich. Toby, however, was richer and more titled, a fact Michael hated.

"I had heard you are interested in investing in the Hall Road consortium, Lord Michael?"

"I am." Lord Michael frowned. "How is it you know that?" The man's polite facade slipped.

"My friends are behind it. You know them of course, Lords Hamilton and Stafford."

He visibly paled. "I had not realized they were involved."

"Yes, we are involved, in fact it is our consortium," Toby said holding the man's gaze. *Therefore, you will never be part of it.*

"Tobias!"

He turned to see who had called him, and found Lady Petunia waving at him a few feet away.

"Michael, I am being summoned. Excuse me." With a brief bow, he walked away, knowing he'd left the man seething, and feeling a great deal better for it.

"Ladies," Toby said, bowing to Anthony's three aunts. "May I be of assistance to you in some way?" They were all seated against the wall on a chaise.

"Draw a chair up before us, Tobias. We wish to discuss a matter with you," Lady Petunia demanded. She was the one who usually gave the orders out of the three of them.

Toby wondered if Anthony had told them about Florence. He would be more than happy with these three in the child's life as they would dote on her. In fact, when she had settled into life with him, he'd make sure it happened.

He located a seat, and placed it down before them, which was directly in the path of people wanting to skirt around the edges of the room, but he knew better than to argue.

"Now, we have decided..."—*four words that never went well for anyone*—"that it is time for you to marry."

"Oh... ah." Toby had been speaking for many years. Since he was one? Maybe earlier, he had no recollection, but right then everything he'd learned was suddenly a jumbled mess in his head.

"And to that end, we have drawn up a list, dear," Agatha, who sat directly to Petunia's right, said.

These three were creatures of habit. The way they dressed, how they sat, and how they planned their attacks. He'd seen it before. Petunia always started, and then the others joined her.

"Lovely ladies, all three of them," Lavinia said.

"I don't want to marry," Toby said with as much force as his dry throat could muster. He should marry, now Florence would be in his care, but he was not doing so just for the child. When the time came, if the time came, it would be with someone he'd carefully chosen.

"And yet it is time," Agatha said.

"Why now is it time?" he asked when he could have just said no, absolutely not. The problem here was, these women had saved him and his two best friends, one of whom was their nephew, and because of that, he would always love and watch over them. Toby would never be rude to them, but he'd not believed he'd have a need to until now.

"We have seen how happy our nephew is," Petunia said. "It fills our hearts with joy."

"Joy," Lavinia parroted as if he'd not heard.

"And as we think of you like we do Anthony, we have decided that it is time to help you find joy."

"Not Jamie?"

"We're starting with you, as he is not ready," Petunia said with a cat that has the cream smile on her face.

"Now, the three women on this list are here this evening." Agatha held out a small square of paper, then waved it before him until he took it.

"Don't read it now, save that until later, and we shall see you soon to get your thoughts. There are plenty more lovely young women we could have added to that list, but we had no wish to frighten you," Lavinia said.

"Ah, well." Toby looked at the paper in his hand. "I am, of course, honored you consider me as you do, and you are all very important to me also." They beamed at that.

Sweet silver-haired assassins, he thought.

"But I have no wish to wed."

"Anthony was the same, dear, and now look how happy he is," Petunia said.

They all looked as one to the right. Toby followed their eyes and found Anthony and Evie standing together. He was smiling at something she was saying, or just at her. It was enough to make him feel nauseous.

"I can say with all confidence I never want to look at a woman like your nephew is looking at his wife, ladies," Toby said.

"Oh, posh to that, of course you do, and we are going to ensure that happens."

If there was one thing he'd learned in the years these women had been in his life it was that they did exactly as they wished, no matter how much protest you put up. He could tell them about Florence, but he didn't want them turning up at his townhouse until she was ready to meet them.

"And now I must leave you as I am due to dance with Miss Levine."

"Wonderful," Petunia said. "But she is not on the list."

He walked away vowing to have a chat with Anthony and get him to tell them he was not about to marry for love. When he did, it would be an arrangement born of mutual respect but no emotion.

"Where are you going with that scowl on your face?" Jamie asked intercepting him. "You look intent on murder."

He thought about his next move. If he spoke to Anthony, Jamie would hear, and then he'd be angry that Toby hadn't told him.

"You don't think there is enough going on in my life to look like I am intent on murder?"

"Absolutely, and yet you have the best social face of anyone I know. Therefore, it must be dire indeed to have made you scowl like that in public. Is it Florence? Are you worried about her?"

"No, she will be sleeping by now."

"I know this is hard on you, Toby," Jamie said. "Give it time, my friend, and she will adjust to you."

"She looks at me like I will hurt her. I hate it, and yet don't know how to change that."

"It will take time," Jamie said again.

"I know, but it is hard to see fear in her eyes."

His friend squeezed his shoulder.

"I was just given a list by the aunts."

Jamie frowned. "What list?"

"A list."

"Still none the wiser."

"It has women's names on it, Jamie," Toby said patiently.

His friend's eyes widened. He then looked left and right.

"What are you doing?" Toby asked.

"Looking for them. They may have a list for me."

"Apparently you are not ready."

"What? Why not?" Jamie demanded.

"You want a list? I can give you mine."

"No. But why am I not ready?" His frown was fierce now. "Mind you, after my dance with that vixen Miss Alice Hamner I am inclined to agree.

Miss Hamner was Liberty's friend.

"Don't tell me she didn't swoon with joy to be dancing with you—"

"Yes, thank you," Jamie cut him off. "The woman had far too much to say for herself."

"Perhaps the aunts think you are too immature to have a wife?" Toby annoyed his friend.

Jamie's frown eased. "There is that. I'm heading to supper. Do you want something sweet to ease your foul mood like me?"

"Very much so."

They walked, passing guests as they did so, and stopping occasionally to talk. Lady Tabitha gave Toby a shy smile. *Was she on the list?*

Everyone was primped and pampered for the ball, and this was a setting as familiar to Toby as any in his life. He and his friends had entered society together, and each had done what they needed to survive and outrun their past.

Anthony had taken that to excess in his own way. Gambling, spending time with doxies, and other vices. Jamie had his exercise and enjoyed beating people with his boxing gloves when things got bad for him. Toby couldn't confirm it completely, as his friend would not speak on the matter, but Anthony and Toby believed he also went to the streets late at night and participated in bare knuckle fighting. They'd seen the evidence on his face sometimes, and the way he winced when he moved.

Toby had once been a man who lost himself in women, but that changed after Bidham—after seeing Liberty again—and especially since Florence had moved into his townhouse. He suspected life would never return to what it had been, and to his surprise, he didn't mind that nearly as much as he should.

CHAPTER FOURTEEN

"LIBERTY, SMILE."

"I am, Alice."

"Are you?" Her friend tilted her head to the side. "It looks to be more of a scowl."

"Absolutely not." Liberty angled her body so she was looking at her friend and the wall behind her, rather than searching through the guests for Tobias, which she'd found herself doing far too much lately.

She huffed out a breath and forced her lips up.

It had been seven days since she'd spoken with him in the chocolate shop. Unfortunately, she'd run into him everywhere. It was almost like now they'd become reacquainted, if that was what you could call it, they were being hurled constantly into each other's paths.

There was the bookstore she loved, where she'd found him in the children's section for some unknown reason. Did he have children in his life? She couldn't imagine where from. She'd been there shopping for a gift for her mother to give a friend's granddaughter. Their eyes had clashed, and Liberty had turned around and walked back out the door.

Then she had been out driving with Edward, and he'd seen a sweet shop. The carriage had stopped, and Liberty had dashed in to buy them something sugary. Toby had been there and the bags of sweets before him on the counter had been vast. Liberty hadn't even greeted him. She'd simply raised a brow and walked deeper into the shop hoping he'd leave. He had.

"Had there been small children present tonight, you would terrify them with that look, Liberty."

"Yes, thank you, Alice, for your input." Liberty stopped scowling.

Alice Hamner and Liberty had been friends since they both entered society. Three seasons on and both were still unwed. Liberty, because she wasn't popular, and Alice, because she was being sponsored by her aunt and uncle, and did not have a large dowry, therefore unless a wealthy man fell madly in love with her, chances were she'd struggle to marry well.

Liberty thought that a travesty as Alice was beautiful inside and out, plus she had a wicked sense of humor that often had her swallowing down a bark of laughter.

"I am helping your family to rid themselves of you by making you an excellent prospect for some rich peer to wed," Alice said.

She, like Liberty, knew how to play the society game with polite smiles and social chatter. Where her hair was red, Alice's was black as a starless sky. Porcelain skin, and the perfect rosebud mouth. She had emerald eyes, and to Liberty looked like a doll, but not even her beauty had lured a suitor to offer for her.

"I have decided that one day soon I will leave London and return to my village, where I shall have ten cats, and take in knitting," Alice said.

"You can't knit," Liberty added. "And who will you live with?"

"I will learn, and I will find a position with a family who needs a companion."

"You can come and live with me. I will put you to work cleaning floors," Liberty said.

"I would prefer that to this, and my uncle's deep sighs every time he is forced to pay a bill for my clothing, as they are not without funds, but not flush either. Do you know, Liberty," Alice added, looking at her.

"What?"

"I think being a woman with no means of earning her own money, and at the mercy of a penny-pinching uncle and aunt, is worse than cleaning your floors."

"I'm sorry, Alice." Liberty took her hand, hearing the desperation in her friend's voice. "We shall both retire to Father's estate and live there in peace. Will that suit you?"

Her friend smiled, but there was sadness in her eyes, and a tinge of desperation.

"It will be all right, Alice." Liberty vowed silently to make it so. Her family would always support her, but Alice did not have that luxury.

They stood in silence, watching the dancers. Most evenings Alice and Liberty hugged the walls or wandered together. They were happy chatting about many things. Anything from reading, and the silliness of society, and especially a select few of its members.

"That is a lovely dress, Liberty," Alice said. "Pale green is the perfect color for your hair."

"Well, my mother doesn't think it's lovely. In fact, I am to have a fitting with Miss Battlemore."

"No!" Alice gasped. "I hear that woman is an absolute tartar."

"Apparently, while I had believed they were not determined to see me wed, in fact, I was wrong and they are, so mother is starting with restyling me.

"I'm sorry. Perhaps you are right and we should simply run away to one of your father's estates." Her friend then looked over her shoulder, frowning.

"What?"

"Lord Corbyn is making his way toward us, Liberty, and it is you, not me, he is looking at."

Liberty squinted to bring Tobias into focus as best she could. It certainly seemed like he was coming her way, but why? They had never danced together before, and nor had he sought her out. Did he have something about the occurrences in Bidham to discuss? Yes, that had to be the reason, and dancing would be the best way.

"I'm sure I don't know why he would ask me to dance," Liberty said.

She felt Alice's eyes on the side of her face. "What aren't you telling me, Liberty?"

"Why would I not be telling you something when you know everything about me?"

"Not everything," Alice corrected. "No one can know everything about a person, even a friend."

"Do you remember I told you I hurt my head, Alice?"

"Yes."

"Well, Lord Corbyn was involved in that," she said, not sure why she was telling her friend this now.

"Good Lord, really. I want every detail when he's finished dancing with you, Liberty. And then I want the reasons why you have not told me the truth about that day before now."

"Alice—"

"Ssh. He's close. Do you see him?"

"I am not blind," Liberty whispered. "He's just a bit blurry."

"He's wearing a black jacket, and his waistcoat is black with a gold pattern. Very nice it is too. Lord Corbyn is an exceptionally handsome man, Liberty."

"Is he?"

She felt Alice's eyes on her again.

"I really cannot wait to hear this story you have to tell, Liberty, as your tone suggests to me it will be a good one, but right now smile, and make it look less like a grimace," her friend hissed in her ear.

"Good evening, Lady Liberty, Miss Hamner," a deep voice said seconds later.

"Lord Corbyn," Alice said, dropping into a curtsey.

Liberty did the same.

"May I have this dance, Lady Liberty?"

"I have no wish to dance," she blurted. "I don't dance often."

Suddenly, she felt panicky at the thought of being close to this man again.

"It's a waltz, and not overly taxing, surely? Even without your glasses."

Alice nudged her.

"Very well." She placed her hand on the arm he held out. Found a tight smile for her friend and then let him lead her to the floor. He turned her into his arms, and soon they were dancing.

Liberty had never danced with Tobias. She'd heard he was an excellent partner, Alice had assured her of it, but they'd always kept their distance, and she'd been content with that.

In truth, Liberty rarely danced at all. Her leg—and the fact she often didn't wear her glasses—made her seem clumsy, so she'd turned down far more partners than she'd accepted.

The feel of his hand on her back should not be shooting heat through her as they had layers of material between them. Her fingers in his felt delicate, and she'd never thought of herself as that before.

"Why are you dancing with me?" Liberty had never been one to talk around something that needed to be said. "Do you have news about your investigations into Bidham?"

"Are you going to the Bidham fair, my lady?"

"I am, yes." She went every year, as did her family, because while Corbyns had been associated with the village longer, her father was a duke, and they were happy to have him attend, even if they had yet to ask him to open the event. But then a Corbyn had done that since its inception. *Then this rat had walked away from the village, and me.*

He sighed, loudly, and it had her looking up into his deep brown eyes.

"I know I have no right to ask you to do anything, but I will ask this of you. Have a care, Lady Liberty. Something is afoot in Bidham, and I am going to find out what. But with the death of Sally—"

"You believe it is connected?" she interrupted him.

"I don't have a solid reason to believe that, but, yes, I do," he said. "Now, I am planning to go to the fair, but things have come up."

"What things?" Liberty asked before she could stop herself. "Don't answer that. I don't want to know."

"I'm not telling you anyway," he said calmly.

Now she really wanted to know.

"I wish to help with the investigation," Liberty said.

She watched his jaw clench and waited for the refusal, not that she'd listen to him, but Liberty knew it was coming.

"Ask questions, my lady. I believe people may tell you what they will not tell me in the village."

"Because you walked away from Bidham."

He nodded. His eyes had returned to over her head, but now dropped to meet hers. "Exactly, and I no longer hold their confidence."

Something hung in the air between them then. Unspoken words. Words neither would ever share, and especially not here. After so many years of hating this man, it felt odd to be close to him. To have him touching her. Liberty did not want to feel the moorings of the anger she'd harbored toward him for so long slip, but they were.

She'd watched him, of course, as best she could with no glasses. Seen him flirting and women fawning all over him.

"Why don't you wear your glasses if you need them?" he asked her suddenly. "You're always squinting, spilling drinks, or walking into people, Lady Liberty."

"I do not walk into people," she protested.

He held her gaze for long seconds, and Liberty felt the need to squirm, but as she was an adult, she simply kept her expression blank.

"You were the least clumsy person I knew and yet I have witnessed with my own eyes the times you've thrown champagne over people, and wondered why. Now I know it is because—"

"Thank you, I have no wish to hear your words," Liberty interrupted him.

"When did you start wearing them?"

"That is none of your business," she said and thankfully the music chose that moment to stop. He escorted her back to Alice, who was smiling prettily, a particular talent she'd learned and Liberty had yet to master.

"Ladies," Tobias said bowing. He then walked away, and Liberty drew her first deep breath.

"Come along, we shall enter the supper room and load our plates. Then, I want the entire story as it unfolded between you and Lord Corbyn," Alice said.

She would not tell all of it, but some. The bits that had cut her deeply would stay with just two people. Him and her.

Chapter Fifteen

IT WAS AN odd thing to suddenly have Liberty back in his life, Toby thought as he joined his friend. Just as it was odd he was now guardian to a small child and her dog. Odd and unsettling, and yet when he thought of Liberty and Florence, a small kernel of warmth flared to life inside him. One had every reason to hate him, the other didn't.

"Come, I am hungry. We shall go to the supper room and eat," Jamie said. "And you can tell me about that dance you just had with Lady Liberty."

"No, I can't," Toby added, looking for her, but she was not where he'd left her. Was she dancing with someone else?

They walked down the hall to the supper room to find other guests already there. The table was groaning with the weight of food on top of it. Jamie grabbed two plates and passed one to Toby. He was soon loading it with patties and cakes.

"Lord Corbyn."

Turning from the table, Toby found Liberty's father behind him. A man he'd once known well. They'd shared meals together, and he'd spent hours in his house with his daughter. With him was his wife, another whom he'd once been close to.

"Duke, Duchess," Jamie said, bowing. They'd not spoken a great deal in the years since he'd turned from Liberty, and he'd wondered if she'd told them of that day, but dismissed that thought because the Duke of Talbot would never have talked to

Toby again if she had.

"Will you attend the Bidham fair this year, Lord Corbyn?" the duke asked.

"I will, yes," Toby said. *I hope,* he added silently, thinking of Florence. Surely his friends were right, and she'd love to attend.

The man's smile was wide, as was his wife's. "Well now, that does make me happy," he said. "As it will the village."

"I'm not so sure about that," Toby said honestly.

"They will soon forgive you, but the hurt runs deep. The Corbyn family has been important to the village of Bidham for many years."

Toby nodded. "I know, and I'm sorry for my absence for so long, Duke."

"I'm sure you had your reasons." He held out his hand and Toby shook it. "On behalf of Bidham, welcome home, Lord Corbyn."

The words made his throat tighten. They were standing in a supper room in London, and Liberty's father had just welcomed him home to a village many miles away. Why did that make him want to weep like a babe?

"Enjoy your food, and we will look forward to seeing you at the fair," the duke said, then he and the duchess left.

"There," Jamie said coming back to his side with a laden plate. He was pointing to two chairs. "Quick, before we have to offer them to anyone."

"You are a gentleman," Toby said. "Should a lady require one, we are duty bound to offer."

"Eat fast then, and I have several questions for you while you do."

"I'm sure you do," Toby said dropping a crab patty into his mouth.

"First, I want you to open that note and show me the names on it," Jamie said. "Second, does the Duke of Talbot know that something is going on in Bidham, or just his daughter?"

"I'm not sure, but I don't believe he does, or Liberty would have said something," Toby said. *Wouldn't she?*

"So because I am married, I therefore do not get an invitation to join you for supper with my wife?"

Anthony arrived with Evie. A woman with a forthright nature, wonderful spirit, and perfect in every way for their friend.

He had once been a man who didn't smile, and rarely laughed, unless with Toby or Jamie. His aunts, too, saw a different side of him from the one he showed society. All that had changed the day Evie had walked into his life. Theirs was a tumultuous story that thankfully had a happy ending, which many were not afforded in life.

Jamie and Toby now counted Evie as a friend, and would forgive her anything for what she'd done for Anthony.

"You and your wife were looking longingly into each other's eyes, so we left you to it," Jamie said.

"Jealousy is an ugly trait," Anthony said, looking smug.

"How are Florence and Barnaby doing, Toby? I cannot wait to meet her," Evie said looking at the eclair on Jamie's plate. He held it out, and she took it. After a large bite, she hummed out her pleasure.

"Florence is scared, and dislikes me, or more mistrusts me," Toby said. "Barnaby, however, loves me as I take him outside in the morning and hurl sticks for him to bound after. I enjoy having a dog in the house again, even if he sheds his hair over everything."

"How are your staff coping?" Anthony drawled.

"I doubt they'd tell me if they weren't, but so far, all seems to run smoothly." *Except the fact Florence wants nothing to do with me.*

"That poor little girl, how she has suffered. But time will help, I promise you," Evie said.

"I hope you are right," Toby added.

"You would never have given me your éclair." Anthony glared at Toby.

"I like your wife better than you," Toby said. "She helped me pick out dolls and a house, and other things for Florence."

"There is that," Evie said. "Find us chairs, Anthony, and I will get us food," she then added.

"Other food too please, Evangeline," her husband called as his wife headed for the eclairs. She didn't acknowledge him.

"Has Florence spoken to you yet?" Anthony asked.

"No. When I visit the nursery that she never seems to want to leave, she looks at me through her large brown eyes and stays silent. I tell you, Anthony, I was sure my heart was a shriveled, hard muscle inside my chest, but seeing that little girl's pain makes it ache."

"I have no doubt that from the first meeting, we will all feel the same," Jamie said. "Remember, we are there for you, Toby."

"I know, and am grateful for it, and for the fact you are giving her time to settle before you visit," Toby added.

"Yes, well, let's move on to the exciting news of the night," Jamie said.

"What news?" Anthony demanded.

"Your aunts have given Toby a list."

"Now that's exciting," Anthony said, knowing immediately what the list held.

"How is it he knows what is on the list, but you didn't?" Toby asked Jamie, as he searched the room for Liberty. He found her seated with Miss Hamner.

"I knew. I just wanted to make you tell me," Jamie lied.

"I can't believe my aunts have decided they will marry you off next," Anthony said, looking far too happy about the prospect.

"Yes, well, it's not happening. I know I should want a wife because of Florence, but I am not ready."

"If you say so," Anthony said.

"I do say so," Toby added.

"Show us the list," Jamie said.

He pulled it out reluctantly from the pocket he'd forced it into. Opening it, he felt dread grip him. He shut it again.

"What?" Jamie demanded.

"I'm not sure, but I don't think I want to read it. If I read it, then I've acknowledged this list, and what your aunts want me to do."

"You're an adult. No one can make you do what you don't want to, Toby," Anthony said, snatching the list from his grip. He then opened it and was soon laughing. Jamie leaned closer to read the names and joined his friend.

Toby snatched the list back and looked at the three names written in black ink. Reaching the last of the women who would supposedly make him an excellent wife, he understood their laughter.

Lady Liberty Talbot.

TOBY DID NOT stay at the ball much longer after that. His friends had spent the rest of the evening heckling him over the names on the list, and then there was Florence. Worry for her had niggled in the back of his head. Was she all right? What if she woke and needed him, which she'd never done before, but tonight could be that night?

Toby wasn't sure how it had happened, as he'd not even had a conversation with the little girl, but he'd changed since she'd entered his life. He wanted to label it as vulnerable, but as he'd vowed to never be that again, he didn't. But one little girl who carried his blood had done what no one else could. She'd made him feel.

Not quite true. Since Liberty reentered his life, she'd made him feel, too.

Entering his townhouse silently, Toby went to his room and took off his boots, jacket, and waistcoat. Then he did what he did most nights before he retired. He went to stand outside the nursery. Barnaby would be in there with Florence, keeping her safe, but he still hated that she could be in there alone and upset. Her nanny would have sought her bed by now.

There was, as usual, no noise, and that was a sign for him to leave. He hesitated with his hand on the door and then opened it and entered.

Toby didn't see her at first, but when his eyes went to the window, he found her under it. She sat on the floor in a shaft of moonlight hugging the blonde-haired doll under one arm, and Barnaby lying beside her, her other hand on his fur. Her eyes were on him as he approached. Toby did so slowly, unsure of his next move. When he reached her, he dropped to the floor beside Florence, kneeling. She was crying, and his heart burned for her pain.

Barnaby's tail gave a thump on the floor, and Toby ran a hand over his soft head.

"I'm so sorry you are hurting, Florence."

Totally at sea, he went on instinct and continued talking.

"I lost someone I loved when I was young. My brother Mathew. He was my friend, and I missed him so much. I cried a lot too. We used to play together every day."

She looked at him through those sad eyes.

"I was so sad, and I wanted him back. Angry too that my brother had left, and I didn't have him in my life anymore. I felt lost."

Florence turned her head from him, and then she was picking up the black-haired doll. She handed it to Toby silently. He hugged it close.

"Does hugging your doll make you feel better?" And that was possibly the stupidest thing he'd ever said. As if a doll could make her feel better.

"I miss Mummy and Daddy," she whispered in a husky voice. They were the first words she'd spoken to him.

"I know," he said, holding her gaze. "I'm pleased you brought Barnaby with you. I haven't had a dog in many years, and having him here makes me realize how much I miss that."

They sat there looking at each other for a while in silence, and Toby worked through what he wanted to say to her. She was only five years old, so he had to temper his words so she understood them.

"I want to be your friend like Barnaby, Florence. I want us to be friends and spend time together. I don't have a child, or family, but I would like you and Barnaby to be that, if you'll let me."

Toby leaned in closer and wiped the tears from her cheeks with his thumb and she let him, which to him was a win.

"I want to go home," she whispered.

"I know. If you'd like to, I can take you from London soon, and we can go to my home, which will now be yours too. It's in the country, and there is going to be a fair in the local village. Would you like that?

He saw something flicker in her eyes, and then she nodded.

Toby didn't know what was going on in Bidham yet, but he would keep her safe and always at his side when they got there. The fair will be full of people and fun things for her to enjoy, and he suddenly wanted her to experience what he and Mathew had as children.

She climbed to her feet suddenly, and Toby thought she may leave him and return to her room. Instead, she went to the bookshelf. Taking a book down, she returned to him and held it out.

"You want me to read that to you?"

"Yes, please."

"How about we go to your bedroom? You can get in bed, and I'll read it?" It was well past time she should be sleeping; even he knew that.

She nodded.

They rose silently and walked into the bedroom. He helped her into bed and pulled up the covers. His hesitation was only brief, but he remembered his mother kissing him when she came to see him in bed sometimes, so Toby leaned in and pressed his lips to her forehead. He then lit the lamp on the small table beside her bed.

"Here." Florence patted the space beside her and he wondered why now, tonight, she was letting him get closer, but he didn't ask.

More emotion clogged his throat as he settled on the bed and read with a little girl who carried his blood. She lay on her pillow looking at the book, and something powerful gripped him. Right then, he knew he would fight any battle he needed for this child. Not his child, but his blood. She was now his and he hers, and he would keep her safe.

CHAPTER SIXTEEN

"**I** FAIL TO see why I have to come with you just because Helen cannot," Edward said from beside Liberty as they walked toward the park.

"Apparently Father thinks you're an excellent companion, and due to the stiffness in my leg, and inability to see without my glasses, I need someone to keep me from walking under a carriage," Liberty said.

Edward snorted. "You only need them for close up things, and you have barely limped in months."

Liberty loved her brother because he never allowed her to feel sorry for herself, even when she'd had reason to.

"If you are a good boy, I promise to purchase you whatever food you want when our errands are complete.

"Where is Helen?" Edward asked, his long strides keeping up with Liberty's. He was already taller than she which was annoying.

"Visiting her brother." What she was actually doing was following Liberty's orders, to talk to Dudley, and tell him everything they'd seen and heard. Dudley still visited Bidham regularly and chances were, he'd know something. He may also get Sydney to talk about what he was delivering in London, and why.

"Edward, have you noticed anything odd about Bidham?"

Liberty had thought about discussing this with her parents,

but chances were, they wouldn't notice if something wasn't right, anyway. She loved them, but they were a duke and duchess, and often oblivious to the goings on around them.

"Other than the usual, do you mean?" her brother said. "Like when Miss Jack does that skipping, hop step when she walks? Or Mr. Bernhard uses his rooster to guide him down the street, seeing as he's blind?"

"Yes, yes, there are oddities there, I know that. I mean, anything other than the usual odd," Liberty added.

"Now you mention it. Jason Todd told me his older brother was suddenly going to London a great deal, when he never went there because he said it was a stinky, filthy place. I found that odd."

"I'm sure he had a reason," was all Liberty said tucking that information away to think about later. "Now, while we are here, it is father's birthday when we go back to Bidham for the fair. We need to select him a gift," Liberty said.

"I hate selecting gifts," Edward said.

"But you enjoy receiving them, so put your back into it."

He muttered something she couldn't understand.

"I wish we'd brought an umbrella," Liberty said, looking skyward.

"If we went to the murder display that mother refuses to take me to, then we wouldn't get wet."

"What is this fixation with murder and ghoulish things you have, Edward?" Liberty said, looking around her for no other reason, than she felt she should constantly be on alert now when out walking in London.

First, there was having no wish to bump into Tobias again, and second, she needed to look at all drivers of carts, of which there were plenty.

"I am not fixated. I am intrigued. Please note the difference, Liberty," Edward said in a pompous tone.

She elbowed him in the ribs, making him wheeze.

"You have the pointiest elbows," he rasped. "Good lord."

"What?"

"I'm sure that was Cecil Todd driving that cart," Edward said, pointing. "And considering what his brother told me, I think it must be."

"Really? Come along. Let's see where he is going then." Liberty grabbed her brother's arm and started walking faster.

"Why?"

"I'm not sure, Edward, and this stays between us."

He sighed. "Is this one of those brother-sister promises that if I break you will make me suffer for months?"

"Exactly that."

They walked until the cart turned into the exact street Helen's brother had turned into. Standing on the corner, she watched the same men walk out of the building, and then they were unloading barrels.

"What do you think is in those?" Edward asked.

She told him then of the things that she'd learned, and about Helen's brother Sydney.

"Well, that's all a bit odd."

"Extremely," Liberty agreed. "But there is little we can do about it. Come along, let us get that present."

"And then we will visit the murder display."

"That depends on how much you annoy me," Liberty said.

"If that is the requirement, then I would not take you anywhere were our positions reversed," Edward added.

They found a shop that had pipes, walking sticks, and other things their father liked. Selections made, they headed for the park, in the opposite direction from the murder display.

"I will get there, you know," Edward said.

"Oh, I know," Liberty said. "Take Helen with you. She has a delight in ghoulish things also."

"Really? Capital, I'll do that."

"There is a chess competition on in the park. I thought you might like to see that," Liberty said.

"I would, because after all, what is not to like about two

people moving pieces around a board? Excessively exciting."

"I'm not sure when you went from being my lovely little brother to this sarcastic version, Edward."

"I think it started about a year ago. If I must endure you watching chess as it is your favorite hobby, then first you must feed me. Pies, I think," he said, tugging her to the right.

"What do you suggest, sir?" Edward asked the vendor.

Liberty stood back and watched her little brother. He was good with people and would one day make an excellent duke. He had a way about him that relaxed those he met. Unlike her, who tended to make them bristle with very little effort on her part.

"Here is your pie," he said holding it inches from her nose. "Put your glasses on, Liberty, and I will not tell mother."

"Until you want me to do something for you, then you'll use it against me."

"You know me so well."

She selected meat, and he fruit, and they ate them far too quickly, thus burning their throats, and humming their delight at every mouthful.

Entering the park, they then wandered in silence for a while, comfortable in each other's company. Liberty had only achieved that with two people other than family in her life before.

Alice and Tobias. Once she'd been able to sit next to him for hours and neither had needed to speak. Yes, she was a child, but even back then she'd known he was her person. That someone special who wanted nothing more from you than companionship.

"Lady Liberty."

She didn't groan but it was a near thing as she saw the four women coming her way. Clearing Tobias from her thoughts, which he'd been in far too frequently recently, she nudged Edward.

"Brace yourself. These ladies are harmless, but can talk more than Great-Aunt Elizabeth."

"Run then."

"You may not be in society, but I am, and running would be

cause for scandal, brother."

Mrs. Masters, Miss Masters, Miss Louise Masters, and Miss Elsbeth Masters all looked like peas in a pod with their wide faces and blonde locks. Each dressed in varying shades of pastel.

They all curtseyed prettily to Edward.

"Well, I will be over there, sister. I see someone waving to me," he then said, smiling.

The women tittered and Liberty only just resisted rolling her eyes. Her brother would be a charmer when he entered society. Of course, there was no one over there waving at him, she knew as he hurried away.

"Lady Liberty, will we see you at Vauxhall Gardens this week? There is to be a fireworks extravaganza," Mrs. Masters said.

Liberty was never sure how to take these four ladies. Sometimes they were nice, others snippy, and they always talked over the top of each other. Having a conversation with them was like being buffeted in a howling wind. You left exhausted, unsure what had just happened.

"I had hoped to attend, yes," she said.

"Excellent." Mrs. Masters leaned in as if she was going to confide in Liberty. "We have hopes of an announcement that night," she added. Her eyes then went to her eldest daughter, who blushed.

"Well," Liberty said. "That's exciting. I shall look forward to hearing more. I must go, as my brother is now waving for me to join him."

"Of course, of course. There is also another burgeoning romance for my second eldest daughter. A certain viscount, you understand," Mrs. Masters said. She then placed a finger on her lips. "But enough on that matter."

Viscount? Surely not Tobias, but then why did she care? How many other viscounts were there in London this season?

"Wonderful. Good day to you ladies," Liberty said, dropping into a curtsey. She then walked away in the direction that Edward had taken. Squinting, she saw a group of people and guessed it was the chess event taking place. Her brother would likely be there, because it may bore him, but compared to chatting with the Masters women, would prove far more entertaining.

She reached the men ringing the tables and found Edward in conversation with someone. Liberty didn't know the man. Large bristly moustache, and he wore eyeglasses, which she envied him.

"And here she is. Lady Liberty, this is Mr. Hasslebach. He is the one hosting this event. Unbeaten at chess, he is something of a master. I told him you are the best player I knew, and I thought you may wish to join the competition."

"Ah, no, thank you," she said shooting her brother daggers.

"Of course, you are a woman, so chances are you'll lose," Edward added.

Mr. Hasslebach looked shocked at his words.

"I have no wish to play now, Edward," Liberty gritted out.

He made a clucking sound under his breath that had her back stiffening. Really, was there anyone who could annoy you more than a sibling you loved with every fiber of your being?

"Well, it is highly irregular for a woman to want to challenge, as we have never before allowed—"

"I'll do it," Liberty said before she could stop herself.

"I thought you might," Edward said, looking smug. "I knew that highly irregular and women comment would do it," he added, leaning in to whisper the words into her ear.

"You are a sneaky rodent," she whispered back.

"It's extremely lucky you love me then," he said, wriggling his nose.

"Come along, Lady Liberty," Mr. Hasslebach said, looking uncomfortable.

"She is a duke's daughter, sir, if that makes the pain of her competing in your chess competition easier to bear," Edward said in a hard tone.

"It's all right, brother." Liberty patted his arm. "I'm used to men believing women are a distant second to them."

"They're not," he said. "Beat them, sister."

She leaned in to kiss his cheek.

They took her name and then she stood in line behind a man who smiled at her, which settled her nerves slightly.

"I'm not sure I should do this, Edward. Mother will not be pleased."

"She is not here, and don't tell me you constantly don't do things she has no wish for you to."

"Someone could see and report back to her."

"We will say it's your look alike. Now you need to do this for your fellow womankind, I will find an excellent vantage point where I can glare at people if they question your right to be here."

"And I suppose it will be close to where that vendor is selling bags of roasted chestnuts?"

"Very likely."

She stood there watching the four tables set up. All occupied by men. She would definitely need her glasses for this one. Opening her reticule, she put them on and felt the tightness in her temples ease. If there were indeed hell to pay when her mother found out, which she surely would, she may as well get told off for wearing her glasses, too.

Ten minutes later Liberty was seated across from a bear of a man who smirked at her. She smiled back sweetly, and then focused on everything she'd learned in all those chess books her father had in his office. The ones she'd pored over for hours, and then sat at his chess board and put into action.

"I will go easy on you, madam."

She simpered, well, thought she did, as it wasn't something she'd ever mastered. "You are too kind."

Liberty then set about beating him soundly.

CHAPTER SEVENTEEN

TOBY HAD INTRODUCED Anthony, Jamie, and Evie to Florence this morning. She had been shy, but happy enough to take tea with everyone. He'd explained they were his friends, which seemed to relax her slightly. Barnaby had also been a success, and coaxed food out of Anthony and Jamie, which was no easy task.

After they'd left, Toby did what Evie had told him to. With trepidation, and a touch of fear, he'd gone to the nursery to ask Miss Haigh if he could take Florence and Barnaby out for a walk. The nanny seemed pleased and offered to come. He'd said he would be fine and hoped he was right.

Toby wasn't sure if he should be alone with this child's welfare in his hands, but Evie said for them to truly bond, he needed to show her he could look after her alone. He'd protested, but she'd shut every one of his objections down, until finally Toby had given in.

Since the night he'd gone to the nursery after the ball, things had changed for the better between them. He knew that. Florence talked to him now. Not a lot, but if he asked her a question, she answered. She also let him read a bedtime story to her every evening. Toby treasured those moments.

He liked to see her smile and decided it would be his life's work to continue making her happy. Another thing he'd realized for certain was he now did indeed need a wife, but he would have to make that selection carefully, as Florence's happiness was paramount to any decision.

"It's a nice day for a walk in the park," Toby said as they left the house. Holding out his hand, he held his breath until her little fingers slipped into his. Her hand was the most precious thing he'd ever held.

Him. A man who once needed no one, and in fact fought against that closeness, now wanted it with his ward. It was her innocence and vulnerability that brought out his protective instincts. He would never let her suffer as he had.

After wandering for a while and chatting to her about what they saw, to which she'd answered occasionally with a nod or smile, Toby noticed a group gathered in the park and headed that way. The day was mild, and Florence wore her little jacket over her dress and bonnet in a matching shade of rose pink, looking cute.

They reached the ring of people and eased into a space. The young man to his left shuffled sideways to accommodate them. Barnaby then sat on Toby's foot. Clearly the grass was damp.

"Lord Corbyn," the young man then said, nodding.

He tried to put a name to the face. It was the eyes that gave him away. Liberty's brother Edward.

"Lord Talbot," Corbyn said, bowing. "Allow me to introduce you to Miss Florence, my ward, and her dog Barnaby."

Florence looked up at Liberty's brother and then dropped into a credible curtsey while still holding Toby's hand.

"Well, he's a fine looking fellow," Edward said, patting the golden head while smiling at Florence.

He felt yet another jolt of pain in his chest looking at the boy, because it made him think of the brother he'd lost too soon. Liberty and Toby had often discussed Edward and Mathew, and the men they'd one day become.

"Do you enjoy chess, Miss Florence?" Edward asked.

"I have never played," she said.

"And you, my lord?" Toby asked him.

"We are neighbors, Lord Corbyn. My name is Edward." He

had that straightforward way of speaking his sister had once used. "And no, chess is not my game."

"And I am Toby. Are you here alone, Edward?"

"No. Liberty is about to play."

Toby's head snapped around so fast it was a wonder he didn't strain something. There she was, seated at a nearby table, glasses perched on her nose, a small frown pulling at her brows. She wore her favorite shade of pale blue, a deeper blue pelisse over it, and a matching bonnet. A few fiery curls had escaped to frame her face, and his chest gave a traitorous squeeze at the sight.

Sweet, he thought. Something about this woman got to him, and he suspected part of that was due to the connection they'd once shared.

"The man who organizes this had no wish for Liberty to participate, which was enough to spur her on to do so," Edward said. "She's taking that man apart. I knew she would, because he smirked at her. Not a sound notion, Toby. As you know my sister, you'll understand what I mean." The boy then held out a bag of hot chestnuts, which Toby slid his hand into, because hot chestnuts were a particular favorite of his. He then bent down to give Florence one.

He stood beside Liberty's brother and watched her play, with Florence now leaning on his legs. She was crunching chestnuts and feeding bits to Barnaby. What surprised Toby was how comfortable he felt in that moment with these two, and the dog.

"I'm not a lip reader, you understand, Toby, but I think my sister's opponent said something pitying to Liberty because she's giving him her sickly-sweet smile," Edward said.

Toby remembered that smile.

"Suffice to say, she will want to beat him soundly after that."

Looking around them, Toby saw mainly men watching. A few were frowning and muttering and pointing at Liberty. A woman in their midst was not making them happy.

As if sensing him looking at them, several turned his way, and Toby sent them a hard look.

"You and my sister were once friends," Edward said softly.

It wasn't a question, but a statement. "We were."

"I was young, but I remember you because you had a younger brother and when he came with you to visit, he often played with me."

Toby swallowed the lump in his throat those words produced.

"Please allow me to say how sorry I am for his death."

"Thank you," Toby rasped.

Florence touched his fingers briefly, almost as if she was reassuring him.

"When we nearly lost Liberty, I wondered how I would cope," Edward said.

The solemn words had Toby's blood running cold. *Liberty had nearly died?*

"When did she nearly die?" he forced out.

"Just before she was to enter society, she had an accident and fell off her horse," Edward said.

She could have broken her neck and he would never have known.

He was about to ask another question when the man Liberty was playing against let out a roar as he rose to his feet. "You should not have been able to beat me!"

"Look after Florence, Edward," Toby said. He then climbed the rope that penned the chess opponents in and was standing beside the man before Liberty could get out of her chair.

"Problem?" he said with a calm he was not feeling. *Liberty had nearly died.* He couldn't shake that thought from his head.

"She should not have beaten me!" The man spoke in a thick accent that Toby thought could have been Russian.

"Because I am a woman, therefore I cannot beat you?" Liberty said, in a tone that boded trouble for the man as she regained her feet.

"She—"

"That's Lady Liberty to you, and be warned," Toby said, eyeing the man. "If you say anything further which does not include congratulations, then I will take that as an insult to her."

"I am quite capable of handling this," Liberty fumed.

The man glared at her, then just when Toby thought he'd have to teach him a lesson in manners, he stormed away.

Liberty rounded on Toby. "Why are you here? You should not have stepped in. What if someone notices?" Her eyes were shooting left and right.

"I don't care if someone sees. He should not have spoken to you that way, my lady," Toby snapped.

"He stepped in because that man was threatening you, Liberty. You should thank Lord Corbyn," Edward said, arriving with Florence, who was now holding his hand, and Barnaby.

Her teeth snapped together, and then her eyes fell to the child.

"Why are you holding a child's hand, and who does that dog belong to?"

"She is my ward, and lives with me." Toby smiled at Florence reassuringly. "Florence, this is Lady Liberty, and she is Edward's sister. That is Barnaby." He pointed at the dog.

"You have a ward?" He could see the shock on her face.

"Come this way if you please, Lady Liberty, and I will introduce you to your next opponent," a man with a spectacular moustache said to Liberty.

He could see she had many questions, but they would wait. Now she had another man to beat. This one was older, with thick gray hair and a smile, which thankfully he directed at her.

Toby, Florence, and Edward walked back to where they'd been watching, but the crowd had grown and Florence could not see over the heads. Bending, he asked, "Would you like me to lift you into my arms so you can see?"

She nodded.

It felt awkward, but he managed it. Lifting her high, Toby held her against his chest. When her little arms looped around his neck, the lump in his throat nearly choked him. Barnaby once again settled on his foot.

Edward then held out a twist of paper. Florence took a lemon drop, as did Toby.

"What really happened between you and my sister all those years ago?" Edward said as they watched the man make his first move. "I asked her, but she refused to tell me anything other than you had grown apart."

Clearly Liberty's brother had the same forthright nature she'd once had.

Toby kept his eyes on the game. Watched Liberty move pieces around the chessboard after careful consideration. He didn't remember her playing chess when they were young. Liberty had always wanted to be outside, riding or walking, but apparently she was good at it.

"I may have been young, but I saw her the day she came home from your house," Edward said softly, and Toby thought the only way he could get him to stop was to walk away, but as he wanted to watch Liberty, he stayed. "Saw her lying on her bed sobbing as if her heart had been ripped from her chest. I climbed on with her and lay beside her. We stayed there all day not talking. She clutched my hand and wept."

He'd said the words softly so only Toby could hear. Florence was loudly sucking on her lemon drop.

The thought of Liberty weeping for him burned inside his chest. Toby didn't want that pain. Had worked hard to not feel.

"I hated you. Vowed I always would do so."

"Then you shouldn't have offered me a lemon drop," Toby said, because he had no idea what else to say.

"I also have more roasted chestnuts, so you may not get one of them."

"I am, of course, desolate."

"As I've grown older, I've begun to understand that everyone does something for a reason. You and my sister were best friends; even I could see that. So something had to have made you turn from her."

"Edward, what happened is in the past now. We cannot go

back and right the wrongs even if we should wish it."

Toby felt Edward's eyes on the side of his face, but he did not speak again. They stood in silence then and watched Liberty play.

"When did she start wearing glasses?" Toby asked minutes later.

"After the accident. Have you not noticed the changes in my sister?"

He had, but believed they'd come with age. The more sedate pace she walked and danced. The eyeglasses. How she'd lost her zest for life... well, at least in society. When he didn't speak, Edward continued.

"As I explained, Liberty had a riding accident. But perhaps this is not my story to tell, and she would be angry with me if I did."

"She's never going to tell me, Edward," Toby said, refusing to beg the young man to continue, even though he wanted to hear what happened.

"Very well, but if you say you heard this from me I will call you a liar."

"I won't."

"Liberty was riding hard, as she always did. This day more so, as she'd told me that riding in such a manner would not be tolerated when she reached London for her season. We think a bird flew up, but my sister does not remember. She fell and rolled down a hill."

No one looking at Toby would know what he was thinking in that moment, and he was glad he'd learned to school his expression into one of cynical boredom.

"She broke her thigh and hit her head. Liberty was unconscious for days. When she woke she was different," Edward said.

"Different?"

"Her eyes wouldn't focus and she had to learn to walk again. I helped her," Edward said. "She was bedridden for months and suffered terrible headaches. Then one day, Father brought in this man. His name was Dr. Valerie. And he got her out of bed and moving again. He applied warm cloths to her leg and had Helen rub in ointments."

And I didn't know she was suffering. There was no going back, Toby reminded himself, tightening his arms around Florence. Only forward.

"Thank you for telling me."

Toby stood and watched his old friend win the next two matches. *Liberty could have died.* That thought kept circling inside his head.

"She's playing Mr. Hasslebach, in the last match," Edward said. "My guess is he's not happy about that."

"That man has whiskers covering his mouth," Florence whispered to Toby.

"It would be hard to eat don't you think?" She agreed with a nod.

"He's scared he's going to lose." Edward held out the second bag of roasted chestnuts for Florence.

He liked this young man. Liked his forthright nature and dry sense of humor, which was probably because that was exactly how Liberty had been as a young girl. He also liked how easy he was with Florence.

Toby, standing there holding a small girl, with a dog sitting on his foot, chatting to Edward, would shock the people of society if they saw him at that moment.

The thought didn't worry him at all. In fact, he found he liked it very much.

CHAPTER EIGHTEEN

"A BREAK WILL be called before the final, where I will play Lady Liberty," Mr. Hasslebach said loudly.

Liberty looked to where Toby still stood with her brother and his ward. *Toby had a ward.* If she hadn't seen the little girl, she would not have believed it possible. When had she come to live with him?

He held her high in his arms, and hers were around his neck, which told Liberty she was happy to be there. She searched for a maid, or nanny, and saw no one nearby, just Tobias and the child, plus, the golden Labrador sitting on Tobias's foot.

Where was the girl when she'd seen him traveling from London the day her carriage wheel had broken?

She had so many questions, and no wish to ask them of him. No wish to spend time with that man if she did not have to. He disturbed her, and those feelings she'd long shut away were rising. Especially seeing him smiling at Florence. That smile was one he used to use with her. She hadn't seen it in many years.

Liberty looked at Edward, who was stroking the top of the dog's head, seeming comfortable with the man who had crushed her that day many years ago. She started toward her brother... not Tobias.

"I am going to purchase a cup of tea. My throat is parched, Edward," Liberty said in a harsh tone. The little girl looked at her wide eyed.

"Soften your tone, Liberty," Edward said, looking at the child.

"Sorry. Hello, Florence," Liberty said, forcing a smile onto her lips. "My name is Liberty. It's very nice to meet you." It wasn't the child's fault that the man holding her had become her enemy.

"Have you been eating my brother's lemon drops and roasted chestnuts?"

"Yes," Florence whispered.

Edward held out the bag of nuts to her. Liberty took one. "I suppose you ate all the lemon drops, too?" she said instead of, *How is it possible you are a ward to this sweet little girl, Tobias?*

"All gone I'm afraid. Florence has a taste for them," Edward said.

"He ate them," the girl then added, pointing to Edward.

"Not all surely?" Liberty teased her.

"Nearly all," Florence said solemnly.

"Would you like me to get your tea for you, seeing as I have been basking in your success, while the men around me groan loudly?" Edward asked.

"Excellent. I am useful for something, then, and I can get my own tea," Liberty said.

"I knew you would come in handy at some stage," her brother said with a cheeky smile. He then handed his chestnuts to Tobias. "I suppose you want tea too, my lord?"

"No," Liberty said as Tobias said, "Yes."

"Would you and Barnaby like to come for a walk, Florence? You can help me carry the cups," Edward said, ignoring her.

"Yes." The little girl wriggled to get down.

Toby lowered her to her feet gently. He then dug into his pocket and handed her some money. "You can pay for our tea with this, Florence."

She nodded, eyes serious, and then took Edward's hand and walked away.

"Why are you talking to my brother?" Liberty rounded on him when Edward had walked away. "What game are you playing?"

"Those are the questions you want to ask me when I've seen your eyes on Florence?" he said calmly.

She closed her teeth with a snap.

"She is my cousin's child. He and his wife recently passed away, and I am now her guardian and the owner of Barnaby."

She wanted to ask how he, a man who appeared to care for little but himself, could care for a child, but she didn't. The kind boy she'd once known was hopefully still inside him. Plus, she'd seen him holding the little girl gently. Those weren't the actions of a callous man, surely?

"Now about Bidham," he continued. "I think it is definitely smuggling that is taking place there. But I also believe the village is under threat. I sent a man to investigate. No one would talk to him. But the magistrate, who was called in to deal with Sally's death, said it was murder and that, to his mind, there is something odd going on in Bidham."

She felt the pain lance through her at the thought of Sally's death.

"I'm sorry her death upsets you, Liberty."

"That is neither here nor there," she said, watching Edward and Florence walk away with Barnaby. "But I need to tell you something, my lord."

"As I am standing before you, now is as good a time as any," Tobias said.

She glared at him. "We don't like each other, and I'm fine with that. So once this is done, we will carry on with our mutual animosity."

"I believe I told you I don't dislike you—"

"Stop," she hissed. "No one speaks to me the way you did. Ignores me the way you have, and can say they don't dislike me." She then inhaled through her nose. "It matters not anyway. What I wanted to say is that Edward and I just saw Cecil Todd driving a cart similar to the one Helen's brother was driving, and he stopped at the same place. He and two other men I'd seen before then unloaded the barrels."

"Tell me you didn't go back to the warehouse and ask more questions."

"Not that it is any concern of yours what I do, but I did not."

"At least in this you are showing sense." His dark eyes were narrowed now.

"I continually show sense, unlike you," she snapped back.

"No good can come of continuing this conversation, so I will ask you where exactly is this warehouse location?" Tobias said.

He was right, no good could come of them arguing. Their only focus should be Bidham. The problem was Liberty felt irrational around this man. Before she could speak again, her brother and the child returned.

"She put honey in yours because I told the lady serving that you had a sour disposition, Liberty," Edward said. "Florence also got some in hers, but that was just to make her sweeter."

The little girl had a small smile on her face as she looked at Edward.

"I'm not entirely sure why I love you," Liberty muttered taking the mug.

Edward handed Toby his.

"Tell him where that place was Cecil drove the cart to this morning, Edward. I think Mr. Hasslebach wants to begin, and as I want this over before mother hears about it, I will see if I can beat him quickly."

"Liberty," Toby said.

"What?" She looked at his left ear.

"Have you noticed since you started playing that the crowd has grown and changed?"

She looked at the people now two deep around them and saw the women.

"You are championing these women; don't forget that," he said.

"I expect you to win, Sister, and when you do, I will heckle the men in the crowd," Edward said loudly. "I believe in you, Liberty. Plus, Florence told me she wants you to win. Apparently, her mother was excellent at chess."

"Was she?" Tobias asked, looking down at his ward. She replied with a nod.

"Thank you for your belief in me, Edward." She then bent to talk to Florence. "And thank you for your support too." The little girl patted her cheek.

Leaving Tobias, Edward, Florence, and Barnaby, she went to where Mr. Hasslebach now stood beside the table they'd play at.

"Good luck," he said, but Liberty didn't feel like he really meant it.

Twenty minutes later, Liberty was sure Mr. Hasslebach was trying to put her off her stride. He was humming and tapping his fingers. Liberty despised tapping as much as she despised someone crunching loudly nearby, which her brother constantly did.

It was also the height of rudeness to do what the man was doing, and he would know that. But Liberty knew his actions were because she was good at chess, and he was in danger of losing.

The match was close, and Liberty had to shut out all the noise and distraction, especially the fact that her brother stood with her enemy... perhaps enemy was harsh, but the man had crushed her.

"Go on, Love, you show him," someone in the crowd called out.

Mr. Hasslebach glared at the woman.

"Stuffy old goat," she muttered.

"Excuse me, but there is no need for name calling."

Liberty tried to shut out the exchange taking place a few feet from her as voices rose.

"Exactly that, madam. He is a stuffy old goat."

Those words had come from Edward.

"You men aren't happy because that lady is beating one of you," a woman said.

Concentrate, Liberty, she reminded herself as the debate raged on.

"I fear she's right, Polebrook," came the deep words of Tobias.

That man, Liberty thought. She wished he'd exit himself from her life once again. She hated that her heart beat a little harder when he was near.

Focus!

Recalling her favorite chess book, Liberty made a move that had Mr. Hasslebach inhaling sharply.

A loud crunch told her Edward was closer and still eating chestnuts. Liberty refused to look at him or Tobias and that sweet little girl.

"She won't have the pluck to finish it," a man said.

"She's had the pluck to do so, thus far," Tobias said.

Mr. Hasslebach countered, and she moved again. The concentration was making her head ache, which sometimes happened, and the doctors said may go on forever, or one day stop, which was frustrating, but Liberty had no time to worry about that now.

Focusing on the pieces on the checkered board before her, she worked through her next moves in her head. When Liberty saw the pathway, she made her first move. She knew Mr. Hasslebach had seen it too because he made a choking, coughing sound in his throat as if to clear it.

"Checkmate, I believe," Liberty said quietly two moves later. Mr. Hasslebach gasped.

"She just said checkmate!" a woman's voice cried.

"How is that possible? No one beats Mr. Hasslebach."

"You have read *The Elements of Chess*?" Mr. Hasslebach asked when he could speak. He was studying the board.

"I have, yes."

He rose then and held out his hand. Liberty rose too and shook it. Then pandemonium broke out, but only from the women watching. They cheered and clapped, and a few even hugged each other in excitement. Many of the men in the audience looked angry.

"I never watched it before, but I'll be sure to now if women can play and win!"

"I say she has to have cheated," a male voice said.

"Agree."

"No one has been able to beat Mr. Hasslebach. How can she? A woman."

Liberty ignored the words. She was used to people's opinions where women were concerned; she and others faced them daily.

"Take that back," Edward said in a loud voice, which drew her eyes. Her brother was now standing toe to toe with a much larger and older man than him. Liberty moved closer, but before she could reach her brother, Tobias appeared, nudging Edward to one side. He then handed him Florence.

"She won that match using skill, and the fact you would say otherwise, Lucas, speaks more to your character than hers," Tobias said in a hard, cold voice. "Now apologize for your words at once."

The crowd had turned from the chess game to watch Tobias and Mr. Lucas, who Liberty had danced with a few times, and didn't like at all. She'd agreed with Alice when she'd said his eyes were too close together.

"I say, Corbyn, we were just chatting," another man said, but she couldn't see his face as he stood behind the crowd.

"If Lady Liberty were a man, she would call you out for what you just said, Lucas. Apologize at once."

Liberty held her breath, waiting to see what would happen, and then Mr. Lucas muttered an apology to Tobias, who looked mean enough to punch him.

"It is not to me that you need to say sorry, Lucas," Tobias then said, looking at Liberty now. "Come closer, my lady," he said holding her gaze. "Mr. Lucas has something he wishes to say to you."

She didn't want to come closer, or make the already-created scene worse, but she knew she had no other option. Liberty approached, wishing herself anywhere but here.

"Well done." A few of the women called out to her as she walked. "Congratulations, Lady Liberty." Lady Yarrow, who was a close friend of her mother's spoke these words. She was going to be in so much trouble when this news reached her.

"Say the words, Lucas," Tobias said when she stopped beside him. A muscle ticked in his jaw. She remembered seeing it a time or two when they were children, and it had been she back then who had provoked him.

"I'm sorry for my words, Lady Liberty." Mr. Lucas looked like he'd swallowed a mouthful of ten-day-old haddock.

She nodded. He then bowed and walked away with haste, taking his friends with him. They threw quelling looks at her over their shoulders.

Oh, this was bad. Her parents would surely hear, and then when she stepped into society she would be the center of attention, which she loathed.

"I'm sorry, Florence," Tobias was saying then as he took the girl back in his arms. "For raising my voice." She patted his cheek as if to say she forgave him.

The sight of this handsome man holding that sweet little girl, with the dog at their feet had a few women nearby smiling, but not her. *You loathe him,* she reminded herself.

"Did you have to humiliate him?" She looked at Tobias after shuffling sideways and putting some space between them.

"Yes. I would have punched him if there weren't a crowd, and Florence wasn't with me," Tobias said, now calm.

"I'd like to have seen that."

"That will do, Edward. You are becoming entirely too bloodthirsty," Liberty said.

She should thank Tobias for standing up for her honor, but what she'd rather do was walk fast in the opposite direction. But she was no coward.

"You did not need to step in, but thank you just the same for it."

"If that was you being grateful, it was a pathetic attempt." His brown eyes held something she'd not seen in a long while as they looked at her. There was a wicked glint in them now the anger had gone.

"It is the only one you are getting. Now come along, Edward. It will be a miracle if mother doesn't hear about this."

"Oh, she'll hear. I just saw Mrs. Minton," Edward said, looking happy considering they would both be in a world of trouble when they got home.

"My lady, this is yours."

Mr. Hasslebach came to her side, holding out a chess piece for her. "The winner of this competition keeps it until the next tournament is called."

She took it. "Thank you, and of course I will return so you can win it back," Liberty said, feeling sorry for the man now. He looked like a lost puppy. Clearly, it hurt that she'd beat him.

"I've never lost that piece to anyone," he added solemnly.

"Don't do it." The words were whispered in her ear as Liberty moved her hand to pass it back to Mr. Hasslebach.

Liberty ignored Tobias and clenched her fingers tighter around the chess piece. How dared he tell her what to do.

"My sister will, of course, be happy to challenge you at your earliest convenience, sir," Edward said.

Mr. Hasslebach pulled out a card and handed it to Edward with mournful eyes, instead of Liberty, who would actually be the person he needed to contact. He then walked away. Without a backward glance, Liberty did the same, needing to put some distance between herself and Tobias Corbyn, and his sweet-faced little ward.

CHAPTER NINETEEN

"WILL YOU NEVER learn?"

"What? I'm just fencing with him," Tobias said swishing his blade back and forth. "I'm quite good at it, you know."

His friends had lured him out of the townhouse today to exercise, telling him he would grow lazy if he did not. He'd agreed to come, but not about the lazy comment. He was busier than ever now Florence and Barnaby lived with him.

Life for Tobias was settling into a rhythm. He was now comfortable in leaving Florence at home for a few hours at a time, and she was more comfortable around him. They walked in the gardens daily with Barnaby, and he shared meals with her. He'd also taught her to slide down the banister, which had produced a genuine laugh from his ward.

The dog had also infiltrated the Corbyn household. He'd caught Chadders out the window handing Barnaby a large bone yesterday.

Tobias had also thrown himself into investigating what was going on in Bidham, and why a few of the villagers were turning up in London... well, two of them anyway. Edward had told him he'd seen Cecil Todd, and Liberty and Helen, Sydney, Helen's brother, delivering barrels to that warehouse. He'd gone there to investigate.

"Jamie's fitter than both of us, and we have yet to beat him,"

Anthony said, drawing him from his thoughts.

"You have grown soft since your marriage to Evie," Toby said, lunging to the left and right. "The hard, unfeeling man you once were has gone, and in its place is this whining creature who talks about his feelings." Jamie, who was stretching his muscles beside him for some reason, snorted. The man was always moving.

"You are hardly one to speak. Since Florence entered your life, I've seen a definite change in your rakish behavior," Anthony said.

Which he couldn't deny.

"Back to this Bidham business. You say that warehouse definitely had barrels in it, and little else?" Anthony asked.

Toby rolled with the change, as that was their way. They were always discussing two things at once, while annoying each other.

"Something didn't feel right there," Toby said.

"Tell us again exactly what happened when you went to the warehouse alone, without one of us for backup," Jamie said.

Toby rolled his eyes. "I am quite capable of asking a few questions in daylight, alone," he carried on before they spoke. "I told them I'd come to inspect the shipment of goods I ordered." He'd gone along with Liberty's theme of pretending to be there for another purpose. Not that she should have been there at all, infernal woman.

"The man who opened the door told me they were not holding anything for Lord Corbyn. I pulled out the piece of paper I'd had the forethought to write with the address for this warehouse on, and handed it to the man."

"That was quite clever considering it was you who thought of it," Anthony said crossing his legs at the ankles, relaxed, which was something he'd once rarely been.

"Very amusing. I looked in the doorway and saw all the barrels, and then the man returned so I stepped back outside."

"How many men in there?" Jamie asked.

"Five."

"No one you recognized from Bidham or society?" Anthony asked.

"No."

"We probably need to go back after dark and have a good look around," Jamie said.

"Agreed," Toby said.

"Are you fighting Corbyn, Stafford?"

The man who had asked that question dropped down beside Anthony.

"We are, Raine. Do you wish to take on the loser?" Toby asked.

"God no. I just had a match with my youngest brother." The man looked around him. "He's gone, thankfully, and I can now acknowledge the ache in my thighs and arm, but that is after taking him apart. Old age, you know, it comes to all of us."

The Earl of Raine had three brothers, all younger, and Toby had never known a single one of them to take a backward step when a forward one was on offer.

"Indeed, well you sit those aging bones here beside me, Raine, and we will take a wager on the match," Anthony said.

Soon bets were placed by more than the two lords seated in the front row.

"My aunts paid me a call," Anthony said when Toby handed him his jacket and began rolling up his sleeves.

"How lovely for you," Toby said.

"They are quite convinced one of those three women is to be your future wife, Tobias, especially given that you have Florence in your household now. I tend to agree, in fact—"

"One more word and I will skewer you," Toby snarled. He then stomped away to where Jamie was still lunging. "For pity's sake, man, you look like a... actually, I have no words for what you look like."

Jamie looked from Anthony and back to Toby. "What did he say to annoy you?"

"Nothing," Toby snapped. "Stop lunging and start fencing."

"En garde then, my surly friend," Jamie said.

Toby cleared his head and focused. His friend liked to attack. He fenced like he did most things, with skill and speed.

"Excellent parry, Corbyn!" someone called out as he took offensive action to deflect Jamie's attack.

"You have improved," Jamie said, barely out of breath.

"Or you're slowing down," Toby wheezed, lunging.

"Nice riposte!" Anthony called.

They turned, they lunged, and they retreated, and soon Toby's shirt was sticking to him and he'd forgotten all about the irritating Liberty Talbot... damn, she was back. Jamie took advantage of his mind wandering and struck.

"You were doing so well for a while there," Anthony said, wandering over while Toby bent at the waist sucking in air. "I almost believed you'd beat him."

"He lost focus," Jamie said now swinging his blade from side to side as if he'd not just fought Toby. "I saw it and struck. I wonder what he was thinking about?"

"I detest you," Toby said when he could breathe again. His friend smiled.

"Well done, Lord Corbyn."

Toby took his time turning to face the man at his back. Lord Michael was with his two friends this time. Mr. Patterson and Lord Sybil. Both were as oily and mean spirited as him, for all they portrayed a different facade to society.

"I had my money on Stafford of course. He was the sure bet." Lord Michael said.

"Would you care to have a match, Michael?" Anthony said, his eyes narrowed and angry.

Anyone from their time in Blackwood Hall created that reaction in the three friends.

"I'm afraid I don't have the time today. I just wanted to congratulate you, Stafford, and commiserations, Corbyn." The smile was genuine, but Toby didn't return it.

Perhaps Michael was not as villainous as some involved, but he was complicit because he'd known and done nothing to stop the beatings and torture. Therefore, he would always be the enemy as far as Toby was concerned.

"Yes, well, it is not everyone who can do something as physical as fencing, Michael," Jamie said.

"Indeed, there is a certain set of skills required, and not everyone can master them," Anthony added.

Michael's eyes narrowed at the deliberate insults.

"Indeed, I believe gambling is more your thing?" Toby added.

"And chess," Anthony said. "Not as stressful on the heart."

It was rare they came out and deliberately annoyed someone from their time at Blackwood, but that did not mean they hadn't sought revenge. In fact, they had. Calculated and deliberate, they had gone after those who had harmed them in subtle ways that would never lead back to the three of them.

"I can fence quite admirably," Michael protested, his pleasant expression slipping slightly. "I just do not have the time to do so right now."

"Of course you don't." Toby sounded smug. "Don't let us hold you up."

"Good day," Lord Michael said with a stiff bow.

"Rat-faced bastard," Toby muttered after the man had left.

"You know, we've never really looked into his affairs. The man appears to keep his nose clean, and I've not heard his name linked to any business dealings. Perhaps it's time we dug deeper?" Anthony said.

"Agreed," both Jamie and Toby added.

Jamie wandered off to do more stretches and Anthony to speak with someone else, and Toby moved to watch two more fencers do battle. He stood behind a group of men he wasn't well acquainted with but they were on nodding terms.

"I'll court her because she'd come with a title and wealth, but there are others I'd prefer," one was saying.

"Oh indeed. Miss Little is exquisite, and it won't be a hardship to take her to bed, but she's not going to come with as much money as others."

"Close your eyes when doing the deed, Bilcoe."

This caused raucous laughter among the three men. Toby didn't think he'd ever been like that... hoped he and his friends had never discussed a woman as if she were a commodity to acquire. Yet, he knew that was the way of things. A woman in society had one role. To marry and marry well. But he would not have that expectation for Florence, Toby vowed. He would see her happy in whatever choice she made. There would be no marriage to a man just because it was expected of her.

"Not that I've seen them, you understand, but I believe she has nice breasts. It's the hair that worries me," one of the men said.

"Indeed. It suggests a fiery temperament even if there has been no evidence of one."

"Still, a duke's daughter is not to be sneezed at, even if she is a little long in the tooth."

Toby pushed upright off the wall, as he went through all the duke's daughters currently in London. There were only two. One who fitted the hair comment.

"I saw her limping once. I wonder if there is an issue with her limbs."

"She squints too."

"Late to society and still unwed. You have to wonder why?"

"If the hair is a problem, you could just make her wear her bonnets all the time, even in the bedroom."

That anyone would not love Liberty's hair enraged Toby. It further enraged him they spoke of her limping as if it was a fault. The squinting too, all of which had come about due to her accident Edward had said.

"I shall have to give it some thought. The money and title would be welcome, but I'm unsure I could spend the rest of my life with her."

"You'll have a mistress, so once you have an heir, you need

never lay with her again."

The rage was swift and fierce and robbed Toby of his sanity. He stayed where he was behind them, attempting to calm down. It didn't work, which was something else that seemed to have changed inside him recently. His emotions flared out of control with ease, especially if there was a threat or insult to someone he cared about.

"To stand there and openly discuss a woman so anyone can overhear is beyond contempt," Toby snapped. The words had the immediate effect of quieting every other noise around them. All eyes turned to him.

"L-Lord Corbyn!" The color drained out of the face of one of the men. "I was just—"

"You were speaking about Lady Liberty, weren't you?" No one answered him. "Weren't you?" Toby thundered.

"Problem?" Jamie appeared.

"I-we did not mean—"

"I heard every word," Toby growled advancing.

Anthony stepped into his path.

"Were I you, Lockwood, I would run, because that particular look in my friend's eyes does not bode well for anyone."

"I am not finished," Toby snapped trying to step around Anthony, but as Jamie was suddenly there he couldn't. "Move."

"We meant no insult to Lady Liberty," Lockwood called.

"Every word you spoke was an insult!" Toby roared as the three men fled. "Look in the mirror! None of you are a catch any woman would willingly want!"

"Stuff him into his jacket, and let's go," Anthony said.

Minutes later, Toby found himself on the street, rage still gripping his body. He searched for the three men who had insulted Liberty and couldn't find them.

"I wanted to punch them," he muttered.

"They are silly young men, but harmless," Anthony said.

"They were rude and insulting, and not just to Liberty. It is uncalled for."

"As we have been before," Jamie said.

"We were never insulting," Toby gritted out. "Women have it hard enough. They should not be subjected to such behavior."

He felt his friends' eyes on him, and looked the other way.

"So, I think we can cross two names off that list," Anthony said. "She will be excellent with Florence as will her younger brother."

"What are you talking about?" he snapped.

Anthony looked at him with a raised brow.

"I will not be marrying her," Toby said, but the words held little strength, and he told himself that was because he'd just had a rigorous fencing match, even if it was a lie.

CHAPTER TWENTY

"MISS BATTLEMORE, THIS is my daughter Lady Liberty."

She was reading in her room… well, actually Liberty was once again thinking about the perfidious Lord Corbyn and wishing she wasn't, when the door was thrown open. In walked her mother and a woman she'd heard about but never met. Short, round, and with an expression that would curdle custard. Miss Battlemore wore a beautiful peacock-blue dress, and she styled her blonde hair perfectly atop her head.

"She needs an entirely new wardrobe," her mother added.

"I don't need an entirely new wardrobe," Liberty protested, rising. Her peace was over, it seemed.

"It is time," Miss Battlemore said.

Seeing as they'd never met, and she'd not seen any of the clothes Liberty wore, she wasn't sure how the woman had come to that conclusion.

"My clothes are fashionable," Liberty protested. "Elegant even," she added when both women looked at her.

"I know they are, dear, but still you are unwed."

"Mother!" Liberty protested.

"Good luck, Miss Battlemore," her mother then whispered on her way back out the door.

"Remove your dress if you please. I wish to study your figure."

There was a trace of an accent there, but Liberty didn't think it was French like a lot of the seamstresses in London.

Helen started unbuttoning her dress from behind. "She looks like a right one," her maid whispered.

"You will not leave me alone with her," Liberty whispered back while Miss Battlemore opened her large bag after lowering it to a side table.

"Clothing should enhance not hide," Miss Battlemore declared, coming to study Liberty now clad in only her chemise. She then walked around her twice, and then did so again the other way, her eyes running up and down Liberty's body. "You will wear my creations adequately," the woman then declared.

Over the next thirty minutes she was measured, looked at from all angles, and draped in materials. Helen was enlisted and any fear she'd had of Miss Battlemore had soon eased, and she was happy to discuss styles with the woman.

"Do I get a say in any of this?" Liberty felt she needed to ask.

"Tell me, Lady Liberty, when you were last fitted for your dresses, did you tell them you wished for colors that accentuated your lovely hair?"

"I do dress in colors that suit my hair," Liberty protested.

"My dresses will promote it, as they will your lovely figure."

It was not often someone said her hair was lovely.

She nodded, unsure what to add to that. Ten minutes later Miss Battlemore had gone, promising to have a dress ready in time for the Talbot ball.

"Mother wants to speak to you in Father's office," Edward said, appearing in her doorway.

"About what?"

"I don't know, but brace yourself. She looks angry. My guess is she heard about the chess game."

"Botheration," Liberty muttered. "I thought I'd got away with that as it was two days ago now."

"Yes, well, good luck. I'm for the kitchens. I believe biscuits have just been baked."

"You don't want to support me?"

"Definitely not," her brother said.

"At least bring me a biscuit back. I'll likely need it," Liberty muttered.

He kissed her cheek and left. Liberty sometimes wished she had Edward's life. He'd marry whomever he wanted one day, and could really do as he wished without repercussions.

"Such is the life of a woman," she muttered, heading for her father's study.

The door was open, and her mother stood behind her father, who was seated at his desk. The picture was one of solidarity, which didn't bode well for Liberty.

"You wished to see me?" Liberty said as she walked inside.

"Close the door, daughter," her father said.

She did as she was asked.

"Sit, please," he then added, giving her a smile.

"Do not smile at her."

"She is my daughter, wife. I can surely smile at her."

"Liberty, you were seen playing chess with your glasses on!" her mother shrieked with more force than necessary, as she was seated close enough to hear should she wish to whisper. "How could you make a spectacle of yourself like that where anyone could have seen you… and did!"

"Most people would be proud of what I achieved by beating Mr. Hasslebach who has yet to be beaten in his tournament," Liberty said.

"Proud! You wore your glasses in public, and played chess… with men!" her mother shrieked.

"And won."

"And that is supposed to appease me?"

The shrill tone made her wince. "I'm quite sure I don't know what to do with you. Perhaps you could step in, my lord?"

"Liberty, we only wish for what is best for you, and your mother thinks what you are doing is not that. Personally, I'm happy you beat that Hasslebach. He's been lording it over everyone at the chess club for—"

"Happy?" his wife demanded. "Your daughter embarrassed herself and us. I want you to censure her. It will be a miracle if all of society doesn't find out. Marrying her off is hard enough, but—"

"Yes, well, thank you for reminding me I'm not up to society's high standards, Mother. At least I can rely on you, my own parent, to ensure I know my limitations."

"Liberty—"

"Perhaps, for once in your life, you could accept me as I am, like you do Edward," she interrupted her mother. "But of course he's your son, so he can do whatever he wishes," she added bitterly.

She'd fought hard to be everything her parents wanted her to be when in society, but it was exhausting, and clearly, she failed.

"We are not discussing Edward, Liberty. I forbid you to wear your glasses again in public."

"Calm down," her father said.

"I have a headache every night," Liberty said. "I can't see where I walk, or read anything. I have tripped over so many things I am now thought of as clumsy. Is this what you wish for me, your daughter, Mother?"

"I wish for you to be married!" her mother shrieked.

"And the cost doesn't matter?" Liberty said, all fight leaving her. She was suddenly tired of all of this.

"What cost? You are a duke's daughter and live in luxury," her mother demanded.

"That will do," her father said.

"And because I have all of that I am therefore happy, and expected to wed a man whom I have no wish to spend the rest of my life with?" Liberty asked.

"What man?" her mother demanded. "From where I am standing, no one is offering for you, and considering—"

"Enough!" Her father cut his wife off.

Liberty rose from her chair and left the room, closing the door softly behind her.

AFTER A FEW hours spent in her room, with her door locked, Liberty climbed into the Talbot carriage that was to take her to book club. Her mother awaited her inside. They then spent the journey in strained silence.

Relieved when they arrived, Liberty stepped down first, and entered the townhouse leaving her mother to follow, or not, as was her wish.

They were greeted with sweet, faintly musky smelling kisses on the cheek by the three women who lived here, after being escorted through a house with more furniture than required, and each delicate side table or cabinet full of figurines and topped with vases of flowers.

Her mother slipped past her when they stepped into the parlor and found a seat beside Lady Petunia.

"Hurry it along, Lady Liberty. No point in standing about the place when there is excellent seating before you." A firm shove followed these words in Liberty's back. Turning, she found Alice and her aunt.

"Aunt, must you herd everyone about the place? They are not pieces on your chess board."

Mrs. Hamner was tall, broad shouldered, and never walked anywhere. She stomped. Her husband, Alice's uncle, was built the same way. No-nonsense people who didn't have a gentle bone in their body. Liberty felt sorry for her friend having to live with them. But then Alice was no shy, retiring debutante, either, and could stand up for herself.

"Good evening, Mrs. Hamner, Alice."

"Uncle beat her with a move she'd never seen before, which annoyed Aunt," Alice said.

Mrs. Hamner sniffed. "You must come and play us both, Liberty. I heard about your victory in the park."

Liberty shot her mother a look to see if she'd overheard. Her lips were in a hard, disapproving line which suggested she had.

"My advice is keep your distance from my aunt, Liberty, as she will simply want to interrogate you about chess," Alice said, tugging Liberty toward a sofa.

"Lady Liberty," Lady Petunia called from her place beside Liberty's mother. "There is space here for you." She then patted the seat beside her.

"Oh, ah… I had thought—"

"At once, dear," Lady Petunia said, and there was no doubting the threat in those words.

Liberty shot Alice a wide-eyed look. Her friend smirked and walked to the sofa alone.

"There now, isn't this comfortable?" Lady Petunia said after Liberty had taken the space beside her.

"Lovely," her mother agreed through her teeth.

"I was talking with our nephew's friend, Lord Corbyn, and remembered that you live minutes from him, Lady Liberty."

"We do," her mother agreed.

"Lovely boy Tobias. Kind, sweet natured, and extremely handsome," Lady Petunia added. "And to have taken on that dear sweet little Florence without a thought shows his true character."

"Child?" her mother asked.

Lady Petunia then launched into a detailed explanation as to why Florence was now living with Tobias.

"What a kind-natured young man. He and my daughter were close as children," her mother said, thawing slightly.

"Well now, how lovely."

Lady Petunia then proceeded to talk about Tobias for a further ten minutes with her mother dropping in her own compliments about the boy she'd once known. Of course, her parents were not aware of everything that had happened between her and him. Even so, a bit of loyalty here would be nice.

"Well past time he married," Lady Petunia added.

Oh, hell no.

"Well past time my daughter was married," her mother muttered, which she and Lady Petunia heard.

"Yes, thank you, mother," Liberty said, mortified.

"Ladies, if I could have your attention," Lady Agatha, Lady Petunia's sister said, clapping her hands, much to Liberty's relief. "It is time to discuss the book."

For three seasons she'd muddled along doing what had to be done, or more importantly what her mother wanted her to do, and now suddenly, this year, everything was changing. Tobias had reentered her life… reluctantly. Not only that, suddenly she needed to have a complete new wardrobe, and her parents were pushing for her to marry. There were also the goings on in Bidham to worry about.

Why now?

"I for one thought it repetitive, and were I many years younger, perhaps then I may have enjoyed it," Mrs. Hamner said.

Alice looked pained. "You cannot be serious, Aunt. It was a delightful read, with humor and touches of seriousness that had me close to weeping."

Liberty's friend never wept, so that was said purely from a theatrical standpoint.

"Poppycock!"

"If I may interject, Mrs. Hamner."

And so it began. A heated debate that lasted through two pots of tea, and several plates of dainty sandwiches and cakes.

"I believe the dialogue and character development is the best I have read in many years," Liberty added after she'd swallowed the mouthful of truly delicious lemon tart. "Elizabeth Bennet is wonderful—"

"Hardly realistic," Mrs. Hamner cut in.

"Very realistic, and for many of us," Alice snapped.

"Agreed," Liberty said, glaring at her mother.

"Well, I do believe it is your turn to select the next book, Mrs. Hamner," Lady Petunia said quickly, looking nervous.

"*The Mysteries of Udolpho*, by Ann Radcliffe," Alice's aunt said.

"I hope it is not too scary," Liberty's mother said.

"It is a work of fiction, Mother," Liberty muttered.

"Wonderful. I love a robust discussion, and tonight's was that," the third of Lord Hamilton's aunts, Lavinia, said.

"And you'll keep in mind what I said," Lady Petunia added as she escorted Liberty and her mother to the door.

She looked at the woman, trying to remember of all the things she'd said tonight, which one she should keep in mind.

"Lord Tobias. Wonderful man and just perfect. Plus, there's the child now, so his need is greater."

"Perfect for what?" Liberty asked. Her mother tittered at that. Clearly, she knew what he was perfect for, and if he married her daughter, then nothing else mattered. Not even the fact he'd treated her terribly.

"Why, for a marriage to you, of course, Lady Liberty. Have a safe trip home."

CHAPTER TWENTY-ONE

VAUXHALL GARDENS HAD always been somewhere Toby enjoyed. Loud noise, plenty of beautiful women, and outrageous entertainment. Tonight, he wanted to be anywhere but here. First there was Florence, who he knew was asleep, but he was happier if he was in the house while she did, and second there was Liberty, whom he could not stop thinking about.

"Why are you morose?"

"What?" He shot Jamie a look as he wandered with him through the gardens.

"You're morose."

"I am not. I'm weary. Please note the difference. I have a child to care for. They are exhausting, if wonderful. There is also not a morose bone in my body, and I'll thank you to remember that," Toby said, looking around him for Liberty, which was something he did far too often. "Morose is for people who can find nothing to entertain them." He sent his hand in an arc. "Does this look to you like I am not entertained?"

Since the chess match, and the revelations her brother had told him about the accident, which Edward was sure would infuriate his sister, Toby had watched her closer.

There was the Heather musicale, where she'd arrived late, and moved to a seat several rows in front of him, slowly. Which he now knew was her not being cautious, but likely due to her leg. *Was she still in pain because of it?*

Last night he'd seen her at the Sowter ball, exquisite in a lavender dress, which to his mind was cut too low in the bodice, and watched her dance, but just the once, and a waltz like she had with him. He wondered if she chose that dance because if she fell, whoever was her partner would hold her up.

I want to be the one holding her up. The words slid into his head before he could stop them.

"Morose," Jamie said again.

"I have things on my mind," Toby said. "You are not intelligent enough to hold things inside your head, so it doesn't happen to you."

"Harsh. Ah look, there is Lady Luton looking at you longingly."

"Excellent alliteration." Toby followed his friends and found Lady Luton, whom he'd had a liaison with after her husband passed six months ago. She gave him a smile that could only be termed smoldering.

"She is giving you a come-hither look."

"Let's go the other way," Toby said, herding his friend to the left like a lost sheep.

"Why?"

"You're full of questions tonight," Toby said.

"Something is off with you. Anthony said as much yesterday."

"You and Anthony are discussing me now?"

"We always discuss you, because then we don't have to look to closely at ourselves."

Toby snorted. "I have a child living in my house. That is a huge responsibility. Surely you and Anthony understand that."

"Yes, and of course that would be unsettling, but there is also Lady Liberty," Jamie said and this time his voice was serious. "I think she is on your mind."

"I am a rake and a libertine, and as such, no woman takes up space in my head," Toby lied.

"If you say so, but you no longer are those things since Florence arrived," Jamie said.

Toby added nothing to that.

"Come along then. We are to meet the newlyweds and watch the fireworks. But if you wish to speak about anything, you know I am all ears."

"I do, and I don't want to speak about anything."

They walked on in silence, passing guests excited to be here for the display about to begin. Toby tried to remember a time he was last excited and failed.

"I'm just going to walk for a while. I'll join you shortly, Jamie."

His friend looked at him. "Very well, but don't get into any trouble, as I will not be there to save you."

"I shall try," Toby drawled.

He walked away from the guests and down a path. Veering left, he went down another that was less frequented by society members, unless they wanted a few minutes alone to do things they shouldn't, and then it was the perfect destination. Darker and only lit by the occasional torch, it was full of shadows and places to hide.

People had been attacked here often, but that didn't worry Toby. He could look after himself, and to be honest, a scuffle might take the edge off the unease that was constantly riding him.

Liberty's accident could have killed her, and that thought had settled inside his head. He'd seen her for three seasons, and not once had he thought the choice he'd made to push her away from him that day the wrong one. So why was he doubting himself now? Why had hearing about her accident rocked him?

A squeak of outrage to his right had Toby stopping. He could walk on. It was none of his business if a couple or a woman alone was in there. But what if it weren't innocent? What if she had been lured there?

Developing a conscience was hell, and he blamed Liberty and Florence for that too. If someone was hurting one of them, he'd want a man to step in and stop it. Step in and protect them.

Just the thought made him feel ill.

Toby looked at the trees behind which there was clearly rustling, and then someone appeared. Head down, the woman wasn't running, which suggested she'd not been in any danger.

"Is everything all right, madam?" Toby had to ask, and when she said yes, he'd walk on.

Her head shot up, and their eyes connected. He saw the fear in hers.

"Liberty? What the hell are you doing here alone?" The rage was fast and flooded his body. He stormed closer. "Are you mad?"

Was she meeting someone? A lover? The ugly thought slid into his head, and he had no right to feel the bite of jealousy over it. What she did was her business.

"I am not mad, and you'll unhand me at once," she said, her voice high-pitched.

"What has happened? What scared you?" He hadn't even realized he'd wrapped his fingers around her wrist.

"Let me go at once, and I will return to my parents." She squinted up at him.

"You should not have left them," he snarled. "Why are you not wearing your glasses?"

She made a small shrieking sound, which suggested her rage now matched his.

"Tell me," he demanded.

"My mother has no wish for her daughter to be seen wearing eyeglasses in public." She looked up at him defiantly. Eyes squinting as she tried to bring him into focus.

"My surprise is that you listen to her. Now, tell me, why were you in those trees?"

"I don't have to tell you anything."

"And yet you will. It is dangerous to be alone in such a place. Anyone could have attacked you—"

"I am no concern of yours," she snapped.

Toby didn't know what possessed him to do what he did in that moment. But looking down at her lovely eyes and soft lips in a defiant line, he was soon lowering his head.

"What—"

He kissed her. Liberty, his old childhood friend. The woman he'd turned from, and Toby knew that with the first touch, it had been a mistake.

Her lips were soft, and her body felt full and lush as he pulled her closer. One kiss and he was gone. He'd know now, every time he looked at her, what she tasted like.

One hand went to her head, where Toby angled it to meet his lips, and he took the kiss deeper. Desperate to get as close to this woman as he could. He lost all reason. His only focus was her and this. Placing a hand on her spine, he pressed her flush to his body. Felt every inch of her lush form, from her thighs to her breasts against his.

Her hands fisted on his lapels as he caressed her back. Toby fought with himself to not ravage her lips. Not consume her with the need that was charging through his body. In that moment, he wanted to lay her down and possess her, and it was that thought which had him lifting his head.

"Toby," she whispered, and it was the first time he'd heard his name on her lips since that day. "Wh-what are you doing?"

Christ. He released her and took a step back, so their bodies no longer touched.

"Why did you kiss me?" He heard the uncertainty in her voice.

"I am a rake, remember?" But he wasn't anymore, and never would be again.

Her eyes widened, and she closed the gap between them. He took the slap without moving, because he'd deserved it. And then she was walking away from him. He grabbed her wrist, stopping her. But she didn't look at him.

"I want to know why you were here alone, my lady?"

"Go to hell."

"Again? I believe you sent me there several times already. Now tell me, what has you here on this path without company?"

"I wanted to be alone," she said, chin raised, tone defiant.

"Don't lie to me, Liberty, this is serious."

She glared at him, and then tried to shake free, but he held her in place.

"I will hold you here all night if I must. Someone will come along and find us—"

"All right," she snapped. "I saw someone I thought I recognized. A man from Bidham, and he was walking this way, so I followed."

The anger flared inside him again, thankfully forcing down the lust he'd felt kissing Liberty. He didn't kiss innocents. "I thought you were an intelligent woman."

She tried to pull free again.

"Who did you see?"

"Sydney, Helen's brother. He went into those trees." She pointed over her shoulder. "I followed. He met a man, because another voice said, 'You're late.'"

"Liberty, this is not a game," Toby said as several scenarios of what could have happened to her played out inside his head.

"I stood on a branch and it made a noise. The men went quiet, so I ran," she then added.

Toby tugged her closer until their faces were inches apart. "You will not take any more risks, Liberty. This, walking here alone was foolish. One of those men could have grabbed you."

"Sydney would—"

"He is doing what someone else tells him to," Toby gritted out. "He is likely as terrified as you right now. This is no game for a silly young lady to play."

Her chin raised again, and he raked his eyes over her features.

"Don't treat me like a fool, Lord Corbyn."

So beautiful, Toby thought. So fiery and determined. He'd never wanted a woman more than in that moment.

"Then don't act like one, Lady Liberty. Never walk here alone again, or I will tell your father."

She wrenched free, and he let her, and then she stumbled a

few steps. He reached out to steady her, but she staggered back.

"Don't pretend I mean anything to you," she spat out. "Never touch me again. I'm not one of your paramours, and I never want to be." She turned from him and hurried away.

Toby followed, walking a few paces behind her until she reached a more frequented path. He doubled back to check for anyone lurking in the bushes when she was surrounded by people. He saw no signs of anyone.

Someone could have grabbed her, and no one would have known. The thought terrified him.

Toby found his friends seated in a booth, eating and drinking. With them were Lord and Lady Brighton, and their three daughters. Toby glared at Anthony and Evie. One of the Brightons was on the aunts' list of prospective brides.

Looking around, he couldn't see the elderly women any-where.

"My aunts could not make it today," Anthony said, as if read-ing his mind. "You sit there, my friend," he added, waving Toby to the seat next to the eldest Brighton, Angela, who was suppos-edly someone who would make him an excellent wife.

"Good evening, my lord."

"Miss Brighton," he said, taking the seat and managing not to glare at his friends. Jamie sat beside Lord Brighton, happily conversing about horses.

Toby looked for Liberty and found her with her mother and father in the booth beside theirs. At her side was Mr. Williams, and the way he was angling his body toward Liberty had a lance of jealousy spiking through him.

"Are you well, Lord Corbyn?"

"Pardon?" The word came out with a definite snap to it be-cause Miss Brighton's eyes widened. He forced a smile onto his lips.

"You made a noise," she said.

"Sorry, just clearing my throat," he added with forced polite-ness. His eyes went back to Liberty. She looked miserable. He amended that to sad and hated he'd played a part in her current mood.

Their eyes caught and held for long seconds, and she looked away first. Her hair glowed from the lamplight behind her. He'd seen her for three seasons, but only now was he really seeing her. Her beauty and spirit. *I also know what she feels like.* Her curves pressed to his body. Her lips beneath his.

"Are you looking forward to the fireworks display, my lord?"

He dragged his eyes from Liberty and back to Miss Brighton.

"I am. I have seen them before and enjoyed them very much," he said, slipping into what he did best. Society chitchat was like breathing to Toby. It was never personal, or tugged emotion out of him, and never took a great deal of thought.

Miss Brighton was sweet and polite. He enjoyed an enlightening conversation with her about star formations, a fact that surprised Toby. She was beautiful too, and had all the attributes that a future Lady Corbyn would need. She would make Florence an excellent mother. But he felt absolutely nothing for her and knew he never would.

He looked at Liberty again. It was no longer Williams seated beside her. But Lord Michael. Everything inside Toby rebelled at the sight of that man close to her. He wanted to storm the distance between them and pummel him with his fists.

And this happens when you start caring for someone.

Christ. Did he? He knew Florence was important to him, but now Liberty? *Of course she is, you bloody fool.*

"I hope to study the stars more in-depth. I wish to look through a telescope also one day," Miss Brighton said.

"Yes, I believe they are intriguing," Toby said, as she launched into a detailed breakdown on just how intriguing.

He watched Liberty laugh at something Michael said. Surely her parents didn't believe the man a suitable husband for her?

Toby talked and drank and no one watching him would see the anger simmering beneath the surface every time he looked at Liberty and Michael. He knew women married men older than them, but the thought of that man touching or kissing her made him nauseous.

"The display is about to start. Come along," Evie said after they finished their meal.

They all walked to where the fireworks would start.

"What has your hat band too tight?" Anthony asked from his left, while Jamie moved to his right.

"Earlier, I found Lady Liberty coming out of the trees beside one of the less frequented walks here. She told me she was there because she was following someone. Her maid's brother, who is a Bidham local, and the one she saw driving the cart that day in London. She heard another man greet him, but she alerted them she was there, so had to flee."

Jamie whistled. "Did they see her, do you believe?"

"I don't know, but we can't discount it," Toby added.

"It may pay you to keep a closer eye on her until we know what is going on," Anthony said. "I didn't like seeing Michael seated next to her tonight. Surely they don't think him a match for Lady Liberty?"

"I will speak to her father if I believe that is a possibility," Toby said.

"Or," Jamie added, dragging out the word, "you could marry her yourself."

"You can't be serious?" Toby hissed.

"We are, because we believe you care for her," Anthony said.

"How is it you believe that when you've barely seen us together?" Toby scoffed, but his heart was thudding hard inside his chest. "She is far too sweet and innocent for a libertine like me, and I care nothing for her."

"If you say so," Jamie said.

Toby only just bit back the need to say something else. Instead, he made himself look at the first burst of lights filling the night sky and not search for Liberty.

CHAPTER TWENTY-TWO

"Y OU'LL PARDON ME for arriving late, my lord."

"Think nothing of it, Mr. Scully."

"I've just arrived back from Bidham, and thought you'd like the information fresh, as it were," the man said. "There's definitely something going on there, my lord."

Toby sat in the chair behind his desk, and the private detective he'd hired, Mr. Scully, across from him. The man was large, with a solid body that few would want to take on in a fight, he was sure, and his size came in handy in his occupation.

"What did you uncover, Mr. Scully?"

Toby sat back in his chair as the man spoke. This had been his father's office, and his before him, and there were touches of them everywhere, but he'd also added his own. Like the enormous world globe he rotated on the corner of his desk when he was thinking.

"They're a tight-lipped lot, those villagers, but I spent time in the Gill, and spoke to a few of them. Mr. Jasper told me that the village was no longer as it had been. That dark days lay over Bidham, and he feared would for many years to come."

"But he did not elaborate on what those dark days entailed?"

Mr. Scully shook his head. "Miss Maddon, who takes in sewing, said she feared for the people in her village, and then looked ready to cry. About broke my heart, especially considering she'd given me tea and sugar biscuits."

"I've eaten those biscuits," Toby said before he could stop himself. Something else he was doing these days. Saying what was actually inside his head. "They're delicious."

"That they are," Mr. Scully said. "When I pressed her, she wouldn't speak again, so I left."

"And what of the others you questioned?"

"It was like that with everyone I tried to get information out of. I tell you, my lord, it was as if someone were standing over the village threatening these people if they spoke out of turn."

No one threatened his people, Toby thought. *And yet because you have not cared enough about them, you've left them exposed.* The thought left a sour taste inside his mouth.

"Did you see anyone suspicious?"

"Four men. All walked away as I approached, but they were watching me, my lord. I'd wanted to chat with the Ackers family after the death of their daughter, but they weren't in the village, or so I was told."

He couldn't imagine what it would be like to lose a child. Florence had been in his life for such a short time, but she was now part of it... part of him. To lose her would destroy him.

"Thank you, Mr. Scully. I am grateful. If you hear anything further, please let me know. I have given you two more names I wish you to investigate, and the location of the warehouse they were seen delivering barrels to."

After the man had gone, Toby wrote everything he remembered about what was happening in Bidham. The list was growing.

The clack of nails on the floor outside his door was followed by Barnaby pushing it open the and wandering in, tail wagging.

"Hello, what have you got in your mouth this time?"

Removing the maid's slipper, he lowered it to his desk and looked at the dog. "Do not steal anymore footwear, Barnaby. Are we clear on that?" The dog sat and held out his paw as if to shake on the deal. Toby didn't buy it. He'd steal another shoe by midnight.

Leaving his office, Toby went to visit Florence with the dog, and read her yet another story.

"That was a big yawn," he said after he'd finished. She gave him a sleepy smile, and then sitting upright, wrapped her arms around his neck. The shock held him rigid for seconds, and then he settled his arms around her, holding her close.

"Thank you for my hug," he said into her hair.

"Thank you for being my friend." She then kissed his cheek and lay back down in her bed.

Emotion nearly choked him as he regained his feet. Bending he kissed her softly, and then pulled up the covers.

"Sleep well, Florence, and thank you for being my friend too."

He left the nursery smiling and went to his room to change for tonight's event. His manservant was there, waiting for him.

Tonight was the Talbot ball, where he would see Liberty, as it was her family hosting the event. The smile fell from his lips. He'd kissed his childhood friend, and now wished vehemently he hadn't, because he couldn't stop thinking about it or her.

"If you could raise your chin, my lord."

He did as his manservant, Joseph, ordered, and the man tied his neckcloth. He'd been with Toby for many years, and he realized he knew very little about him. *Which says what about you? Your own misery and demons have solely preoccupied you to the point of ignoring everything and everyone else in your life.*

Toby knew members of society rarely interacted with their staff unless it was in the usual course of things. Bring tea please, or no, the black jacket. Thank you. But he wondered then about his staff. Were they happy? For some reason, that bothered him right then.

"Have you ever been in love, Joseph?" He wasn't sure why those particular words had been the ones to come out of his mouth, or who was more shocked by them. Toby for saying them, or his manservant for hearing them. But he rallied. The man wasn't someone to fall about the place in shock, like Agatha, one of Anthony's aunts. The woman was forever shrieking if she saw a mouse or spider. Toby had rescued her a few times himself by removing a threatening insect.

The man hesitated. "Speak freely, Joseph."

"Well, my lord, I am to marry Miss Pratt."

Toby's eyes shot to him. Of the same height as him, he was a military man, with shoulders that were always straight, and shoes polished to a shine. He was far neater than Toby, a fact Joseph bemoaned as he was responsible for how his master looked. The problem was, Toby disliked neckties, waistcoats, and suit jackets. He was most comfortable in shirtsleeves and usually wandered about his town house dressed that way. This did not please his manservant.

"Miss Pratt, my maid?" He brought her to mind. Short, with a shy smile, but that was all he came up with.

"Yes, my lord."

"How is it I did not know that my manservant is marrying my maid? Further to that is how did I not know you and she were… close," he added when nothing else came to mind.

"Chadders likes to keep belowstairs things there, my lord, so as not to interfere in your life."

Because I am a selfish bastard. It was a night for revelations of a personal nature it seemed.

"I'm happy for you both," Toby said. "When is the wedding?" *Did he have married quarters here in his townhouse?*

"Two months, my lord."

"And you will live here?"

"We will."

"Excellent." He would have a word with Chadders about the forthcoming nuptials.

There was never anything more confronting than realizing you were a spoiled man who had lived his life upstairs, while those below just got on with it, and seeing to his every need. Especially as they'd all been so accepting of Florence and Barnaby.

"Joseph."

"Yes, my lord." He was picking up the waistcoat he'd draped over a chair.

"Is all well belowstairs?"

"Well, my lord?" He held it out.

"Happy. Are my staff happy and well?"

"Chadders had gout in his foot last week, so putting on his shoe wasn't easy," Joseph said as if they talked like this all the time, which they most definitely did not. Their conversations were usually brief and on the color of his waistcoat.

He'd kept himself distant for too long before Florence arrived and ignored things he should not have. That was about to change.

"But Mrs. Snow the housekeeper is excellent at healing, and he's feeling better," Joseph added.

Toby tried to remember if he'd seen his butler hobbling and couldn't.

"Of course, Jane has gone now."

Toby looked at Joseph. Saw the worry in his eyes.

"Jane being?"

"She worked in the kitchens, my lord. Mrs. Luke, your housekeeper, dismissed her."

He may be oblivious to a lot of what went on around him, but he knew when something was off. Joseph was not happy about Jane's dismissal.

"And why does this bother you so much?" Toby said, sliding his arms into the black evening jacket.

"Because she didn't steal from the staff, like Mrs. Luke said she did. Now Stephen is threatening to leave."

And this is why he didn't involve himself in the running of his household. It was complex and had many moving parts.

"And why is Stephen upset that Jane has been dismissed?"

"Because he's her brother."

"I have a brother and sister working on my staff?" His manservant nodded solemnly.

"Why did Mrs. Luke say that Jane stole if she didn't?"

Joseph's lips drew into a line.

"We've come this far. Tell me the rest," Toby said, bending to pull on his highly polished evening shoes.

"It's a delicate matter, my lord, and I have no wish to cause more trouble."

"What you tell me will stay between us," Toby said, wishing he'd never asked. Being a self-obsessed individual had its benefits, he reminded himself.

"Mrs. Luke said that Barnaby was a hairy beast, and something should be done about him, and that Miss Florence is causing a great deal of work. Jane told her that wasn't true, and it was wrong of Mrs. Luke to speak that way."

Toby only just refrained from pinching the bridge of his nose.

"Do the staff have a problem with my ward and her dog?"

"Not all, we love them," Joseph said, and Toby knew the words were genuine.

"Does the staff want Jane back?"

"Yes, my lord, she's a lovely girl."

"And what of Mrs. Luke?" Joseph looked down at his feet, which he never did. He always made eye contact. "Joseph?"

"She likes things her way. If you cross her, then life can be very difficult."

"I understand that the dog and child have created more work. Do I need more staff?"

He shook his head slowly. "Mrs. Luke is not good with change."

"If you were me, what would you do about this?" Toby asked.

"But I'm not you, my lord, if you'll pardon me for being so forthright."

"I understand that, but if you were, what would you do?" Toby said patiently.

"I'd reinstate Jane and talk to Mrs. Luke about her ways."

"Ways?"

"Her manner. She's too brisk and opinionated."

"Shouldn't my butler have something to say on this matter?" Joseph looked pained.

"Let's have it," Toby said, waving his hand. "We've gone this far."

"He's too soft. It's Mrs. Luke who really runs everything."

He hadn't known that either. Toby thought Chadders was tough when required.

"Please inform Mrs. Luke I wish to speak with her in my office tomorrow morning. Then tell Stephen to have his sister Jane return to work the day after. Now, I am going to a ball, which right now seems a lot less complicated."

"Thank you, my lord." Joseph bowed.

"In the future, I would like to be notified of all the goings on. Can I rely on you to ensure that happens, Joseph?"

The man smiled... actually smiled. Toby couldn't remember the last time he'd seen that expression on his manservant's face.

"I will, my lord, and thank you."

"Right then. Good evening, Joseph. I'm sure there is a warm cup of tea and some of that superb vanilla cake in your immediate future. Whereas, I will eat small crab patties and pretend to like the people I am talking with."

"Surely some of them you like?"

He smiled as his friends slid into his head. Evie too, but there was also now Liberty. "Some, yes."

Joseph hesitated as he reached the door. "The household staff really do love Miss Florence and Barnaby, my lord. Never fear, that is not the case. They will be as loyal to them as they are to you."

"Thank you, Joseph."

Toby always checked on Florence one last time before he left the house, and Barnaby opened an eye as he entered the room. He slept beside her on the bed, something Miss Haigh did not like, but Toby allowed because, with the trauma this little girl had suffered, he wanted her to feel safe.

Smiling down at the sight of her lying on her side, hands under her chin, Toby felt it again, that fierce surge of emotion that he was coming to define as love. Patting the dog's head he left, quietly closing the door behind him.

Walking along the halls of his townhouse seconds later, Toby poked about inside his chest and thought that he felt lighter. For so long, he'd carried a heavy weight there. Blackwood had nearly destroyed him.

"But it didn't," he muttered. He'd let it define him, and that was a sobering thought.

"Good evening, Chadders." Toby greeted his butler when he reached the front entrance. "How is the gout this evening?"

He enjoyed the look of surprised pleasure on his butler's face, and thought again, what a selfish bastard he'd allowed himself to become.

"It is a great deal better, Lord Corbyn. Thank you for asking."

"Excellent, and now, like I just told Joseph, take your tea and ensure there is a wedge of vanilla cake with it."

Toby walked out his front door sure that his butler's jaw had just dropped open, and felt like whistling. He didn't, but it was there.

A loud meow had him looking down. The biggest gray cat he'd ever seen sat there staring up at him.

"What are you doing here?" Toby asked, dropping to a crouch. He'd always loved animals because they never wanted more than a pat and food from you. But they, too, were something he'd shut out of his life until Barnaby had turned up with Florence. "Are you the neighbor's cat?"

Did the Waltons have a cat?

The animal had matted fur and was missing half an ear. Toby didn't think the Waltons, who were first class snobs, would have a cat like this one.

"My lord, is something wrong?"

Looking over his shoulder, he saw his butler standing on the front steps.

"Take this cat to the kitchens and feed it, Chadders." Toby picked up the animal, and it purred loudly as he handed it to his butler. "I'm sure it will leave as soon as it has eaten," he placated his servant.

The butler took the cat in stunned silence and retreated inside without another word. Toby looked at the sky and wondered if it was a full moon, as his actions in the last hour were different from those he'd undertaken inside his townhouse in the last ten years.

Reaching his carriage, he nodded to his driver and then looked at the young footman holding open the door.

"Are you Stephen?"

The man nodded. "Yes, my lord."

"Jane's brother?"

The young man nodded again.

"Well, she is being reinstated, but I'll ask you to keep that to yourself until I have spoken with Mrs. Luke," Toby said, wondering if he were making things worse or better in his household. He hoped for the latter. Would he have to dismiss Mrs. Luke? The thought actually made his head hurt.

Stephen smiled. "Thank you, my lord, and I will say nothing, but Jane will be pleased."

"You're welcome."

Toby got inside his carriage then before he made any more rash decisions that involved his staff and animals, and told himself for the rest of the night he would once again be the cold, formidable Lord Corbyn, and then he thought of Liberty and sighed.

CHAPTER TWENTY-THREE

IT WASN'T FAR to the Duke of Talbot's house. Sitting back, he allowed thoughts to come and go. He had been going through the motions of existing for too long. Appeared to be happy and live his life as he chose, but in fact, it was the opposite. He'd been hiding in plain sight. Now he had a child, a dog, and hopefully not a cat. Him, the eternal bachelor; the thought was a sobering one.

He'd written to his mother yesterday, outlining all that had happened. No doubt that would send her into a frenzy, and she'd appear in Bidham when he arrived there soon.

Liberty slid into his head then. She deserved the truth from him, but Toby knew that in telling her he would have to speak of his days at Blackwood House. He hated talking of that time. It made him vulnerable, and he'd fought hard to never again be that. But perhaps to heal he must? What did he want from Liberty Talbot? He didn't have an answer, but he knew it was something.

Looking out the window he noted they were passing the street where she had recklessly spoken to that man in the warehouse, after both she and Helen had seen her brother delivering something there.

He tapped on the roof, and the carriage began to slow. Toby intended to take a quick look around, just to be sure nothing was out of place. Unlike his last visit, the property should be empty at this hour—or so he hoped.

"Is something amiss, my lord?" Rory asked after he'd stepped down.

"I just need to check on something. I will be only a few minutes if you will wait here, please."

Entering the lane, he looked about him, which wasn't easy as no streetlamps lit the area. But his eyes adjusted, and Toby made his way to the building at the end. He walked along the first side to the window, but could see nothing inside, so he continued around the warehouse.

Nearing the rear of the building, he saw light coming from a partially open door. Stopping beside it, Toby listened.

"We've had people here asking questions."

"Doesn't mean they know anything."

"Doesn't mean they don't."

"The women came, and they're from the village, his lordship said. Then there's the nobleman poking around. Plus, we know a man was questioning the villagers. So far, they're too scared to speak, but that may change."

"His lordship says to keep things as they are. They won't speak, not after what we did. They're scared."

"This next shipment is big… the biggest. He wants everything to run smooth, so don't get the wobbles now."

"I'm not. It's them nosing around that worry me."

"He'll take care of that. He's a right mean one when he needs to be."

Toby studied the building, looking for a way inside. Those words had left him cold with fury. Were the women they'd spoken of Liberty and Helen? Had they murdered Sally Ackers to keep the Bidham locals quiet? Who was this nobleman they spoke of? He needed answers to those questions, and he needed them now.

"What the bloody hell do you want!"

Toby turned at the words, but not quick enough and something came down hard on the back of his head. He staggered, but did not go down. The sound of running feet told him that whoever was inside that warehouse would be outside in seconds. Toby would be outnumbered.

He lashed out with his fist and connected. The recipient went down, and he ran back toward the carriage. The thud of feet told him they were following, but he could see Rory now.

"Is all well, my lord?"

"Make haste, Rory, I am being followed. To the ball, please!"

"At once."

Toby climbed inside as they sped away. Pulling off a glove, he touched the lump forming on the back of his head, but there was at least no blood. He should probably go home, but something stopped him, and he knew it was Liberty. He needed to warn her to have a care now after what he'd learned tonight. If anything happened to her, he would never forgive himself.

Resting his head on the back of the seat, Toby closed his eyes. Those men were talking about Bidham, but who was his lordship?

He would go to the ball and tell his friends what he'd over-heard, and if the dull ache now throbbing in the back of his skull didn't ease, he would leave. He thought about Florence then. She was his responsibility and if anything had happened to him tonight, who would look after her?

Tomorrow he would set that right. He'd make Anthony and Evie her guardians.

Forcing himself upright, as the carriage slowed to a crawl behind the others lining up to stop before the Duke and Duchess of Talbot's townhouse, he took several deep, slow breaths.

Were his eyes unfocused? Blinking, he tried to clear them. The door opened, and he stepped down, looking at the house before him.

He'd never attended a ball here before. In fact, he'd never stepped foot inside the London Talbot residence. Large and imposing, as befitted the duke's standing in society, it was impressive, and rose three stories in gray stone. Looking up, slowly, as movement did not help the pain, he wondered which room Liberty slept in, and saw a face pressed to the window, then a hand.

He waved back as Edward looked down at him. That tug inside his chest was still there, but less fierce now as he thought about Mathew. He, too, was something he'd forced down deep inside. Toby hadn't allowed his little brother to live on after his death. His memory had died with him, and that wasn't right. Florence, too, should know about him.

Stepping in through the large front doors, he joined the queue of people waiting to greet the hosts.

"Lord Corbyn? You know my daughter, Miss Waltham?" The man in front of him turned to speak with Toby.

"Of course. Good evening." Toby bowed, and smiled at the woman, although it was likely more a grimace.

A man of good fortune, titled, and single, was a hunted species in society. He didn't blame the young women, and knew their purpose was solely securing a good match. Was it right? Possibly not, but as it had always been that way, Toby doubted it would change anytime soon.

"Well now, this is good timing," a voice said from behind him. Turning, he looked at Anthony, who had his wife at his side, both looking ridiculously happy still, he noted.

"Hello, Toby. That is a fine waistcoat."

"Good evening, Evie, you look lovely."

"Friend here," Anthony drawled as Toby kissed her cheek.

"Anthony." Toby bowed deeply. He would get his friends alone soon and tell them what had transpired, but not here, where anyone could be listening. Whomever this lordship was could walk among them, and he did not want him alerted they were on to him. "My night has improved vastly with your appearance in it," Toby added.

Anthony harrumphed.

"We are excited to be journeying to Bidham in a few days," Evie said.

"Don't. Seriously, Evie has the household in an uproar, and is obsessed with packing this and packing that," Anthony said.

"Good evening, I have arrived so you can all rest easy," Jamie said appearing.

He'd like to be resting, Toby thought as the dull ache in his head had him wanting to sit somewhere in a dark corner and close his eyes.

"That is untrue," Evie protested. "I just like order, and there is nothing wrong with that. Good evening, Jamie."

"Are you to open the fair, Toby?" Jamie asked after he'd kissed her cheek.

"I have, and yes, I will. It seems they may forgive me for turning my back on the village."

Evie, Anthony, and Jamie looked at him with varying expressions.

"What?" Toby said, knowing exactly why they were staring at him. He would like to say it was the blow to the head that had loosened his tongue, but after that business in his townhouse with the staff, he couldn't. He knew he was changing, and unlike before, would embrace it. *It was time.*

"You never talk of your past," Anthony said.

"None of us are open books," Toby added. "Now move along. We are in a receiving line and holding everyone up.

Jamie stepped around him, then stared into Toby's eyes. "You look different."

Were his pupils dilated?

"Exactly how do I look different when my body is the same?"

"Your eyes are squinty. Has something happened, Toby? Are you in pain? Florence—"

"Is well and tucked up in bed as we speak."

Toby nudged him back a few steps.

Anthony turned to study him. He then said softly, "What has happened?"

"Not here," Toby said, realizing they wouldn't believe him if he kept denying it. "After we have greeted the Talbots, I will tell you."

They walked a few more paces and then he could see their hosts. Liberty stood beside her mother, and her expression was polite, but he knew her well enough, even after all these years, to know she hated being the center of attention.

His eyes traveled down from the top of her sunset locks, pinned on top of her head with something that sparkled. She smiled as another guest greeted them. This one was genuine, and everything inside Toby that wasn't already clenched did so. She was beautiful.

"Your Lady Liberty is looking lovely this evening," Jamie whispered in his ear.

He refused to punch his friend right here in front of some of the more voracious society gossips, but the need was there. *He was jealous.*

Liberty was wearing white, but the bodice was lower than she usually wore, and showed off the tops of her lovely breasts. Beneath the bust was an overskirt in sheer blue that opened down the front. Around her neck was a matching satin ribbon.

"Your mouth is open," Jamie whispered.

"Shut up."

"At least the color is returning to your cheeks," Anthony added. "Did you eat something off today? Is that why you look as you do?"

"I told you I will tell you everything soon. Shut up."

Toby kept his eyes on Liberty, and he let the feelings inside him come. His friend, and so much more. What he'd done had forced her from his life, but he wanted to rectify that. Wanted her back.

She squinted then, attempting to focus on something. Liberty should be wearing her glasses, and it was wrong of her mother to not allow that. She could easily walk into something and hurt herself.

Her hands hung at her side, one clenched in a fist. Why had she not married before now? Liberty was as beautiful as many, and more so, Toby believed. The accident had her entering society later than others, but she was a duke's daughter. Clearly the bachelors like him were fools not to see she was worthy of their attentions.

She bent slightly at the waist to hear something a guest said to her, and Tobias watched Mr. Parker leering down her bodice.

"Did you just growl, Tobias?" Anthony asked.

"No."

But he had, because he wanted to be the one to look at her breasts, and knew he'd lost all rights to Liberty Talbot many years ago. *But that was about to change.*

CHAPTER TWENTY-FOUR

LIBERTY LOATHED BEING on display like she was now. Standing beside her mother and father, greeting every guest who entered their townhouse to attend the Talbot ball. Yes, she'd been in society for years, and yes, most nights someone was looking at her and either picking her appearance apart, or criticizing her for being an old maid, but this was different. She had to smile and say the right things continually until this infernally long receiving line was done with.

There was also the fact that she couldn't see a great deal. If she squinted, that brought things into focus more, but still, it wasn't easy.

"Smile, daughter."

"I am smiling, Father."

"Is that what we're calling it?"

"It would help if I could see," she muttered.

"Ah, Lady Samson, how lovely you look this evening," he said, as if he'd not spoken those words multiple times already. The woman he'd just complimented preened, so Liberty knew he'd sounded genuine.

"I forbid you to wear your glasses," her mother hissed seconds later.

"It saddens me that wearing my glasses makes you ashamed, Mother, when without them I am basically blind."

"Liberty," her mother said, clearly shocked at her words. "It is not that at all."

The entire conversation was taking place in harsh whispers, and likely this was not the place, but she still felt a need to say the words.

"I would rather see than reach my bed with a headache and sore shins from walking into things," Liberty muttered.

"Be quiet, both of you," her father said under his breath.

Shooting the line a look, Liberty gauged how long she would have to stay here before slipping away to find Alice, who had already arrived with her aunt, who thankfully had won at chess and seemed in a pleasant mood.

Studying the ones closer, she stiffened as she saw Tobias was next to greet them. He'd kissed her at Vauxhall Gardens, and she'd been able to think of little else. Squinting, she noted he looked pale. Even in this light, she could see that. *Was his jaw clenched?*

"Good evening, Tobias," her father said.

With him were Lord and Lady Hamilton and Lord Stafford.

"Duke and Duchess," Tobias said.

Liberty watched him bow, and when he straightened, wince. He didn't look right, and his eyes seemed odd and squinty. But then again, that could just be the light and the fact she couldn't see clearly. Was he ill? The thought should not have made her stomach clench; however, it did.

"Lady Liberty," Toby said, reaching her next.

"What's wrong?"

"Pardon?" He straightened after bowing, and she could see clearly something wasn't right now. His eyes definitely looked odd.

"What is wrong with you?"

"Nothing is wrong with me," he denied, but the words held little strength. "Good evening." He then walked away, and Lord Stafford greeted her.

She debated for all of five seconds before asking, "What is wrong with Lord Corbyn?"

"As to that, Lady Liberty, I am unsure, as he has yet to tell me. But clearly something is, if you noticed it also." His eyes followed the tall form that was heading for the doorway which led to the ballroom. "I shall follow and get it out of him."

"Lady Liberty," Lady Hamilton said, greeting her next with her husband.

"Lord and Lady Hamilton." Liberty dropped into a curtsey, but her eyes were on the door that Tobias had just walked through.

"I know that you and Tobias were close friends, my lady," Lord Hamilton said.

If the words shocked her, she didn't show it. "Once, long ago, my lord," she said.

"Perhaps one day you could ask him again why he turned from you, my lady? He could do with another friend in his corner, especially now he has Florence," the man said. He then smiled and walked away with his wife, leaving her reeling.

She'd had doubts, of course, about why Tobias had done what he had to her, and they'd intensified recently. *Should she ask him? Would he tell her the truth?*

Liberty went through the motions of greeting the guests, but her head was whirling with thoughts of Tobias. *Was he all right?*

"Smile," her mother hissed out the side of her mouth. "Good evening, Lord Michael."

Liberty forced her lips upward as the man bowed before her.

"Good evening, Lady Liberty. I hope you will have room on your card to dance with me."

"Of course she will, won't you, dear?" her mother said.

"I would love to dance with you, my lord," Liberty said, attempting to sound enthusiastic.

"May I say you look beautiful this evening, Lady Liberty."

Lord Michael really was a nice man. Even if what he'd said about Tobias had annoyed her, which made no sense because, until recently, her thoughts had hardly been flattering either.

"That man would make you an excellent husband, Liberty,"

her mother said when he'd walked away. "Handsome, distinguished."

"Old," Liberty added.

"Yes, well, you cannot afford to be picky, dear. The clock is ticking."

She looked at her mother, who had spoken that entire sentence with a smile on her face, her social mask firmly in place.

"And yet the clock can tick for him?"

"Ah, Prudence, Agatha, and Lavinia, how wonderful to see you," her mother said loudly. "I am so pleased you have come."

"As we are pleased to be in your splendid house," Lady Agatha said.

"Lady Liberty," Lady Prudence said. "You look lovely this evening. Is that a new dress? It's not your usual style, but I like it."

"It's one of Miss Battlemore's," Liberty's mother said before she could. "Wouldn't you agree it's just right for her?"

"Perfect," Lady Prudence agreed.

"Excellent, well, I'm glad my clothing is making you all happy. If you will excuse me, I see a staff member trying to get my attention. You stay, Mother. I will deal with it."

Before her mother could stop her, Liberty had walked away. Opening a door just before the ballroom, she slipped inside and kept moving.

She knew what her mother was about. Knew Liberty's marriage was her focus, but it angered her she had no say in the matter. If she'd stayed there a second longer, Liberty would have said something she'd regret.

Life had run along the same way for years. Now it had tilted, and she didn't seem able to right it again. It was him, of course. Since the day he'd rescued her after her carriage wheel had broken, Tobias had been everywhere she was. Then there was Florence, his ward, who he'd genuinely seemed to have an affection for that day in the park. How was it possible? The cold, aloof Lord Corbyn was now raising a sweet little girl?

Liberty's head was not on straight, and she needed to take a few moments before she entered the ballroom. Walking down the hallway that ran off it, she encountered a maid.

"Is all well, Anne?"

"Yes, my lady."

Damn, she'd hoped for an actual emergency.

"Excellent, well come to me if you need anything."

The girl bobbed a curtsey and hurried off.

She made herself enter the ballroom then. Skirting the edges, Liberty searched for Alice. Instead, she saw Tobias. He was just heading toward the open door at the end, leading to the terrace, and down into the gardens.

It took her two seconds to decide to follow. Nodding, smiling, and acting like she knew exactly where she was going and why, Liberty didn't stop to chat. She walked out the door.

There were a few people out here but not many. Again Liberty smiled and kept walking. The terrace wound around the entire left side of the Talbot townhouse, but few would walk farther than where she now stood, as there was no light. Plus, it was a chilly evening in London.

Looking around her, Liberty searched for Tobias and saw only shapes. Pulling out her eyeglasses from the handy pocket she'd insisted Miss Battlemore sew into her dress, she put them on.

Walking into the darkness farther around the terrace, she located Tobias. Leaning on the balustrade, he had his head lowered between his hands. He was the picture of defeat, and she didn't like how that made her feel.

"Are you unwell?"

He straightened, and she heard the hiss of his breath at the movement.

"Good evening again, Lady Liberty. You should not be out here alone with me."

"Why are you out here alone when you have just arrived? Why are you wincing when you move, and why do your eyes appear squinty?"

"Which question do you wish an answer to first?" His words sounded raspy and off as he straightened to turn and lean against the balustrade, as if he needed it to hold him upright.

"What is going on, Lord Corbyn?" Something hit her then, and she did not like it one bit. "Are you meeting someone here?" The realization that it could be a woman had cold slithering through her body.

"You think I would have a secret liaison at your family home?" The words were no longer calm. "Your opinion of me is indeed poor."

"I don't know you," she said in a low, angry voice.

He didn't answer that, instead turning from her to look out to the night sky.

"If you are not meeting someone, then are you unwell, my lord? Do you need me to collect your friends to assist you?"

"I don't need you to collect anyone." He was still looking at the sky.

"Why are you looking at the sky?"

"I like it."

She took a deep breath and counted to ten.

"So you still do that, too?"

"What?" She had only reached five.

"Count to ten when you are trying to calm down."

"No," Liberty lied. "Have you found anything more out about Bidham?" If he didn't want to answer her about what was going on with him, then she'd ask him about that.

"You need to go back inside, my lady." He turned, and then swayed.

Liberty closed the distance between them and took his arm. "Come, you need to sit down, as clearly you are not well, and like my father, refuse to acknowledge it."

"I am well," he gritted out.

"I can see that," she mocked him. Liberty tugged his arm and led him to a seat her father had placed on this side so his wife could sit here and look over the gardens in private. "Sit at once,

Lord Corbyn." She nudged him down into it.

His breath came out on a heavy sigh as he lowered himself onto the wooden seat.

"What is going on, Lord Corbyn?"

His sigh was loud. "I hit my head before coming here, and in fact I probably should have gone home, but I didn't." He spoke the words slowly, as if they pained him, and then frowned, as if confused by having said them to her. "I fear it is not getting better, but worse."

"You should have returned to your townhouse," Liberty said, wondering what she should do now. What if he became unconscious?

"In my defense, it was not this bad earlier, my lady."

Liberty looked around her and found the door that led into a small parlor. Trying the handle, she was relieved when it opened. Entering, she hurried to the sideboard and found the tray that held a brandy decanter. Liberty poured some into a glass. Hurrying back out the door, she was relieved to find Tobias still where she'd left him. She sat beside him.

"Sip this."

"I remember that about you too," he said, taking it.

"What?"

"The bossiness."

"I beg your pardon, but I am not bossy." She leaned closer to study his face, checking his eyes.

Liberty's father was a widely read man, and he often ordered medical books. In one, she'd read that dilated pupils were not good after a head knock.

"Your pupils have dilated."

"I like you in your glasses better than without them." He didn't sip, but threw back the contents of the glass, then lowered it to the seat beside him.

"I said sip."

"I've never been very good at orders." He turned to look at her, and then his hands were on her shoulders, and he was tugging her close. So close that their faces were now only inches apart.

"Let me go, Lord Corbyn."

"Considering the pounding in my skull, you would think I could. But I can't. Not after that kiss we shared, as I've thought of little else."

This kiss was soft. Just a brush of his lips on hers, and Liberty felt her limbs go weak and tried to fight the urge to lean into that large body.

He made a sound low in his throat and then took the kiss deeper. Clutching handfuls of his jacket, she held on. She wanted to climb into his lap and take everything he gave her in that moment. Liberty swallowed a whimper when he eased back, after brushing a last soft kiss over her lips.

"Don't kiss me again," she whispered, getting to her feet and backing away from him. "Please." The word came out as a plea. "We are not friends."

"Do you only kiss friends, then?" he asked.

"Don't toy with me, Lord Corbyn. I am not one of those silly women who falls all over themselves to get your attention. Nor the other sort."

"Other sort?"

Fiery color heated Liberty's cheeks. They both knew what other sort she alluded to.

That made him snort, and then wince. "I did not kiss you because I thought you were anything but exactly who you are. The friend I hurt and owe a long overdue apology to."

The words shocked her. He wanted to apologize. Would he tell her why he'd said what he had that day?

"When did you hit your head?" Liberty said instead of demanding that apology now.

"I went to see that warehouse again you and Helen visited. I thought if I went at night it may be empty. It wasn't."

"And you said I shouldn't have gone there in daylight? Yet you went alone at night?" Her voice had risen, and he winced.

"I beg of you to lower your voice, Liberty."

"Lady Liberty," she whispered.

She couldn't make any sense of this. Tobias was here in her home. Tobias had kissed her again. The man who she had vowed to loathe until she drew her last breath was now looking vulnerable. *He wanted to apologize.* What did it mean that just looking at him made heat bloom inside her chest?

"I'm sorry that I did not know about your accident, Liberty." His eyes locked on hers.

"Pardon?"

"Your brother told me about the day you fell from the horse. About how long it took you to recover, which is why you did not enter society with the other debutantes your age. Why you wear your eyeglasses."

Dear God, Edward, why?

"I just wanted to say how sorry I am that I didn't know about it."

"Why now? Why are you talking to me like this now, after all these years? I don't understand," Liberty said, going for honesty.

He sighed loudly. "I'm not sure I know how to answer that, Liberty. I'll just say that things are changing and taking me with them. I've seen what I've become, and suddenly I don't like that man very much."

They stared at each other for a long time, and then she said, "I'll find one of your friends to help you."

"I don't need them. I will leave and return home." He got to his feet before she could stop him.

"Do not go anywhere alone from now on, Liberty, and don't investigate what is going on in Bidham further. I believe whoever is behind this business knows both your and my identities. Therefore, it is dangerous for you to be anywhere alone. Until you hear from me, leave the house with company… please."

She had so many questions, but instead just nodded. He walked away from her then, and this time it was Liberty who fell on the seat and stared out at the night sky.

CHAPTER TWENTY-FIVE

TWO DAYS AFTER the Talbot ball, Toby woke feeling a great deal better.

His manservant had taken one look at him that night and asked what was wrong. After he'd told Joseph, he had gone to speak with his cook, who was excellent at healing, something else he'd not known. He'd returned with something for his head that had made him thankfully fall into a deep dreamless sleep.

Pushing himself upright, Toby leaned on the headboard and thought about Liberty and that kiss. He wanted that woman with a desperation he'd never felt with another. A simple kiss and he'd lost the ability to think rationally. For years he'd ignored her, but no more.

He remembered what he'd overheard at that warehouse. Liberty wasn't safe, and he had to make sure she understood that. Make sure she didn't take any further risks.

"Enter," he responded to a tap on the door. What surprised him was that it was Florence and Barnaby standing there when it opened. She was still wearing her dressing gown and slippers.

"What's happened? Are you all right?" He'd taken to wearing a nightshirt to bed since she'd entered his household in case she needed him.

She came in with one hand on the dog, and the other clutching a book, to stand beside his bed looking up at him with those big eyes that would always get her whatever she asked for.

"You did not read to me yesterday."

"I'm sorry about that, Florence. I was unwell."

"Miss Haigh told me that."

"So you came here with your book to ask me to read to you now?" She nodded solemnly.

"Have you had your morning meal?" Florence shook her head.

"Good morning, my lord." Joseph appeared in the doorway behind the little girl. "And Miss Florence and Barnaby," he added.

"Good morning, Joseph."

Barnaby jumped onto the bed and draped himself across Tobias's legs.

"Ah, it appears we need a tray of food, as Miss Florence has yet to eat her morning meal," Toby said. "Also, could you just check on Miss Haigh, please?" Clearly, the slight tinge of panic in his words resonated, and his manservant fled.

"I like this book."

"Well then, perhaps we should read it."

Florence rarely came right out and asked for anything. She wasn't outspoken yet, but he was sure that, given time and confidence in her surroundings, that would come. But she did like to spend time with Tobias.

"But you'll have to come up here with Barnaby," he added.

She held out her arms, and Toby lifted her up to settle beside him.

"Don't mind me," he muttered to the dog who made a sound in his throat as he moved his legs.

Toby took the book and began to read. When her little head rested on his shoulder, his heart felt like it was too big for his chest. He often thought about his cousin, and what their life had been like. A life where Florence had her mother and her father.

I will keep her safe and happy, cousin.

"Good morning, my lord." His butler appeared in the doorway carrying a large tray, as if it was entirely normal to see his employer, Florence, and Barnaby in his bed, dressed in nightwear.

"Good morning, Chadders." He then looked at Florence. "What do you say to Chadders?"

"Good morning."

His butler beamed at the child. He then laid the tray over Tobias's legs above the slumbering Barnaby.

"How do you feel this morning, my lord?"

"Much improved, thank you."

Taking the mug of steaming black coffee, he inhaled the scent and then gulped. Florence took a finger of toast smeared with jam and bit into it.

"A note arrived at the rear door early this morning, Lord Corbyn," Chadders said, producing a piece of paper from his pocket and handing it to Toby. "Also, yesterday Lords Stafford and Hamilton called. When I explained you were sleeping, they said they'd return today."

"Thank you."

He'd told his housekeeper yesterday morning that her behavior was not acceptable, and things would need to change. She'd not looked happy about this, so he'd added that Toby could always hire a new housekeeper, to which she'd replied that would not be necessary in a tight voice. He didn't think peace would reign immediately, and would have to keep an eye on things until it did.

While Florence ate her toast in small precise bites and looked at the pictures in the book he'd been reading, Toby opened the note.

Be warned that if you or Lady Liberty continue to meddle in what doesn't concern you, the consequences will be dire for someone you love.

Toby folded the note and placed it under his pillow. He then took the book from his ward and began to read once more. When Chadders returned, he gave him the tray. Getting out of bed he pulled on his dressing gown.

"I will be back shortly, Florence. Don't eat all the toast."

She nodded, jam smeared on her chin, which would no doubt end up on his bedding, but right then he didn't care.

Reaching his study, he wrote three notes. One to Liberty, the other two to his friends. Finding his butler once more, he handed them to him.

"I need these taken at once to the recipients, Chadders. Then I want to leave for Hawthorne tomorrow morning with Miss Florence early, as the sun rises. Could you please notify the staff and have the preparations for our departure brought forward."

"I will see to things at once, my lord."

"Thank you. I understand this will cause everyone a great deal more work, but it is important."

"Of course." His butler bowed and then left.

Retrieving Florence, he took her back to the nursery, where Miss Haigh now was. He could see the nanny was surprised to see him wearing his dressing gown, but she didn't mention the fact.

"My Lord, forgive me, I didn't realize Miss Florence had come to see you."

"All is well, Miss Haigh. We just had breakfast together. We are leaving for my estate Hawthorne early tomorrow morning now. If you will ensure everything is sorted for our departure, please."

"Of course."

"Please do not leave the house today, Miss Haigh. This is very important."

The woman looked confused but nodded.

After kissing Florence's cheek, Toby went back to his rooms and changed. *He had to keep them safe... all of them.* He cared about people now, and not just his friends, and he would let no one hurt them.

"You can't loll about on my bed all day, you hopeless animal," he said to Barnaby when he retrieved the note he'd put under his pillow. The dog ignored him and closed his eyes. Seconds later, he was snoring.

⇶⇷

TOBY WAS SEATED in the parlor he used to greet guests, going through his plan while drinking his second cup of coffee, when Anthony and Evie arrived, with Jamie on their heels.

"What the hell is going on?" Anthony demanded stomping into the room.

"It's early," Jamie muttered, heading for the large tray of refreshments Toby had ensured was ready for his guests' arrival.

"Good morning, and all will be revealed as soon as Lady Liberty has arrived."

"I told them you would not have asked us here so early without reason, Toby," Evie said coming forward to kiss his cheek.

"Sit, eat and drink, and I hope—"

"Lady Liberty is here, my lord," Chadders said, appearing in the doorway.

"I will return shortly," Toby said.

"Take your time, and we will enjoy the tea tray," Jamie added with his mouth full.

She was standing in his front entrance, staring up at a painting. Bonnet swinging from her fingers, looking so sweet he felt his heart sigh. *Mine,* he thought instinctively, and did nothing to squash that need. With her were Edward and Helen.

"Good morning."

She spun to look at him, and he was pleased to see she wore her glasses. Edward and Helen both smiled, and Liberty glared.

"What is the meaning of this, Lord Corbyn? Your note said, 'I believe you and your family could be in danger. Come to my townhouse at once.'"

"And here you are. Lovely to see you again, Edward. You also, Helen, and I am pleased you followed my advice, Lady Liberty, and did not travel alone."

"Actually, I caught my sister trying to slip out of the house in a sneaky manner."

"It was not sneaky, Edward. I was leaving by the front door with my maid," Liberty protested.

"Sneaky. When I asked where she was going, she gave me a vague explanation that made no sense," Edward continued, clearly enjoying needling his older sister.

"I said I was going for a walk," Liberty snapped.

"So I pressed her, and she did that thing she does where her lips appear stuck together."

"Ah yes," Tobias said. "I remember what that looks like."

"No, you do not," Liberty protested, looking from Edward to Toby.

"I demanded to know what was going on, and she said as this could include me, I could accompany her, but I was to refrain from annoying her by asking questions she couldn't answer."

Toby had a feeling Edward had perfected the art of getting under his sister's skin. She bared her teeth at them, and he wanted to grab her and kiss her until she slumped against him as she had the night of the ball.

"How is your head, Lord Corbyn?" It was more a demand than a polite enquiry.

"Better, thank you, my lady. If you will come this way, we have much to discuss before we leave for Bidham in the morning," Toby said.

"Are we?" Edward asked. "Wonderful."

"We are not going for two days," Liberty said.

"Your plans have changed."

She was still arguing with him when they reached the parlor his friends sat in. With them now were Florence and Barnaby, who seemed happy to see Edward, because she waved, before going back to the book Evie was reading to her in a chair by the window.

Keeping his voice down so the child did not hear, Toby explained about what had happened to him the night of the Talbot ball.

"And you are just telling us now?" Jamie demanded. "What

possessed you to go there alone?" His friend looked angry now.

"Exactly, especially as I got told off for doing the same in daylight hours with Helen," Liberty said looking a little smug now.

"You are a woman," Toby said holding onto his composure.

"And yet, no one struck me on the head," Liberty added.

He wanted to grab her and kiss that smug look off her face.

"If you will be quiet, I will tell you what else has occurred," Toby said.

"There is more?" Anthony demanded.

"I received a note this morning, which is why I sent word I needed to see you all. This note," he added, holding it out to his friend. The others huddled around to read it.

"Dear Lord," Edward whispered.

"Quite," Jamie added.

"But whoever sent that note will surely be there in Bidham also, as that is where the barrels are being smuggled in," Liberty said.

"It will be easier to keep everyone safe there. London is too busy, and there are too many possibilities for someone to harm one of you," Toby said. "It is best to leave as soon as possible."

"But how will we know who is behind this?" Edward asked.

"I will leave two men in London to investigate and am hiring a further four to go on to Bidham," Toby said. "They will watch over you when you leave the house."

"But my parents?" Liberty said. "How will I get them to leave when they have engagements and had not planned to travel to Bidham yet?"

"I will pretend I have a chest inflammation and need the country air," Edward said. "They will come on in a few days and stop at Lord and Lady Haversham's on the way, and so will be safe."

"We will all travel together," Anthony said, looking at Evie, who still sat with Florence. "If we are together, no one will stop us."

"Agreed," both Jamie and Toby said.

"Is it really necessary to take such extreme measures?" Liberty asked.

"Yes," Toby said, looking at her. He could allow nothing to happen to this woman. Now wasn't the time to think of the future, but one day soon, Toby thought.

Chapter Twenty-Six

"I STILL CAN'T quite believe we got out of London without our parents suspecting anything. Mind you, I am an excellent actor," Edward said from the seat across from Liberty.

"I hate lying to them, but needs must. Do you think they will be safe, Edward?"

"They are traveling three hours to friends, where they will stay for four nights. They will be fine, Liberty," her brother said.

Looking out the carriage window, she saw they were leaving the outskirts of London.

"Father didn't like us going after that business with you being held up by highwaymen, but with a driver and another, both armed, he seemed happier. Plus, the carriage behind with yet another footman and two maids."

"Yes, that appeased Father," Liberty said.

"He likes you, you know," Edward said, his voice hoarse from all the coughing he'd had to do to convince their parents he was indeed unwell. He unwound the scarf his mother had wrapped around his neck.

"Who?"

"Tobias."

"No, he does not." Liberty refused to acknowledge the thought that her brother's words could be the truth.

"Yes, he does."

"He hurt me, and I'm not forgiving him, and I have no wish

to speak on this matter again," Liberty said.

"All I'm saying is, ask him why he did what he did, because it's likely after all this time he will tell you."

She looked at her brother lounging on the seat across from her. Long legs rested beside Liberty.

"Why are you so willing to forgive him for hurting me?"

"I hate he hurt you. Never doubt that, Liberty, but I also know he's a good man, and if he is the right man for you, then you need to forgive him if you can."

Shocked, she looked at her brother. "Right man for me? How can you say such a thing? We don't like each other."

He raised his hands at her shriek. "I have seen the way you look at him, Liberty, just as I have seen the way he looks at you. There is more than dislike there."

Her heart was suddenly thudding hard inside her chest at his words. Her and Tobias? Surely it wasn't possible, and yet hadn't he kissed her, and hadn't she wanted more? When she'd learned he was hurt, Liberty's fear was genuine. There was also that odd feeling she got in her belly when she saw him. *Did she, in fact, care for Tobias deeply?*

"Very well, I will speak on it no more," her brother said, mistaking her silence for anger and not what it actually was. Shock.

Liberty looked out the window, her mind whirling, until they reached the location where the other carriages would be. As they halted, someone threw open the door, and there he stood—Lord Corbyn, his imposing presence filling the space. The man she now realized she no longer disliked.

"Good morning. I trust your chest inflammation is not causing you too much distress, Edward?"

"I am coping, thank you, Tobias," her brother said with a cheeky smile.

"You are well, Lady Liberty?"

She nodded. "Thank you, yes."

"Excellent, then let us be on our way while Florence is content and Barnaby does not need to get out and sniff every blade of grass before finding the perfect one to do his business."

They stopped for lunch at an inn, and all were ready to get out of the carriages. Edward was a hopeless traveling companion, as he spent all his time sleeping, which left Liberty with too much time to think.

Would whoever had written that note to Tobias really come after them if they did not walk away from the investigation? To threaten a peer like that terrified her. Whomever it was must not fear the ramifications.

"My back feels broken," Edward said when he'd opened the door and climbed out.

"Seeing as you are so old and infirm, do you mean?" Liberty took the hand he held out to her. "We have only been traveling for a few hours. God forbid we journey to Scotland one day."

Her brother shuddered at the thought. "I have a ferocious hunger, so make haste, sister."

Liberty watched Tobias lift Florence into his arms out of the carriage and keep her there. He received a smile from the girl, then a kiss on the cheek.

"Hello, Barnaby," Edward said as the dog bounded up to them.

Liberty bent to scratch his ears and received a lick on the cheek for her troubles.

"There can't be much leg room in there with the dog, two adults, and a child," Edward said to Tobias, who stood with Florence's nanny.

"We are coping admirably, aren't we, Florence?" He jiggled her in his arms, and she giggled.

Liberty remembered then how gentle he'd been with his brother, Mathew. Had losing him been the first step in changing Tobias? One day she would ask him, Liberty vowed, but not now. Now they needed to get everyone safely to Bidham and find out what was going on there.

"How are you today, my lady?"

"Well thank you, Lord Stafford," Liberty said as he moved to her side.

"I wonder as we are all in this together, and you and my best friend are close, that we should be on first name terms?"

"Well, as to that, we're not close... not really," Liberty felt she needed to clarify the connection.

He smiled down at her. She didn't know this man well, as she didn't know all of Tobias's friends, but had a feeling she may have misjudged him as a rake and libertine also, when in fact there was a great deal more to him.

"I think you could be wrong there, my lady." He waved a hand before him for her to enter the inn behind the others. "However, I'm sure that will work itself out, given time."

"There is nothing to work out."

"My friend is changing, and that is not all because of that sweet little girl in his arms. Some of it is due to your presence back in his life."

"Oh no." Liberty shook her head.

"Yes," he said, and then walked inside the inn.

She followed, wondering if Lord Stafford's words could be true.

Edward had Florence now in his arms and was wandering around, pointing out things to her that hung on the walls, when she entered.

"Your brother is a wonderful young man, Liberty," a deep voice said from beside her.

"Yes, he is." She walked away from Tobias then, and sat next to Lady Hamilton at a table, wanting some space between them.

There was little conversation as they ate, everyone just wanting to reach their destination safely.

"Liberty, would you mind switching places with Florence and Barnaby?" Edward said as they made their way back outside to the carriages. "She wants to read her favorite book with me, and Barnaby likes to hear the story too, I believe."

"Absolutely not." That would put her in the carriage with

Tobias. "She can continue the journey with us, of course, but—"

"Which would leave Tobias traveling alone. That hardly seems fair," Edward said.

She could read nothing in his eyes, but knew he was up to something. "Not alone. He would have the child's maid."

"The maid goes wherever the child does, sister."

"No, Edward, and in this I will not be challenged."

"There is no need to use that snooty tone with me."

"There is every need, brother," she whispered furiously. "You know how I feel about that man."

"I thought there was a thawing," Edward said calmly.

"No, Edward. End of story. Do not ask me again, and I do not take kindly to whatever this game is you are playing."

"Problem?"

"No, Lord Corbyn. There is no problem." Liberty walked to her carriage, and knew that in doing so, Edward would have no other choice but to follow.

Looking out the window and away from the door and the man who stood outside it chatting with her brother, Liberty focused on the trees. Of course she didn't see them, but pretended to. How dared Edward attempt to put her alone with Tobias, especially as she was unwed. Yes, there were questions she wanted to ask him, but if someone saw them together and her mother heard, there would be hell to pay.

The carriage dipped as her brother got in. She didn't look at him, not wishing to get into an argument about his need to read a book to Florence. He was silent as they left the inn.

The countryside rolled on as far as the eye could see. In the distance, the land rose and fell in a series of hills and valleys. She enjoyed being out of London and back into the wide-open spaces.

"Edward, I have no wish to spend any time alone with Lord Corbyn."

"Now that's a shame."

The deep words had her head whipping around. Beside her sat Tobias. Liberty's mouth opened and closed, but she literally had no words.

"Take a breath, Liberty, before you speak."

"You." She jabbed a finger at him. "How dare you be in my carriage… alone with me." He winced at her screeched words. "You had no right."

"I just want to talk to you, Liberty."

"No… no, no, no." She rose to bang on the roof. Hands grabbed her and forced her down onto the seat opposite.

"Just listen to me. That's all I ask of you." His face was calm, but she saw in his eyes he was anything but.

"Don't touch me!" She shook free of his grasp.

"Please, Liberty. Just hear what I have to say," he said.

"This is wrong. If anyone were to see us—"

"Who will see us?" he demanded.

Liberty couldn't overpower him, so she sat and crossed her arms.

"Speak then, and I will stop the carriage, and then we will once again ride as we were."

He looked at her for long moments, and something made Liberty hold her breath. Was he going to tell her why he'd spoken to her that day as he had? Why he'd turned from their friendship? Now that was a possibility. She felt nervous. She'd held so much rage and pain inside her for Tobias.

"It took me only a few days before I realized that my life would be hell living within the walls of Blackwood House."

CHAPTER TWENTY-SEVEN

HE SAT WITH his hands clasped loosely in his lap, giving the appearance of a man who was relaxed, yet he was far from that. In fact, just thinking back to that time made nausea swirl in his stomach.

"How so?" Liberty asked.

Toby had told Edward he needed to speak with his sister, and being alone in the carriage was his best chance of getting her to listen to him. He'd agreed, after Liberty's brother had told Toby he'd have several things to say to him if he hurt her.

"This is not easy for me to speak of, Liberty, but I owe you the truth so you understand why I did what I did. Why I sent you away."

Her lovely eyes were fixed intently on his. Looking at her, knowing she was just inches from him, eased some of the tension inside Toby.

"I met Jamie and Anthony on the first day I arrived at Blackwood House. We were new, and it was natural we became friends. All from wealthy, noble families, and eager to start this new adventure."

Toby felt his fists curl on his thighs but couldn't stop it. He had to do this for her… for them.

"From the day we entered that place we were beaten and subjected to things I cannot speak of even years later, Liberty."

"No!"

"Yes. It was prolonged, vicious, and broke us." He couldn't look at her… not yet.

She made a sound like a wounded animal, and he felt her move to take the seat beside his, but Toby was back there, deep in the memory and could do nothing to comfort her.

"My parents wouldn't listen when I wrote to them. Father had lived in Blackwood while at school, and said I needed to just get on with things. When I came home for Mathew's death, I could say nothing then, as they were grieving."

"As were you, Tobias," she said, taking his fist in both her hands. Holding it tight, giving him her support.

"I went back, and endured it for years, and then one day Anthony's three aunts came to visit him. Our housemaster, who was the evilest of all our tormentors, told him he was not to speak a word of what went on behind closed doors. But they knew something wasn't right with their nephew. He broke down and told them."

"Thank God," she whispered.

"Two of them stormed into Blackwood, and they told the housemaster that if this treatment did not stop, they would make him pay dearly. Not only that, but they would also speak to each of our families and detail everything that was happening. They would not stop until the school's reputation was destroyed."

"Tell me that put an end to this hell you lived?" Liberty whispered from beside him.

He opened his hand and held her fingers between his.

"It did. We were ignored from that day on."

"I'm so sorry, Toby."

He turned to look at her finally, their faces close. "I said those hateful things to you because I was broken inside, and I knew I would hurt you if I stayed your friend. Something in me changed at Blackwood Hall, and for a long time, I believed I would be no one else. The rage and fear were so fierce they consumed me."

"Toby." She whispered his name, anguished on his behalf.

"I couldn't get close to anyone but Anthony and Jamie, or I

would hurt them… hurt you."

"I'm so sorry, Tobias. If only I'd known, I would have—"

"No. I didn't want anyone to know," he said gripping her fingers.

"And now?"

"Now I have a reason to be different. Now I have a reason to live," he said slowly.

"Florence," she whispered.

"And you." He pressed his lips to hers and she didn't pull away. "I have realized since you came back into my life—"

"Toby—"

"Yes, you are back in my life," he insisted. "I want that." *I want you.*

"You hurt me." The words brushed his lips, her eyes so close now he could see the flecks of gold. "And for so long, I vowed never to forgive you. My hurt changed to rage. So many times I thought about what I'd say to you one day."

"What would you say to me?" He touched her cheek.

She shook her head. "It no longer matters."

"It matters very much to me, Liberty." He wanted her with a desperation that rocked him, but this time Toby did not fight that need. He didn't push down the emotion.

"I gave you something I've never given another person," she said.

"What did you give me?"

"Everything. Trust, friendship, and yes, love." He saw the truth in her eyes and realized just how much he'd hurt her.

"When you went away, I knew you'd come home, even if it was years later. Perhaps that was naive of me," she said. "But I always believed that deep inside you would be a part of my life."

"I'm sorry, Liberty."

"No. I'm sorry, because I didn't see what had happened to you, only my pain. I should have tried harder to understand, but thought only of myself."

He ran his eyes over her face, mapping every inch. His old

friend had grown into a beautiful woman. *His woman.* The rightness of those words settled deep inside him.

"I hate those men for what they did to you, Toby. Were they made to pay for their acts?"

Toby cupped her cheek, running a thumb over the warm soft skin. He could get used to touching Liberty Talbot.

"Some have paid, others we are not finished with."

She looked worried.

"There are ways to do things when it is not obvious who is doing them, Liberty."

"I am pleased you are punishing them, although I doubt it goes anywhere near close enough to what they did to you."

He smiled at her anger on his behalf.

"So you forgive me just like that?"

Her sigh was small. "I'm not sure it will be that easy. After all, I've carried anger toward you inside me for many years, but I will be happy to not feel tense, like a cat out in the rain whenever you are close."

"I'm truly sorry, Liberty. More sorry than I can say, but all I knew was anger and shame back then and not how to deal with what I'd endured, and how it had left me feeling."

Her fingers tightened around his. "There is no shame on your part," she said, her eyes full of fire. "That is all on them, those that hurt you and your friends."

"I have no right to ask you to trust me not to hurt you again, Liberty."

She studied him through those cool blue eyes for long seconds. He felt exposed but didn't look away. In that moment, he did something he hadn't before. Allowed himself to be vulnerable for her. His old friend, who he knew meant a great deal more to him now.

"I trusted the boy you were," she whispered.

"But not the man I have become?"

"I don't really know the man you are now."

"Do you want to?" The tension inside him climbed as she

stared at him.

"I do," she whispered.

More of the ice inside him thawed. Losing Liberty was yet another painful memory he could now let go of.

"And you are wrong, you know, Tobias."

"About what?" His finger traced her cheek.

"You're not broken."

Three simple words and they completely undid him. He felt the sting of tears and swallowed to force them back down.

Liberty tugged her hand free and cupped his cheeks. "You are so much stronger than what that place did to you, Toby. You wouldn't have survived and, yes, thrived in your own way if you weren't."

He looked into her eyes and saw the tears that, as with him, she fought to hold back.

"Do I wish you had dealt with this another way and told me? Yes, but I also know this was your way of surviving what happened to you."

"Liberty," he rasped. He took off her glasses and placed them in his pocket. Then he was kissing her. Deep and desperate, right then he needed this woman more than he'd needed anyone in a long time.

She took everything he gave and returned it. Her hands went to his hair, his to her waist, pulling her closer, so close she was soon in his lap. Where one kiss finished, another started.

"Stop me," he whispered against her lips.

"No." The hands in his hair tugged him closer. Nothing separated them but clothes, and that was too much. His body was hard, his hands trembling with the need to touch and taste her like an innocent youth.

One hand moved, unbuttoning her spencer. Toby's fingers touched the soft skin of her neck. Tracing the curve of her bodice and the swells of her breasts above the neckline of her dress, he swallowed her soft moan.

"I missed you very much," he said, easing back to look at her.

"We talked about entering society and what it would be like for us, and while I knew I'd enter first, that you would be there one day was something I'd always believed. Then you were, and we were strangers."

"I didn't want to enter society," Liberty said.

"Because you knew I was there?"

"You were one reason, but after the accident, everything that had been so easy no longer was."

"I'm sorry you suffered." He stroked her cheek again.

"It was not your fault," she said, her eyes holding his. "We were young when we were friends. I sometimes wondered if in my head I'd made up how close we were. In the moments when I struggled with what you'd told me that day—"

"I have outgrown you, Liberty," Toby said, remembering his words clearly. "I have no further wish to be your friend. From this day forth, we are merely acquaintances. Please do not call here again."

She closed her eyes, and he caught the tear that rolled down her cheek. "Your words were so hard and cold. So final."

"Forgive me, dear friend." He kissed her again, needing to erase the memory of the pain he'd inflicted upon her.

"Yes." She breathed against his lips. A single word that humbled Toby, and then it was her kissing him.

"I want you, Liberty, but have no right to take you." Toby pulled back. "No right to touch and kiss you more than I already have here in this carriage. However, I fear I cannot stop."

"I won't break, Tobias."

"But you are innocent." He traced her full bottom lip.

"I'm also an old maid, and therefore able to make my own decisions."

"Liberty, you could never be an old maid, and you need to move to the other seat right now before I forget I am a gentleman."

She leaned into him, sliding her hand around his neck. "Kiss me," she whispered against his lips, and those two words lit a fire inside Toby. He forgot his good intentions and did as she asked.

Soon the only sound was of their mouths devouring each other again. His hands roamed her body, as hers stroked his neck and tangled in his hair.

"I want to touch all of you," he whispered raggedly.

"I want that too."

He tugged down her bodice, baring her full breasts, and then cupped the soft flesh. Liberty moaned low in her throat.

She was a fire in his veins Toby wasn't sure he'd ever extinguish. The control he prided himself on having fled, and in its place was this burning inside him to take more of what she offered. Lifting her, he lowered Liberty, so she was straddling his thighs.

"Tobias—"

"Toby. I want to be Toby to you again."

"Toby," she breathed.

"I will stop at any time if that is your wish, Liberty. But this burning need to be with you, touch you. It consumes me."

He studied her. Eyes heavy lidded, lips swollen from his kisses. She looked ravished. His hands had pulled strands of her hair free, and with her breasts bare, Liberty looked like every one of his fantasies. His friend, his life, and his love. He kept those words to himself for now, but knew them for the truth.

In that moment, he knew what his future held. It would be with this woman and Florence, and for the first time in many years, Toby felt hope.

CHAPTER TWENTY-EIGHT

EVERY INCH OF her body felt sensitive. Need pulsed through Liberty. Need for the man beside her. Toby was here, and he wanted her as she wanted him. *Her Toby.*

Liberty had never thought to feel passion. Never believed, if she wed, it would be for anything but duty and to create a child. But that changed the minute Toby put his hands on her.

"Touch me again," she whispered as his eyes, heavy with desire, ran over her body. In that moment, she would give him anything. All rational thought had fled, and there was just them and now, and the tension spiraling higher inside her.

He leaned closer, and then his lips were there above the slope of a breast. Her moan had him licking his way down to the peak. His tongue slid over the sensitive bud and Liberty shuddered as sensation coursed through her.

"Toby," she whispered, and he lifted his head.

"Toby, good? Toby, stop?"

"G-good."

"Thank God."

He lowered his head again and laved the taut peak until she was writhing on his thighs. Tension built inside Liberty with every lick. He eased her dress upward with his hands, the heat from his palms leaving a trail of desire and heightening the building tension inside her.

Liberty wanted to feel his skin. Needed to touch him too. Her fingers went to his neck, and then into his hair.

"Toby."

He stopped instantly as she spoke his name and looked up at her with that dark, heated gaze.

"I want to touch you, too."

"You do?"

"Very much." She knew then that while he may give the appearance of a confident man, a man who had a reputation with women, he still carried vulnerability inside him from the hell he'd endured.

Liberty should have felt exposed seated as she was, bared to his gaze, but she didn't. All she felt was an aching need for this man. Her fingers went to his necktie, and she freed it.

"I'm hoping you can retie that."

She smiled but didn't speak as she worked on his buttons next. When she had a few opened, Liberty parted his shirt and then leaned forward and kissed the skin at the base of his throat. Toby's moan was low and deep.

"Liberty," he breathed her name.

She licked the skin as he'd licked her breast.

"Your touch is heaven," he rasped. "For an innocent, you are skilled in torment."

"I may not have spoken to you, Lord Corbyn, but I watched you. Saw the boy I knew become a man. Wondered what lay beneath your clothes."

"I saw you too," he rasped as she placed another hot, open-mouthed kiss on his skin. "And every time I looked at you, I felt that pang of regret."

"Shh." She raised her head and kissed him. His hand went to the back of her neck, holding her closer.

"I can hardly believe I entered this carriage with you hating me, and now you're in my arms," he whispered against her lips.

Then there were no more words, only them, and this.

He slid his hands back up her thighs as he spread his wider, opening her to him.

"I don't deserve your trust, Liberty, but I want it just the same."

She nodded but could not say the words as his thumbs were stroking circles in the soft curls. Sensation, need, it all pulsed through her as his head lowered once more to take her breast into his mouth.

"Toby," she whispered as one finger slid lower and into the damp folds between her thighs. He then stroked it along the seam, making her shudder.

"Just feel, Liberty."

And she did. Every lave of his tongue on her breast, and stroke of his finger between her legs. Soon she was panting and writhing as the tension inside her built to an unbearable height. Then a great wash of pleasure consumed her. Liberty shuddered, her fingers biting into the flesh of Toby's arm.

"Beautiful," he whispered, lifting his head to watch her. "That look is one I will never tire of."

"I have heard of such things, but had not believed them," Liberty whispered.

"Where have you heard of such things?" His smile was small and tight, and she felt the tension inside him. The hardness pressing against his breeches.

"Women talk, my lord. Men are not the only ones who share confidences and gossip, you know."

"I'm shocked," he drawled. "And now you need to get off my lap, because we cannot—"

"We can," she said, doing something she once would never have had the courage to do. But this was Toby. He made her feel strong.

Liberty moved closer to him, so her body was now flush with his, pressing into him. She felt his arousal twitch.

"Now," she said against his lips. "I want you to be the one, Toby."

"No—"

"Yes." Liberty moved, causing friction that sent a delicious spike of heat through her.

"Christ!" He hissed. "I'm trying to be a gentleman."

Her hands went to his breeches. "I don't want you to be a gentleman."

"Be sure," he rasped.

"I am. I didn't even know until this moment I was waiting for you… for this, Toby."

"Liberty—"

"No promises, not yet. I want this for us."

His eyes held hers. "There will be a future for us, Liberty. You know that, don't you?"

Her heart swelled. "I do."

"We will live our lives together, my sweet." He took over unbuttoning his breeches. "Tell me you understand that?"

"I understand."

He freed his length. "Feel me," he whispered.

She touched the hard flesh, and he groaned. Liberty circled him with her fist and stroked, feeling the heat and strength beneath her fingers. Reveling at every sound that came from his lips.

"For an innocent, you are far too knowing," Toby gritted removing her fingers. "This, what we are about to do, will hurt you, Liberty, and while I will make it my life's work to protect you from pain, unfortunately, in this, it is unavoidable.

"It's all right, Toby. I know what happens."

"More of that chat between women?" he gritted out.

"Yes."

"I want you to lift onto your knees, and then lower onto me."

She did and felt the damp head of his arousal at her entrance. Then he was entering her.

"Easy, my sweet."

Liberty focused on the sensations.

"Look at me, Liberty."

Their eyes locked on each other as she slowly lowered, and felt the silken tissues inside her give as he slid deeper. There was a sharp sting of pain as he penetrated her body.

"Christ, you feel good." The muscles in his jaw bunched.

Liberty put her arms around his neck and held him tight. Toby, her friend, and now her love. Later she'd wonder at that. Wonder at how her feelings for this man had changed so rapidly. Or had they just lain dormant?

"Are you all right, Liberty?"

"Oh, yes."

"Then when you can move, I beg of you to do so," he gritted out.

The feel of him was wonderful, even as the pain lingered. She rose, and then down again, and his jaw clenched. She repeated the motion slowly, feeling the delicious tension rise inside her once more. His hands were on her hips, fingers gripping her tight.

"Next time, we will be in a bed," he whispered, his hips thrusting up to meet hers.

A wave of pleasure hit her again as he continued to meet her as she rode him. Thrust after thrust, as the sensations became almost unbearable.

"Now, Liberty, I cannot wait much longer."

She felt the tension peak, and then his thumb pressed inward, finding the small tight bud between her thighs and she scaled that pinnacle of pleasure once more. Her cries muffled in his shoulder as he moaned long and low.

The only sounds for long minutes were the clop of hooves and rasp of their breathing in the small space. He held her pressed to his chest. Arms banded around her back.

"I should not have done that, but I will never regret it," he whispered against her ear. "You're mine now, Liberty. For always."

She had no problem with that, however, she had no energy to take him to task for the high-handed way he'd spoken the words.

"And now we dress, in case the carriages have to stop," he said, easing her off his body and on to the opposite seat. "Use this," he handed her the handkerchief he got out of his jacket pocket, along with her glasses, which he pushed onto her face.

She cleaned and dressed, as did he, but the silence wasn't tense and fraught as it had once been between them. Liberty felt no embarrassment, just a rightness that she was here with Toby. Only when they were both as presentable as they could make themselves did he pull her back onto his lap.

"We have so much to say to each other, and so many years have passed since we were friends, my sweet. But first I want to say that any future with me comes with Florence. She is mine now, as are you."

"And I would have it no other way. I will love her as you do," Liberty said.

He exhaled. "I knew you would, but I needed to ask. Now let me hold you in my arms for the remainder of our journey, where you will always be."

"Yes." Liberty laid her head on his chest as he turned slightly to rest his body more comfortably. "Toby?"

"Liberty?" His fingers stroked her neck.

"Do you speak of Mathew at all?"

He didn't stiffen like he normally would at the mention of his brother, but he felt the heat of pain in his chest.

"I don't think you have grieved properly for him, Toby. Will you let me help you do that? Your brother deserves that from you."

"I know he does." He buried his face in her hair. "I miss him so much still."

"We will talk more about him in the future."

"We will," he said, feeling the rightness in the words. "And my mother deserves that from me as well."

"Yes," she whispered, feeling her eyelids droop. "I love you, Toby." Liberty then closed her eyes and fell asleep in his arms.

CHAPTER TWENTY-NINE

TOBY HAD RELUCTANTLY dropped Liberty at the front door of her family's home yesterday and left. He'd fought the need to take her to Hawthorne with him, but not yet. That day would come soon.

After the brief journey to Hawthorne where he'd pointed out scenery to Florence, they'd arrived. Wide-eyed, she'd taken in the grandeur, even commenting on it being far bigger than the London house. Toby had shown Florence and Miss Haigh to the nursery, and the child's smile had been Toby's reward when she entered. His staff had done an amazing job of readying it for her, and she loved the large rocking horse they'd dragged out of the attic.

He'd spent a few hours with his friends before retiring for the night. They'd pressed him about his carriage ride with Liberty, and all he'd offered was that they'd reached an understanding. Later, lying in his large bed, Toby thought of her—the woman he loved and would marry. For the first time in years, he fell asleep completely content.

The morning had not changed his mood, and after a ride around the estate, and a large lunch, Toby, Anthony, and Jamie had ridden into Bidham.

The fair was tomorrow, but they'd wanted to look around and see if they could get someone to talk to them about the threat hanging over the village. He was determined in this. If they were to help, they needed to know what they were dealing with.

"Florence is changing," Jamie said as they walked down the cobbled street into the village.

"Yes, she's happier," Toby said.

"That little chuckle melts your heart," Anthony added. "My wife informed me she wants a child just like your ward, Toby."

"Well then, you better get busy."

"I better had."

A letter had arrived this morning from Mr. Scully, the private investigator. He'd visited the now empty warehouse where Toby had been assaulted, and while there, he'd come upon a man lurking around the rear of the building.

The man had said he'd come looking for more work, but the place was now empty, and he didn't know where they'd gone. He'd been willing to talk for money, and it had been the first piece of information they'd been able to get from someone involved in the smuggling.

When pressed, he said someone brought the barrels of alcohol to London from somewhere on the coast. He didn't know where.

"It will not be easy to get them to talk, Toby. They won't trust you yet after what they see is your desertion of them," Anthony said.

"I know that, thank you."

"I am just saying, have some patience, my friend."

"The man Mr. Scully questioned could also be lying, Toby," Jamie said. "He could have been there simply to give that information to anyone asking about the smuggling operation."

"Agreed, and that's why we need to get someone in this village to talk to us," Toby said, looking around him for Liberty even though he knew it was unlikely she'd be there.

How was she today, after they'd made love? *Was she happy like him?*

She'd forgiven him, and told Toby he wasn't broken, and today he didn't feel it. Today he felt lighter inside, even as worry for Bidham gnawed at him. He felt hope for a future he'd not once believed he deserved.

"That smile is blinding; put it away at once," Jamie said walking beside him into the village. "The gravity of this situation should not inspire a smile like that."

Flags fluttered in the late afternoon sun at the village's entrance, put there in preparation for tomorrow's fair. Trestles were also being set up, which would hold food and things for sale. He'd loved this day as a child, and spent hours here, usually going home with a sore stomach from eating too much.

"It is not blinding, and I can hardly enter the village scowling now, can I? Besides, women have told me for years my smile is my best feature," Toby said, looking from left to right.

He'd not returned Liberty's declaration of love yesterday, but he would soon. That she loved him, even after everything Toby had done to her, was humbling. Of course he'd known she had to care deeply. Liberty would never have given herself to him if she didn't.

"Ah, but that smile is different," Jamie said. "It's an Anthony smile."

"Is it?" Anthony, who walked beside him, said. "The smile of a man in love, do you mean?"

"That will do," Toby said.

"First Florence is changing you, and now Liberty. You made my life hell tormenting me when I fell in love with Evie, therefore we must now do the same to you," Anthony said, looking smug.

"I have not said I'm in—"

"I saw your face when you stepped down from that carriage, Toby. Something happened between you and your childhood friend on that journey. It was there for everyone to see on both your faces," Jamie said.

He exhaled. "I would rather have this conversation with her than both of you."

"Ah, so there is a conversation to have?" Jamie asked.

Toby ignored them and nodded to Mr. Bridget, who was placing a sign on his fence.

"About time you came back again!" he shouted when he saw Toby.

Toby walked to where the man stood glaring at him. He then held out his hand. It took a few minutes, but the older man shook it.

"You'll forgive me, Mr. Bridget. It was wrong of me to abandon Bidham, but if you'll have me, I'm back now and going nowhere."

The man harrumphed, then nodded. "Very well, you can stay," he said, as if he owned the village. "And it's my hope you'll see your way clear to changing the bad."

Toby leaned in closer. "I'm going to make sure of it, and I'm sorry things have not been easy for the residents. Will you tell me what has been happening?"

Mr. Bridget had always been the man in town who talked the loudest and had the most to say. An unofficial mayor, he was usually the spokesperson, if one were needed. As a child, Toby had been terrified of him.

The older man shook his head. "There are eyes everywhere." He then walked away.

"Come, we need to put an end to this, and to do that, we must know who we are dealing with," Toby said. "I'm not leaving here unless we get someone to talk to us."

He walked, he talked, and no one would speak to him. Toby tried everything, and when that didn't work, Jamie or Anthony stepped in. No one would spill any information, and all appeared terrified when he'd pressed them.

"The threat must be severe indeed to silence an entire town," Anthony said.

It was at the bottom of the village that he saw the man standing beside the bakery. Tom Ackers, Sally's father. His eyes connected with Toby's and then he disappeared.

"I am going to speak to someone."

"Who?" Anthony looked around him.

"There is no time to explain. We must do this fast before anyone is alerted. Enter the bakery and stay there while I go out the rear door. Then we will leave together when I return. Purchase gingerbread."

"Be careful," Jamie said.

"So this is the place where the legendary gingerbread is made?" Anthony said loudly.

"Indeed, it is. Come along and I will purchase you some," Toby added.

They entered, and Toby looked at the man behind the counter. He turned and walked away. Toby followed. They entered the kitchens, and it was there he found a rear door. Tom Ackers stood just inside it with Izack Potter, the bakery's owner.

"My condolences for your loss," Toby said before the man spoke.

"My Sally was murdered, and it was a message for our silence."

Deep grooves of sorrow marked the man's face, and dark smudges framed his sad eyes. Toby could feel his distress.

"But there are those among us that can no longer stay silent," Izack said. "After Sally was found, we received this note."

Toby took the paper handed to him and read the words.

You were told that if you didn't do as I say, there would be trouble for you all. The girl's death was that warning. Heed or more will follow.

"We will ensure that doesn't happen," Toby said pocketing the note. "Now tell me everything I need to know fast, and why the smuggling started?"

A thought had been niggling at him. How could whoever was behind this make an entire village silent?

Tom looked down at his hands. "We were greedy, and I lost my girl because of it."

"A man approached us and said he wanted to bring in barrels

of alcohol." Izack continued the story. "The townsfolk had no problem with making a few extra coins, but soon we realized it was more than just alcohol coming in."

"What else was in those barrels?"

"Opium," Izack said. "A barrel fell off a cart one day and rolled down the street. It broke open, and it was old Mrs. Luther that saw the powder. She knew what it was. We confronted them, and it was then the threats started. Sally was found dead not long after."

Toby knew how destructive opium could be. He'd seen the results on some of society's members.

"We're talking to you because no one else can help us, and we're desperate. The hold they have over us will last forever if we don't stop it," Izack said.

"If we go to the authorities, we will be charged," Tom added. "It's my hope that now you're back in Bidham, that you are a better man than you were, like your father, and will help us, Lord Corbyn."

Toby nodded, knowing he deserved the insult. "I have already started investigations and have found the location in London where the barrels were being delivered."

That surprised them. They then told him everything they knew. Both talked at Toby for the next five minutes.

"And now you need to go as they're watching, my lord, and have eyes everywhere," Tom said. "It's our belief that whoever is behind this is one of you."

"A nobleman?" Toby asked.

"Yes."

"If you hear anything more, find a way to get the information to me," Toby said, walking away. "But trust that I will see this through to its end."

"We want to," Izack Potter said, and Toby could not fault the words, as he'd given them no reason to trust him.

"Do you know when the next shipment is to arrive?" Toby asked.

"It comes every three weeks. They're supplying many around the country now," Izack said.

"They're ruthless, with a huge gang of men, and they're mean and loyal to whoever is behind it," Tom added.

Toby nodded, then went back into the bakery where his friends were talking loudly about how good the gingerbread was. They then all walked out of there eating. It tasted like straw in his mouth.

He wanted whoever was behind this caught, and he would see that done. Only then could he look to a future with Liberty and Florence.

CHAPTER THIRTY

TOBY WALKED WITH his friends down to the end of the street, where it met the water. Thoughts churned in his head as he worked through what he'd learned.

"A lot of work has been done on this dock lately," Anthony said, looking at the wooden structure.

"Look right," Jamie said.

Toby saw the two men standing beside a small building that for years had housed ropes, watching them. They were unfamiliar to him, and something told him they were here to watch over Bidham's inhabitants. Anger simmered low in his belly. Someone was threatening his village, and his people. Yes, he'd not been near this place in years, but that had now changed, and he wanted its inhabitants to feel happy again.

"We could rush them," Anthony said.

"But we don't know if there are others here watching," Jamie added. "We need whoever is behind this operation, not those working for him."

"Come, let's walk. I have things to tell you, but no wish for anyone to overhear," Toby said.

"I've been giving this some thought," Anthony said, "and it's my belief there has to be some place the barrels are being stored nearby. A location that they meet to load them and take them to London."

"They just take them from here, surely?" Toby said.

"If the boats arrive at night or the weather is foul, I doubt that," Anthony added.

"If, as those men I met at the bakery said, there is a nobleman involved, then it's likely he is the one with the property," Toby said.

"Are there any other families locally, other than you and the Talbots?" Jamie asked.

"Not that I'm aware of, but then I've not involved myself in the area for many years," Toby said.

"And look who has just arrived."

At Jamie's words, Toby looked around him and there she was. Liberty with her maid, Helen.

"I don't want her in Bidham without protection," he said, walking toward her.

"Nothing will happen in daylight surrounded by people. Don't overreact, and don't for pity's sake forbid her from coming here," Anthony whispered. "Trust me in this. It will not go well for you."

"He'd probably know better than us to be fair about this kind of thing, Toby," Jamie added.

"I need another piece of gingerbread. Come along, Jamie. We will get some for Florence and Evie too," Anthony said, walking toward the bakery and leaving Toby with Liberty.

He watched the color flush her cheeks as their eyes met. He wanted to forbid her from coming here, but knew Anthony was right. To do so would be folly now, when everything between them was so new. Instead, he leaned in and kissed her cheek.

"Hello, my sweet," he whispered in her ear.

"Hello, Toby," she said as she dropped into a curtsey. The small smile on her face told him she was pleased with his words. "How is Florence?"

"She is well, and at present with her nanny and Evangeline, being spoiled, I am sure."

Toby took her arm and moved her a few steps down the road, as if they were looking out over the water. "Are you all right, Liberty?"

"Of course."

"The carriage ride here, we—"

"I'm all right, Toby, I promise."

"You look beautiful today. I'm glad to see you are wearing your glasses. I have no wish for you to trip and hurt yourself."

"Mother does not mind me wearing them here, where no one from London is likely to see me."

"You don't have to worry about that anymore," Toby said, taking her fingers in his. "Your future is determined."

"Toby—"

"However, we cannot get into that now, as I want to understand what is happening in Bidham, Liberty." She nodded her agreement to that. "Now I need to ask you something."

"Of course. Anything," she said.

He wanted to kiss her again. Lean in and nibble that full bottom lip. No woman had ever consumed him before. It was unsettling.

"Do you know of any other nobleman living in the surrounding area, close to Bidham?" She frowned then, her eyes alert through the lenses of her glasses. "It's important, and I believe connected to what is happening here," Toby added.

She thought about his words for a moment, and then said, "After I saw you here that day, the first time you returned to the village, I came upon Lord Michael when I was leaving. He told me he was here visiting Mr. Landon as he had a telescope, but I'm sure they have nothing to do with this."

"Why are you sure of that?" Toby asked, feeling his anger bite for no other reason than she'd mentioned Michael.

"I do not know Mr. Landon well, but of course Lord Michael is a well-respected society peer, and a good man, even if…"

"Even if what Liberty?" Toby demanded as her words faltered.

"He is not the right man for me," she whispered.

"Has he wanted to be the right man for you?" *Stay calm.*

"Why are you angry with me, Toby?" She was frowning now.

"I'm not angry with you. Please answer the question, Liberty."

Her eyes ran over his face before she spoke again. "I've recently noticed an increase in his interest in me."

The breath hissed out of Toby's mouth. If Michael were involved, had he approached Liberty because she was a local to Bidham? Did he see her as someone he could manipulate? This seemed likely, particularly given that both she and Toby had been seen inquiring at the London warehouse.

Fear ran through his veins at the thought of that man near her.

"You need to listen to me now, Liberty. You cannot have anything to do with Michael," Toby's tone was harsher than he'd intended. Her chin raised, eyes defiant now.

"Toby."

He turned at Jamie's call and noted a man a few feet away. One of the two who'd been watching them earlier. Anthony moved to intercept him, but the man fled, running up the street.

"Was he listening to us?" Liberty asked, eyes shocked.

"Whoever is controlling what is going on here has eyes all over Bidham, Liberty. Promise me you will not speak with Michael again."

"Tell me why I must do as you say?"

"Other than you are now mine, Michael is dangerous to you."

Her blue eyes were almost arctic now as they glared at him. "I beg your pardon? I belong to no man."

He turned fully to face her. "Wrong. You belong to me." He grabbed her shoulders and pulled her close, kissing her hard. Shock had her mouth falling open when he released her.

"What are you doing? Someone will see." She tried to look around, but he held her still.

"I don't care. Look at me, Liberty." She did. "Do you remember what we talked about in the carriage? About the men who inflicted what they did on me, Jamie, and Anthony?"

She nodded, the stiffness leaving her shoulders.

"Michael was a benefactor of Blackwood House and knew exactly what was going on there. He also watched my punishment."

"No," she whispered.

"Yes."

"He told me in London that you were a man of questionable character," Liberty said. Her eyes were now stricken. "Do you believe he is involved in what is happening in Bidham?"

"I don't know, but it's possible, and I'm going to find out for sure. I need to go now, Liberty, but I will see you tomorrow. Do not leave your house until then, and only to come to the fair with your family. Is that understood?"

"Where are you going?" She grabbed his arm. "I want to help you."

"No. We must do this, and I need to know you are safe. If Michael calls at your house, do not let him in. Tell your parents everything if you wish, but do this for me, Liberty."

"My family is visiting with Reverend Nelly today."

"You should have gone with them," Toby said.

"I didn't want to, in case you called." She threw her arms around his neck then, right there in the street, and squeezed him hard. "I love you," she whispered in his ear. "Please stay safe. I don't want to lose you again."

"I have too much to live for now," he said softly. "Trust no one and go nowhere alone. Now, go home at once please, Liberty."

She studied him briefly and then walked to where Helen stood. Soon, they were heading back out of the village.

"There is a tavern," Toby pointed to the Gill. "Go there and await me. I will join you soon," he told his friends.

He walked up the street and watched Liberty and Helen get back into the carriage and roll away. Only when he knew they were safe did he retrace his steps and join Anthony and Jamie.

Toby found his friends at a table in the corner where they

would not be overheard. Searching the interior, he only found two others, both locals. He dropped into the empty chair.

"Whiskey," Jamie said, nudging it toward him.

"Now tell us everything," Anthony said, leaning closer.

Deep in the pit of his stomach, he now knew that Michael was involved in this entire business, and he planned to find out what. He then told Jamie and Anthony everything he knew, including what Liberty had told him.

"Opium," Anthony said. "Well, that actually makes more sense."

"It does," Toby agreed.

"And that Michael could be involved does not surprise me. We know that man is a bastard," Jamie said. "Plus, he's capable of manipulating Liberty to get her on his side. What he doesn't realize is how close you and she are now."

"We need to visit Landon," Toby said throwing down the last of his whiskey.

"Are we to ride up to the front door of Landon's house and ask to look through his telescope?" Anthony asked.

"I don't see why not," Jamie said.

"We don't really know the man," Anthony protested.

"But he's got a telescope, and we, three titled peers, wish to look through it," Toby said. "It is as good a reason to visit him as any."

They left then and were soon mounting and riding away from the village. Toby was still seething with rage over the fact that Michael had come after Liberty. *Bastard.*

"That kiss certainly confirmed what we already knew," Anthony added. "She is the perfect wife for you, my friend."

"I love her." Toby suddenly needed to say the words out loud. Words he should have spoken to Liberty first.

"Well then, there is no more to be said," Jamie added.

"I believe now that Landon will have somewhere on his land that holds the barrels, like you said, Anthony. He and Michael run the entire operation from there, I'm sure of it," Toby said, pushing Liberty out of his head.

"I can't believe an entire village has allowed this to happen," Jamie said. "Why have they not stood up to them before now?"

"Because they were involved originally. If they went to the authorities, then they would also be in trouble… in fact, more so, as the magistrate would likely blame them over any noblemen involved," Toby said.

His friends were silent, thinking over his words for a while.

"I believe you could be right there," Anthony added. "So we need to find the evidence, and who is involved."

"Michael," Toby said.

Jamie growled low in his throat, sounding like a rabid dog.

"Agreed. Let's make him pay," Anthony said.

Landon's property was a fifteen-minute ride from Bidham following the coast road.

"There appears to be another entrance there," Anthony said, pointing ahead of them when they arrived. "It could be worth investigating later and may hold what we are looking for."

"Landon's property will border the cliffs and have a view back to the village," Toby said when they rode through the gate.

"And with the telescope, they can monitor the comings and goings of sea vessels and watch the unloading. Bidham is under constant surveillance," Jamie added.

"Be alert as we ride up," Toby warned.

"What are we going to say to Landon?" Jamie asked.

"That I had no idea he was almost a neighbor until Lord Hampton, who I know was one of Landon's cronies, told me in London that this is where he now lives. I am paying him a call, to enquire if he will attend the fair tomorrow," Toby said.

"That could work," Jamie said.

The driveway wasn't long and soon they were outside a large house that sat back slightly from the cliffs. Dismounting, Toby handed his reins to Jamie, and he and Anthony went to knock on the door.

"Good day to you. I wish to speak with Mr. Landon," Toby

said to the butler.

"I'm afraid he's from home, sir."

"Is Lord Michael visiting?" Toby added.

"He is to arrive this evening, sir."

"Thank you. Please tell both Lord Michael and Mr. Landon that Lords Hamilton, Stafford, and Corbyn called."

The butler bowed after assuring them he would pass on the message.

They walked away knowing that soon Michael would know he was here, and Toby thought that would unsettle the man, seeing as he, Jamie, and Anthony had also been in town asking questions. Then there was the warehouse in London, where he had seen both Liberty and Toby.

Had he been behind the attack on Toby? The man was capable of that and more. Michael would not get near Liberty again; he'd make sure of it.

CHAPTER THIRTY-ONE

REACHING THE END of the driveway, they headed right instead of left. Looking skyward, Toby knew they still had a few hours before darkness fell. But if Landon and Michael were from home, then now may be the time to do some investigating.

"Let's ride in and tether the horses. We can then walk," Jamie said.

They did and were soon on foot, heading along a track wide enough for a horse and cart. It wound to the left through trees, but they saw no houses or cattle. Toby stopped when he saw a big outbuilding.

"An odd place for a building that size, considering there is no livestock nearby," Jamie said. "If there are people inside, it may be better to come back after dark."

"Stay here, and I'll look around. If there is someone there, we will leave," Toby said. He didn't wait for his friends to acknowledge his words but started toward the building. Keeping in the trees for as long as he could, he stepped from their cover as he reached it.

Moving closer, he made his way around the outside looking for a way in, or signs that someone was inside.

"We decided to join you," Anthony whispered.

"Christ," Toby hissed, clutching his chest.

"Something felt off, as if you were walking into danger," Jamie added.

"Who is keeping watch?" Toby snapped.

"The horses," Anthony said.

"We need to get inside, but that door is locked," Toby said. "I can't see anything through that window either."

"There may be another entrance, so keep walking," Anthony urged.

He did, and they found another door at the rear. Trying the handle, this one opened.

"Jamie, you stay out here," Anthony said.

Toby went first. Crouching low when he heard voices, he moved to a row of barrels with Anthony on his heels.

"I don't like that those noblemen were in town. I saw them go into the bakery and not come out for a long time. Then one of them was talking to locals as he walked down the street," a voice said. "That woman was there too."

"Lady Liberty?" another voice asked, and Toby was sure it was Landon. "She will be no trouble. But Corbyn, Stafford, and Hamilton could be."

"After that business in London with them snooping around, and us having to move premises, I don't like it."

"We'll get this shipment off and lie low for a while," Landon said. "If we need to move, then we'll find somewhere else. I'm not giving this up, and I know he won't either."

"The villagers won't turn against us. They have too much to lose. If we must kill someone else, we have to. But it's getting messy," the other man said. "I don't want to spend my days in Newgate."

"This shipment will leave the night after the fair," Landon said. "Michael and I will discuss the issue of what to do about those bloody nobles poking their noses into our business tonight."

"I'm going into the village to get some food. It's good for them to see me," the man said, and then laughed. "I like to keep them scared."

Toby rose until he could see over the barrels and found Landon and a large hulk of a man. He didn't see anyone else. Waving to Anthony as the men started moving to the door, they hurried back outside.

Grabbing Jamie, they then ran around the side away from the entrance. Minutes later, they heard a door closing. They gave it a further five minutes before moving back to the entrance.

"He mentioned Michael's name, but it is not enough proof," Anthony said. "We have to search that building."

"There is a lock on the door now," Toby said.

"Then we go in through the window," Jamie said.

They found a rock and smashed the glass, clearing it away. Toby went in first, with the others following.

"There have to be fifty barrels here," Jamie said, looking around them. "That is a lot of opium."

They found an office and went through a cabinet, taking out several ledgers. It was Toby who found a document with Michael's signature on it detailing that a shipment of opium was to arrive in London, and the date.

"Got him," he said holding it out for his friends to read.

They gathered up everything that would incriminate both Landon and Michael, and left, making their way back to the horses. It was as Toby mounted he remembered something Landon said.

"Liberty said Michael has been showing an interest in her lately. He told her I was a man of questionable character."

"Which is true," Anthony added.

"Landon said Michael is on his way here. You don't think he'd call at the Talbots' first, do you?"

"Did you tell Liberty she needed to be careful of him?" Jamie demanded.

"I told her not to leave her house, or let Michael enter it. Her parents and Edward are not home, however, which means she's alone." Fear gripped him.

"Why would Michael suddenly be a threat to Liberty?" Jamie asked.

"He wouldn't," Anthony said. "Unless he thought she knew something, which she doesn't."

"She knows I suspect him," Toby said. "I'm going to the Talbots'."

"I don't know why Michael would suddenly decide to call on Liberty here. It makes no sense, Toby," Jamie said.

He was right, of course, but something told him to check on her.

"I can see you will not rest until you have," Jamie said. "I will come with you."

"No need. You two go back to Evie and Florence, and I will be there soon. I know you are right, but until I am sure she is safe, I cannot stop worrying."

"Love," Jamie sighed.

"We have no problem accompanying you," Anthony said.

"No. Tell Florence I shall return shortly."

His friends took the evidence, and they parted ways. The ride to the Talbots' was ten minutes, and Toby had to refrain from galloping. He was being foolish, but once he'd checked on her, he'd feel better.

Liberty was now important to him. Did that mean he would worry about her constantly? Was this to be his future? Irrational fear when she wasn't in his line of sight didn't appeal to him at all, even as Toby knew he could no longer live without her.

He knew the Talbot property well, and took the left fork as the driveway split to the stables, where he found the same old crotchety stable master. The man glared at him as he took the reins Toby handed him. Not a word was exchanged. Shaking his head, he walked outside.

The sky was darkening, and while he'd not noticed it before, there was definitely the feel of rain in the air. He let the memories come as he walked. The days he and Liberty had run all over this place. The laughter and promises they'd made to each other.

The house was enormous and built of dark-gray stone, one side completely covered in ivy. Old, like his, and befitting the status of the family who lived within its walls.

He saw the carriage then. It was to one side, so unless someone was looking out the window, it would not be seen. The door didn't hold a crest, so Toby wasn't sure who it belonged to.

"Good day to you," Toby said to the driver. The man nodded down at him. "Who are you driving for?"

"Lord Michael, sir."

"And how long have you been here?"

"We have just arrived, sir," the driver said.

"Thank you."

Heart now pounding hard inside his chest, he walked up to the front door. Had Liberty's family already returned? Why had she let Michael inside when Toby had told her not to?

He didn't knock on the door, but opened it, and let himself inside. There was no sign of the staff, which didn't mean a great deal in a house this size, as they were possibly below the stairs.

Where was Liberty?

"Lord Corbyn?"

The butler, Bernard, who had been here when Toby used to visit, appeared through a door that he knew led to the rear of the house. Toby pressed a finger to his lips and moved to where the man was.

"Is Lord Michael here?"

"No, my lord. Lady Liberty said she was not at home to anyone this evening, so I sent him away."

"His carriage is still outside." The shock on the butler's face was real. "Where is Lady Liberty?"

"She is in the morning parlor upstairs, my lord. I will take you to her."

"I know where it is, Bernard. What I need you to do is find two footmen and arm them. I will then have you and them come to the third floor."

Pulling out his pistol, Toby ran to the stairs as the butler went to carry out his orders. The carpets muted his footsteps as he climbed. Heart pounding, he reached the third floor and stopped.

"How did you get inside our house?" Liberty demanded. "I said I was not home to visitors. I insist you leave at once, Lord Michael." She sounded calm for all she must be terrified knowing what he'd told her about Michael.

"But we are friends, my lady, and I hoped would be more. I called to speak with your father after I have asked for your hand."

"I don't want to marry you."

"You have had several seasons now with no marriage prospects, Lady Liberty. Surely you must find my proposal acceptable?"

Toby's rage grew as he listened to Michael insulting the woman he loved.

"I want you to leave at once, Lord Michael. I will not discuss this with you now, when my family is away from home. It is wrong of you to be here with me."

"Why would you send me away, my lady, when we have always gotten along well," Michael said.

"I have no wish to marry, and after our conversation in London, I know you do. Therefore, I do not want to offend you further by offering hope. You need to leave at once." He could hear the panic rising in Liberty's voice now.

Toby crept forward until he was outside the room. Leaning closer, he looked in and hoped Michael wasn't facing his way. He wasn't. It was Liberty. He eased back, unsure if she had seen him.

"You appear unsettled, Lady Liberty, and after what I learned upon my arrival, I wonder if in fact it is because you know more about me than you should?"

"I do not know what it is you speak of, my lord. Now please leave," Liberty demanded.

"I had no wish for it to come to this, but now it seems I must dispose of you and Lord Corbyn, my lady. Of course, I blame Corbyn. Everything was running smoothly until he found a backbone and some morals," Michael said. "Now I must take charge of the situation before he destroys what I have built."

"You are rambling like a mad man, my lord. What are you

talking about disposing of me and Lord Corbyn?" Liberty sounded furious now.

"Be quiet," Michael snapped. "How much do you know?"

"About what?"

"Don't play me for a fool, Lady Liberty. I saw you at the warehouse in London, and you were seen today talking to Lord Corbyn by one of my men. He overheard some of your conversation."

"I have no idea what it is you speak of," Liberty said, continuing with her lies. "Why are you pointing that pistol at me?" she then asked loudly.

"If you don't tell me what I want to know, I will shoot you here and your family will find you dead on their floor." Michael no longer sounded calm but panicked.

"You are the one who is causing all this harm to the Bidham villagers, aren't you?" Liberty demanded, clearly deciding the pretense was up. "That warehouse in London, all of it, is part of whatever nefarious game you are playing with these people. You are a—"

"If you keep talking, I will shoot you where you stand, my lady. So shut up. I need to think."

"Clearly, not your strong suit," Liberty said. His love had a backbone, and when she was safe, he'd be happy about that. Right now, his veins were filled with ice that she was in that room with a man pointing a gun pointed at her.

"You can't honestly think you'll get away with this? To murder me and then Lord Corbyn would see you hanged."

"I doubt anyone will miss that fool," Michael sneered.

"He is no fool! And ten times the man you could ever be," Liberty snapped back. "You are a gutless coward to have treated him as you did."

Stop provoking him, Liberty. Toby couldn't say the words out loud and alert Michael, but he wanted to. She would get herself shot if she didn't shut up.

Toby turned at a noise behind him and found Anthony and

Jamie. Behind them were two footmen.

"Go," Jamie mouthed as they heard Michael curse, and then Liberty shriek.

Toby entered the room seconds later and found Michael with his arm around Liberty's neck, and a pistol pointed at her head.

"Let her go, Michael. Your scheme is up. Even now the magistrate is on his way, and we have all the evidence we need over you and Landon," Toby said, keeping his eyes on the man and not Liberty.

"Back away, Corbyn, or I'll kill her."

"You're not getting out of here with her," Toby said, his voice hard. "And if you harm her in any way, I will make your death slow and painful. A little like the punishment you allowed us to be subjected to in Blackwood House."

The man's eyes were wide, and moving from left to right, panic clear in the depths.

"It was discipline," Michael said, his voice shaky. "Boys need discipline."

"It was torture at the hands of a select few sadistic and evil men and older boys," Toby said with a calm he was far from feeling. Liberty was in the hands of a man who could, with a single movement of his finger, end her life. *The woman he loved.*

"Let her go now," Toby said, moving his eyes to Liberty, trying to convey to her to stay calm, which wasn't easy he knew with a pistol to her head.

"We are leaving, and you will let us," Michael said.

"Are you to murder two peers this night, then?" Toby asked. "Because my friends, and the staff in this house know you are here, Michael."

"You lie! I slipped in unnoticed!"

"I didn't," Toby said.

"No. I can fix this!" Michael said, the pistol now jabbing into Liberty's neck. "Walk out the door, and we will follow. One misstep, and I will shoot her, Corbyn."

He knew his friends and the footmen would be outside and

likely now hiding. Knew that Liberty's best chance was to walk out of here. Toby made himself turn and retrace his steps. And it was the hardest thing he'd ever done.

"Keep walking to the stairs," Michael said.

"Oh dear!"

Toby turned at Liberty's cry. She stumbled and fell. Michael had to release her or go down too. Toby didn't hesitate, but fired.

"Liberty!" He ran and had her in his arms in seconds. "Tell me you are all right?"

She was sobbing, which he took as a good sign.

"It's over now, my love," he whispered into her hair. "You are safe."

"We are safe," she said into his neck.

Picking her up, Toby carried her back into the parlor, ignoring the man writhing on the floor. He poured a brandy, and then forced it down her throat until her tremors had stopped.

"I can't believe that just happened," she said, her voice stronger now. "He could have shot us. Bastard!"

Toby smiled. Now she was angry, and that made color return to her cheeks.

"I love you, Liberty."

Her hands flew to his face, cupping his cheeks, as she looked deep into his eyes. "I love you so much, Toby."

"Liberty!" They eased apart as Edward ran into the room pale faced. "There is a man bleeding in the hallway!"

"It's all right now, Edward," Toby said as Liberty went to hug her brother. "Your sister is well, and that man deserves to be bleeding on the floor."

The duke and duchess were next to arrive, shock evident on their faces as well as they hurried to their daughter.

"All is well," Liberty said, comforting them.

Anthony appeared next, and Toby knew by the look on his friend's face he was needed.

"I must go now, Liberty. I have to deal with Lord Michael. Unfortunately, the bullet didn't kill him, so we need to get him to a doctor. Then we will speak with the magistrate so Landon can be taken into custody."

"I don't want you to leave," Liberty whispered leaving her family to come to him.

"Soon, I will never have to leave you again." He kissed her softly, and then left the house, knowing that one day she'd be his for always, and he'd never have to walk away from her again.

CHAPTER THIRTY-TWO

"YOU SHOULD HAVE come to us, Liberty, and you, Edward, when you realized all was not well in Bidham."

Liberty looked across the carriage to her father. The Talbots were on their way to the fair. The day dawned clear and bright, and full of hope as far as Liberty was concerned. More hope than she'd allowed herself to hold inside for many years.

"I'm sorry, Father," she and Edward said at the same time, as they had often since her parents had walked into their house to find a bloodied Lord Michael.

"In my defense, I am a child, so it really is far more Liberty's fault than mine surely?" Edward then added.

They all laughed at that, as he'd wanted them to.

"So, from the way Lord Corbyn behaved with you last night, am I to expect a visit from him?"

"Yes," Liberty said battling the blush at her father's words. "He has seen me in my glasses and still wishes to have a future with me," she added.

Her mother sighed. "Perhaps I was wrong there."

"Did you just admit you were wrong?" her husband asked. His wife poked out her tongue in a very un-Duchess of Talbot way.

"I'm glad you are to marry that man, daughter," her father then said. "I always believed he would be your husband one day. Your mother and I never knew what happened between you two or why, but I'm glad you resolved it.

Liberty sniffed back the tears, pressing her face into her handkerchief.

"He will do fine as a brother-in-law, and with him comes Florence and Barnaby, who I will enjoy having in the family very much," Edward added.

The carriage stopped then, and they stepped down and Liberty felt her excitement climb. Toby would be here; she knew he would.

"I always like to see it looking like this," her father said as they took in the village of Bidham alive with activity before them. Color was everywhere they looked. People too, and most appeared to be laughing, unlike yesterday. Finally, the people of Bidham could once again be happy.

Toby and his friends did this.

"Good day to you, Your Graces. My lady. My lord."

"Mr. Bridget." Liberty acknowledged the man who came toward them wearing a flowing cape, as he always did at the event.

"It is a fine day for the Bidham fair."

"Indeed, it is," her mother said.

"I've never seen that man smile," her father said, before wandering off to inspect a table laden with food he could buy.

The sounds of laughter and music filled the air as they walked down the cobbled streets.

"Does it feel different to you here today, Liberty?"

She looked at her brother, but his eyes were on the village before them.

"Happiness," she whispered. "I can feel that today, when recently I have not."

"Exactly that."

Liberty and Edward smiled and stopped to chat with people who wanted to talk. Those who she hadn't conversed with in some time wanted to spend time doing so today.

"They are free," Edward said.

"They are," Liberty said, choking back more tears.

"If you will all come this way!"

Liberty found Mr. Bridget now standing on a small platform. It was he who spoke.

Edward and she made their way to him along with everyone else who was attending the fair. So far, she'd not seen Toby, but knew he would be here. He'd shot Lord Michael last night to rescue her. Then he'd held her close while she'd sobbed out her fears.

The love inside her for that man was fierce. Once, it had been a childish love, but no more. Now it consumed her, and Liberty knew, always would.

"Today we have many reasons to celebrate," Mr. Bridget began. "For so long, a cloud hung over our village, but no more, and the men responsible for removing the threat to Bidham are here today. For the first time in many years, a Lord Corbyn will now open our fair once more!"

She saw him then. His long legs took him up the steps to stand beside Mr. Bridget.

Liberty's heart did a double beat as she looked at the man she loved. Tall, his curls fluttering in the breeze as he held his hat in one hand. Dressed in a deep-green jacket, and green-and-ivory waistcoat, his long legs were in white breeches and his large feet in polished black hessians. Every inch a gentleman... her gentleman.

"Welcome, everyone," he said with a smile. "Before I continue, I would like to apologize for the years I was not here to open your fair. That is about to change from this day onward. You will see me in the village of Bidham frequently, as my ward, Miss Florence, has a taste for gingerbread now, as my brother and I once did."

She sniffed back the tears at his mention of Mathew.

"Very well, we forgive you!" someone called out, which had everyone laughing.

"Thank you. I am humbled to receive your forgiveness,"

Toby said bowing. "Now I would like to declare the Bidham fair open." Loud clapping greeted his words.

Toby's eyes moved through the people gathered and found her. His smile grew. That look felt like warm sunshine running through her entire body. She smiled back, pouring all her love into it.

"I think I'm going to enjoy having him in our family," Edward said. "Especially as he makes you happy, sister."

She did cry then. Edward tutted and took her hand in his, giving it a squeeze.

"I don't remember you being a watering pot. I suppose it must be love."

"I-I suppose it must be."

Toby's eyes stayed on her as he continued to speak. People turned and looked at her, and then smiled when they realized it was Liberty he was looking at.

"And now I have an announcement," Toby said.

"What?"

"I'm about to tell you, Mr. Jasper," Toby added patiently. "I am going to marry Lady Liberty, but as yet I have not asked her."

"I have agreed to the match!" her father yelled from a few feet away.

Liberty was now laughing through her tears.

"Well then, it's about time," Miss Ainsley, also known as Harry, who was once Toby and Mathew's nanny, said.

Cheers went up, and everyone clapped loudly again, as Toby jumped off the stage and came to her.

"Hello, my love." He kissed her.

"I can't believe you said that up there," she said, putting her hands into the ones he held out to her.

"Of course, you can believe it. But, because I want us to start our marriage off on the right footing, I will tell you I spoke to your father before I got up there."

"Toby," she whispered as he tugged her close.

"Liberty." He hugged her gently. "I love you," he said so only she could hear. "Marry me, my sweet. Friend, lover, and soul mate. You are my life."

"Yes," Liberty said throwing her arms around his neck. Why not? Clearly, today was not one for decorum.

"Excellent. Now, let us walk and spend time with our people."

Lord Hamilton appeared with Florence and Barnaby. The little girl went willingly to Toby, clutching the hand he held out to her.

"Hello, Florence," Liberty said. "It is lovely to see you again."

"Hello," she said with a smile that would melt even the hardest heart, Liberty was sure. "Where is Edward?"

"And now we know who her favorite is," Toby drawled. "You only want to find Edward so you can coax sweets out of him, don't you, Florence?"

"Lemon drops," Florence said.

"Come, we will find him, and my guess is that he will already be at the sweets table, which is perfect, don't you think?" Liberty said, taking Toby's other hand.

They walked then, among people who'd known them since childhood, and the day was filled with promise.

"This much happiness is terrifying," Toby said a while later. "But I find that now I have it, I never want to let it go.

"Then we won't," Liberty said. "We are going to make a home filled with love, you, me, and Florence."

"There are also Barnaby and the cat."

"Cat?" Liberty looked at him.

"In London. He has decided to make a home with us, and as long as you are there with us too, it will always be that... a home."

He bent to press a kiss to her cheek, and Liberty knew no more words were needed. They'd found their way back to each other, and nothing would ever change that.

The End

About the Author

Wendy Vella is a *USA Today* and Amazon bestselling author of historical romances filled with romance, intrigue, unconventional heroines, and dashing heroes.

An incurable romantic, Wendy found writing romance a natural fit. Born and raised in a rural area in the North Island of New Zealand, she shares her life with one adorable husband, two delightful adult children and their partners, four delicious grandchildren, and her pup Tilly.

Wendy also writes small town contemporary romances under the name Lani Blake.

wendyvella.com/index.html

www.ingramcontent.com/pod-product-compliance
Lightning Source LLC
Chambersburg PA
CBHW072112300726
48975CB00003B/783